HOME
TO
CAVENDISH

HOME
TO
CAVENDISH

ANTOINETTE TYRRELL

POOLBEG

Published 2019
by Poolbeg Press Ltd
123 Grange Hill, Baldoyle
Dublin 13, Ireland
E-mail: poolbeg@poolbeg.com
www.poolbeg.com

© Antoinette Tyrrell 2019

Copyright for editing, typesetting, layout, design
© Poolbeg Press Ltd

The moral right of the author has been asserted.

1

A catalogue record for this book is available from the British Library.

ISBN 978-178-199-772-7

Printed by Liberduplex, Barcelona

About the author

Antoinette Tyrrell studied English and History at NUI Maynooth followed by a Higher Diploma in Communications. In her early career she worked as a journalist in local radio and for the last fifteen years has worked in public relations. She lives in rural County Kildare with her partner Ahmed. *Home to Cavendish* is her debut novel.

For information on Antoinette's upcoming books visit *www.antoinettetyrrell.ie*

Acknowledgements

A huge thank-you to everyone at Poolbeg, particularly Paula Campbell for seeing the potential in my writing. To my editor, Gaye Shortland, for shining and polishing the manuscript to make it the best it can be. To all the wonderful women that I am so privileged to have in my life. My oldest friends, Mag and Judith, for many years of friendship and fun. Karen and Aisling – we don't get to see each other too often but I love knowing we can pick up where we left off any time. Carmel and Lisa, for your great advice when I'm feeling a bit lost and for always seeing the funny side. The girls at work who were possibly more excited about the book deal than I was, and Áine Matthews for her very helpful advice.

To my extended family, particularly my cousin Philip who has been my one-man PR machine. To the army of phenomenal women that is my family. Thank you to all my wonderful aunts and cousins, particularly my aunts Catherine and Liz and my cousin Colette. It is hugely comforting to know you are always in my corner. My wonderful, fearless sister Martina. Nobody understands you quite like your sister does and I am grateful for your support. My smart and beautiful nieces, Lily and Katie. I love how much you both adore reading! My mother Bridget, who I used to mock as a child for always having her head stuck in a book – until I was bitten by the bug too. Thank you for the endless proofreading of my manuscripts and all the other countless things you do for me.

Thank you to Marwan and Neider for brightening up the house every weekend. Finally, to my partner Ahmed, I love you so much. Thank you for being my biggest fan.

Dedication

To my mother Bridget, who always supports and never judges
— no matter what bizarre ideas we come up with.

PROLOGUE

January 1923

It felt like hours that he'd been crouched down in the wet grass. All feeling had gone from his legs and the cold was seeping into his bones. He wasn't sure he'd be able to stand up – his legs could easily go from under him. His heart was beating loudly, and fear flooded his mind. This wasn't how he had imagined it would be. Brave and important was how he thought he would feel when they had planned and talked about it. Like a real soldier, fighting for Ireland. Now all he wanted was to be at home, home in his mother's kitchen, drinking tea and eating cake, sitting in front of a nice warm fire. Not here, listening to this: a group of grown men, unable to make a decision.

The fighting between them had been going on for the last twenty minutes. If they didn't decide on what they were going to do soon, it would be too late. Someone in the Big House would hear the carry-on of them and the all-important element of surprise, which Johnny O'Neill had told them was their greatest weapon, would be destroyed.

Johnny O'Neill didn't seem so brave now. For all his talk when they had been planning this, it now seemed as if his bravado had deserted him.

'Teach those English bastards a lesson.' That's what he'd said. 'They think we want the crumbs from their table, but they're wrong. Let's see how they like being here with their fine house burning down around their ears. Fuck the Free State! We won't rest until we have a republic and if burning them out is what we have to do – then that's what we're fucking going to do.'

Yet now here they were, Johnny fighting with Barry Cronin.

'Not tonight, Cronin. How were we to know they'd have more English bastards in the house? They'll fight back. We're supposed to burn them out of it but we're not to kill anyone. Those orders come from the top.'

Tadgh shifted uncomfortably as the argument continued and he was sure it was only a matter of time before some of them heard his heart beating and it gave him away. They'd tell him to go home, that a real soldier would never be that afraid. At this rate no house was going to be burned tonight and maybe that was for the best. If his ma reported for work in the kitchen in the morning and the place was nothing but a pile of smoking ashes, there'd be hell to pay. He couldn't think about that though. He was here for a reason: an Irish Republic. If burning this house down was going to help achieve that, then burn the house down was what they had to do.

Then he pictured his ma, working away in the kitchen. There was only her there now and May Ryan from the village. They both worked at the house during the day and went back home each night. It wasn't like the old days any more. His mother had told him stories of the hundreds of people that used to work on the estate, keeping it running so that Lord and Lady Cavendish could live in luxury. If it had been back then, they would not be in this situation. They'd have the information they needed from the locals working in the house. They'd have known who was going to be there tonight. They'd have known if visitors were expected.

Expected or not, there was more than the master and his wife at home tonight. From their vantage point overlooking Cavendish Hall, they'd seen them arrive over an hour ago. All had been going to plan until they heard the thunder of horses' hooves coming up the avenue and then a group of men descended from the two carriages.

Now the place was lit up, a piano could be heard playing, there was laughter coming from the house – and all the while Johnny and Barry kept at it.

Tadgh didn't want to hurt anyone. Burning a house belonging to someone as rich as them was no big deal but he didn't want murder on his hands. Imperialists or not, he didn't want them to die and now it was more than just the master and his wife. What if they'd known they were going to have visitors? What if they had ordered May and his mother to stay late and feed the visitors? What if his mother or May were hurt? If this went ahead, they could be burned alive. He couldn't let that happen. He thought of his poor, kind mother and lovely young May. He had to find a way to put a stop to this now.

But Barry's voice was getting louder and louder. 'Look, we'll do as we planned. We go up, knock on the door and order them to leave. Then we go in, fill the place with petrol and do what we came here to do. It doesn't matter how many of them there are – they're not going to fight with us.'

'You stupid idiot, it won't be that simple,' said Johnny. 'If it was just Cavendish himself, there'd be no problem, but now there's more of them. I counted seven men getting out of those carriages and what do we have? A group of children! We're no bloody army.' Johnny looked at the group assembled around him. Doubt was written across his face.

Standing up, Barry addressed them. 'Right lads, who's with

me? Are we doing this or not? If any of ye are afraid, on ye go, home to your beds. I came here tonight to burn this house and burn it I will!'

Tadgh looked at his comrades and saw only uncertainty. Silence descended upon them. It was made all the more eerie as the clouds overhead gave way and the full moon lit up the night sky.

Suddenly, the front door of the house opened, revealing Edith Cavendish. She was lit perfectly in the moonlight. The most serene and beautiful vision he had ever seen in his life. His heart jumped. Edith wasn't meant to be there. They'd made a plan – she was meant to be in Queenstown, waiting for him. He couldn't do anything that would put Edith in danger. *This had to stop – right now.*

'Fuck it, we don't even have to open the door.' Barry drew himself up to his full height. Pointing his rifle towards the house, he ordered the men to pick up the petrol cans that lay on the ground around them. 'Let's burn these fuckers out of it!'

And they ran towards the house.

Tadgh rushed after them as Edith, seeing the group of men running towards her, turned and screamed for her father.

CHAPTER 1

2002

'*Stop, stop, stop, no, don't do that! I told you to cover it, I told you to cover all the furniture!*'

Elenore Stack rarely raised her voice, but she had learned over the last few months that dealing with builders meant it was now something she frequently had to do. Her home was infested with them. It was as if a plague had come down upon the house – filling it with dust and dirt, plaster, tools, noise and mess.

She knew the builders paid no attention to her. This one she was shouting at was the worst of them all. He now stood in her drawing room with a plank of wood placed on top of the antique Bechstein piano. In his hand was a saw – poised to come down and inflict damage. Her father had bought the piano at auction when Elenore was a child. It had been one of his most treasured possessions.

'*What do you think you're doing?*' she shouted. '*Don't cut wood on my piano! I've told you to mind the furniture a hundred times!*'

The builder looked her up and down. This infuriated her. Not long out of bed, she was dressed in a thin T-shirt and leggings. The tartan dressing gown she was wearing to keep the cold at bay had fallen open and was doing little to conceal her slim build and long legs. Matted blonde hair fell around her shoulders. She knew she didn't look in the slightest bit intimidating. In her early thirties, she was younger than most of the builders. They all seemed to be in their fifties and had made their money in the building trade over many years. She wondered if she would command more respect from them if she were older. She somehow doubted it.

It seemed as though she was fighting a losing battle. She decided a gentler approach might work. She uttered a quick apology. 'I'm sorry. I didn't mean to shout. It's just that the piano you were about to start sawing wood on is a 1903 Bechstein. It's very special. If it were damaged, I'd be devastated.'

The man listened with a smirk on his face. He finally grunted at her which she suspected was the closest she was going to get to compliance. Feeling defeated, she left the room and made her way down to the kitchen which was in the basement. She didn't want to witness any further destruction today. It might just send her over the edge.

The kettle was already on the boil when she got to the kitchen and Donnacha was spooning coffee into a mug. Alfie, her White West Highland Terrier, came rushing over to greet her. He wagged his tail in unbridled excitement. She bent down to pat him on the head and then straightened up to admire the view of her boyfriend as he stood by the kitchen counter, wearing only jeans. She loved it when Donnacha went casual. Used to seeing him in suits, she loved the days when he wasn't going to his office in Cork City and wandered around the house in jeans and a T-shirt.

The view of him, framed by the sunlight shining in from the window high on the wall, was enough to lift her mood. It wasn't often she got to observe him like this; in fact, it wasn't often Donnacha O'Callaghan stood still for long enough to be observed.

Tall and sallow-skinned with broad muscular shoulders and arms well-defined from hours spent in the gym, combined with a mop of jet-black hair, he was like something from a film. Elenore had once spent weeks trying to trace his family history. She was certain his ancestry would be traced back to some sailor who had run aground on the coast of Ireland during the Spanish Armada. Her search had proven fruitless. Donnacha had assured her his good looks were nothing to do with any Spanish ancestors and more to do with looking after himself properly. Yet, no amount of looking after yourself could make you as attractive as that and he knew that was the case. She watched as he moved around. There was an energy about him.

Walking over to her, he placed a kiss on her forehead. 'Did you sleep okay, love?'

She shook her head and made herself a cup of coffee as he took a seat at the kitchen table and began poring over business papers. She sat down opposite him and watched him as she sipped her coffee.

She had hardly slept at all but that was nothing unusual. Nights of peaceful sleep were a far distant memory for Elenore and had been replaced by tossing, turning and worry. She had fallen into a fitful sleep at about four thirty which had finally given way to a deep sleep just in time for her to wake up. For a moment, on waking, she as always forgot. She forgot that things were different now. Forgot that this god-awful building project was under way and that it was necessary, in order for her to survive and hold on to her home.

They had woken her at six, coming in to cause more dust and destruction. She was in a bad mood already. Donnacha had slept the sleep of the dead beside her. Nothing ever fazed him or came between him and his sleep. It didn't matter how much damage the builders did. They never delivered on the things they said they would or had any respect for the house. Yet Donnacha would go downstairs and chat to them as if they were his best friends and they were doing him a favour — when all the while they were charging a fortune and quite possibly destroying her house.

The kitchen was freezing, causing her to shiver. A state-of-the-art new heating system was what Donnacha had promised and what the builders assured her they were delivering. Yet here she was, three weeks after they had started working on it, and the house, fridge-like at the best of times, was giving off the full-blown freezer effect. The original heating system had been temperamental, but it had done its job and kept the ever-present threat of damp at bay. If heat was not restored to the house soon, dry rot would set in and Elenore's worst fear would become a reality.

Her boyfriend's insistence on a new heating system wasn't the only thing bothering her about the renovation. He had also insisted on taking the carpet off the main staircase. Her father had spent a small fortune on a wool Axminister carpet in the 1980s and her mother Violet had said it was going to last a lifetime. She had insisted they all use the concrete stairs at the back of the house which would have originally been used by servants. Her only exception to the rule had been when they had visitors. The less use it got the longer it would last and coming down for breakfast was not an excuse for wear and tear, according to Violet. As it turned out the carpet had outlasted Elenore's mother and father. Until Donnacha got his hands on it, saying paying guests wanted sleek design. Apparently, a carpet from 1981 didn't say *sleek*. The carpet was now consigned to one of the many skips that stood guard outside the grand entrance to the house, leaving the main staircase exposed, waiting to be stripped back and covered with something suitably modern.

The back stairs had always terrified Elenore as a child. She remembered the morning dash from her bedroom, past her parents' room and the nursery, a quick turn onto the winding concrete stairs, concentrating hard on getting to the bottom and past that dark corner at the end where all sorts of monsters might lurk. Then it was past the door that led to the boot room and a final dash in through the oak kitchen door. Then she'd breathe a sigh of relief to find her mother, standing as always making porridge and listening to Gay Byrne on the radio. Violet Stack would turn to her daughter with a smile on her face and every morning the same routine. A kiss on the forehead and the question 'Did you sleep well, love?'

Elenore felt the familiar heaviness in her heart as she thought about her parents. Her mother had passed away four years before, followed not even a year later by the death of her father. Forcing herself not to get lost in sad thoughts, she went to the old radio on the counter. She was almost afraid to turn it on. Her faith in the electricians who were overhauling the wiring in the house had diminished after she had almost got electrocuted on plugging in the kettle a few days previously. Besides, Gay Byrne wouldn't greet her this morning. Instead she'd have to listen to a litany of bad news. It seemed the Celtic Tiger was slowing down, and the news would tell the story of yet another multinational company pulling out of Ireland and moving operations to Eastern Europe.

However, the Celtic Tiger was alive and well in Elenore's house, no matter what the radio said. Anyone looking on would think that money was growing on the stately lime trees that lined the winding avenue to Cavendish Hall. She'd set out with modest plans for the house – just enough work to set up a small enterprise and make it commercially viable. All she needed was to maintain the house and support herself. A bigger-than-average guest house was what she had planned. You couldn't walk half a mile in Ireland these days without coming across a five-star hotel. In her opinion, the country didn't need another one and, besides, she had no clue how to run one. Making hearty dinners like her mother used to do and riding horses was what Elenore knew and she had been sure that such simple things, combined with the charm of the house, was all she would need. America was the market she was after – selling rustic holidays in an authentic Irish country house to lovely wealthy American guests. She'd take them out riding during the day or employ someone local to take them fishing on the bountiful river bordering the demesne. In the evenings she'd light a big fire and provide dinner for them. Five or six people every two or three weeks. She'd done her maths and, given that she could sell exclusivity, she could charge enough to make it work and keep the overheads to a level she could manage. She had hoped some of those guests would become friends and return year after year. She wanted them to love the house just as she did and be charmed by the opportunity to be part of it, if only for a few days each year. She thought of long days hacking around the estate with them and evenings by the roaring fire, drinking wine and learning about their lives. She had a list of stories about her childhood in the house that she could entertain them with. It would involve a lot of work but if things went as she hoped she would be able to afford some help. All she would need would be someone from the village to come in and give her a hand in the evenings. They could help clean up after dinner and set up for the next morning's breakfast. It was vital that her guests felt as if they were being welcomed as part of the family at Cavendish and spending time with the owner would give them that feeling.

Well, that had been the plan until Donnacha came along and took charge with much bigger plans. Of course, he knew what he was doing. Donnacha was a property developer. This is what he did for a living and, with the house as collateral, he assured her that banks would be throwing money at them. On days like today, though, she sometimes hankered for her small plans that didn't involve ripping her family home to shreds. She wished for a future that she controlled and understood how to manage. Donnacha had agreed to pay to get the work started. He told Elenore he wasn't concerned about when she would be able to pay him back. For him, this was a venture the two of them were undertaking together. Once established, they planned that Elenore would look after the day-to-day running of the hotel and Donnacha would take care of the business side of things. But the further into the refurbishment they went, the more out of control Elenore felt. She was beginning to regret her decision to let him take charge.

That thought jolted her back to reality. This wasn't going to be her house any more, nor was it going to be the quaint guest house of her original plans. Of course, they wouldn't be guests now, they would be 'covers' – or was that word only used in restaurants? In any case, it was probably an old-fashioned word not to be associated with the kind of hotel environment Donnacha was planning.

He had even suggested the other day that they might think about changing the name of the house. On seeing the look of horror on her face he'd quickly said it was just a thought and that she shouldn't pay any attention to him. She had laughed to herself afterwards about the notion. For all his big plans, she knew he loved Cavendish. He understood that the soul of this house was the most magical thing about it. It was the feeling you experienced when you walked in the door that would sell this house, far more than any modern upgrades. Donnacha might talk the talk of the man-about-town property developer but Elenore knew he got that about the house. She just had to remind him not to get carried away with plans every now and again.

Looking up from the papers in front of him, he gave her the 100-watt smile that had made her fall for him in the first place. That smile could make you feel you were the only person in a crowded room. He really was one of the most handsome men she had ever met and the fact that he had chosen her never failed to amaze her. What had she done to end up with a man like him? She knew she was pretty but Donnacha had his pick of women. Yet, it was her, Elenore, that he had chosen.

'What have you planned for today, love?' he asked her. Then, before she had a chance to answer, he jumped in with his own plans.

This was one of the many things that appealed to Elenore about him. She really didn't have to talk all that much when she was in his company. Recognising herself as a listener rather than a talker, this situation suited her, even though it was something her female friends often commented on. They wondered if it bothered her that she never really got to say a whole lot in Donnacha's company – nobody did. She didn't mind her friends teasing her like this. They knew she was quite shy and was most at home when outside, in the open air, in the company of Alfie or her beloved horse Jasper. In her mind animals often made much better companions than humans.

Donnacha was outlining his plans for the day. 'Then I have to head in to Cork. I'm meeting with Jerry at twelve and from there I'm going to meet with some idiot from the City Council about the objection that has been lodged against the plans for the office block on City Quay.'

Elenore felt sorry for him. Spending days in meetings surrounded by people one didn't know sounded ghastly to her. Ruefully, she wondered, not for the first time, whether her dream vision of evenings by the fire, regaling genial American guests with family stories, was just fantasy. She didn't really have the temperament or the confidence for it, did she?

Donnacha was talking about all the issues he was encountering in his latest business project and she wondered at the fact that adding the refurbishment of Cavendish to his already busy schedule was not enough to overwhelm him. She was in awe at the endless capacity he appeared to have for work. The project at Cavendish was more than work though. It was something he was doing for their future, to make sure they could keep Cavendish as a family home. It wasn't the real business of property development.

That was building offices and housing developments across Ireland with his business partner Jerry Reynolds. That's where the money was and that's where Donnacha's primary concern lay: the latest project, the one that would make so much more money than the one before it.

Now he had another action-packed day planned for himself.

'I have to go meet with the solicitor then and see what that one is playing at now. Apparently, she's sent another letter. She's looking for some kind of payout on top of the maintenance. Jesus, she has some nerve!'

The 'one' to whom Donnacha was referring was his soon-to-be-ex-wife Karen. The mere mention of her name caused a change in Donnacha's demeanour. Elenore felt sympathy well up in her and wondered for the millionth time how such a great guy as he had married such a manipulative woman as Karen. The two women had never met each other, even though Elenore had been in Donnacha's life for almost two years now, but Aaron, Donnacha's son from his marriage to Karen, was a regular visitor to Cavendish.

It was better she stayed as far away from Karen as possible until the divorce was finalised. That was Donnacha's usual response when she suggested it would be a good idea to meet the mother of the boy who was spending so much time with them. He remained insistent that it wasn't a good idea. 'You don't know her. She's poison and, if she were to meet you, she'd be even worse. Seeing you, seeing how lovely and kind you are, she would just take advantage. I know you don't believe me but she's out-and-out crazy. She'd try to turn you against me, she's that bitter and twisted.'

His loathing of Karen surprised Elenore. It seemed logical to her that there would be some amount of negative feelings between them – that was a normal part of a divorce – but she thought they should be able to get along after all this time. Aaron was such a well-brought-up kid that Karen couldn't be all that bad – she was obviously doing something right. Donnacha had said that there was no one else involved in the breakdown of the marriage. They'd just grown apart. That added to Elenore's puzzlement. Maybe Donnacha was right – perhaps Karen was bitter and twisted – there were some people who were just like that.

'Listen, love,' she said, 'don't let her get to you. It's only a few more months now and the four years will have passed. Then you can go ahead and get your divorce. Once that's done, she'll be out of your hair and we can just get on with our own plans.' Under Ireland's strict divorce laws couples had to be living separately for four years before being granted a divorce. Donnacha was working with his solicitor ahead of the actual divorce date to hammer out a deal that Karen would be happy with, so that when the time came he would be able to move quickly. 'You just focus on Aaron,' she continued. 'Try to keep things alright for him. Try to be civil to each other, at least for Aaron's sake.' She'd tried this line with him many times, trying to make him see reason.

'Jesus, Elenore, how many times have I told you? You don't know her – she's a terrible, terrible person and there's no hope of us being civil to each other. I support her already. I keep her in that apartment. I pay all her bills. I make sure Aaron never wants for anything, but there's no pleasing her.'

'Okay, okay, there's no need to take it out on me. I was just saying.' She didn't add that she had heard all this from him before multiple times.

'Well, don't say. Not everyone is like you, not everyone is forgiving and understanding, especially her. She wants to do everything in her power to make sure I'm not happy. It's not enough that I support her completely, she won't rest until she has everything I own. I worked bloody hard to get all that I have, and I'll be damned if that one gets her hands on it.'

'Calm down, Donnacha!' Elenore could now feel herself

getting annoyed. Fair enough, he was under pressure and having the divorce process drag on for what seemed like ages was a pain for him, but he'd have to learn to control his bad feelings towards his ex-wife. She understood his frustration but wasn't used to anger and raised voices.

Donnacha got up and came over to her, then pulled her to her feet and into a hug. 'I'm sorry, really I am. I'll calm down. I'm just a bit stressed at the moment and I have a tough day ahead. Once it's over we have tonight to look forward to.'

Elenore sighed – she'd forgotten about tonight. She and Donnacha would be attending the Cork Business Leaders Annual Ball. It was an event she'd been to a couple of times when she was much younger, accompanying her father when her mother had been unable to attend. Back then it had been a very different affair. Usually held in the ballroom of one of the bigger hotels, it had been low-key – a dinner and dancing. Her father Jonathan, as owner of Stacks Department Store, would have been invited to say a few words and he would have talked about the great community of business people they had in the city and the work that they did to give back to those who were less fortunate than themselves. There'd be a raffle but nothing too flashy. The top prize was usually a weekend in a Dublin hotel and all the money raised would go to a local charity.

The pleasant catch-up with old friends that had once been the Business Leaders Ball bore no resemblance to the event that they were going to tonight. Last year had been the first time for years that she had gone to the ball and, if Donnacha hadn't pushed her to attend, it would never have occurred to her to go along. Stacks Department Store was no more and Elenore hadn't considered that the plan to turn her house into a glorified guest house qualified as a claim to be accepted as a Cork Business Leader – but Donnacha had insisted.

As Elenore's father had been a leading member of the Cork

Chamber of Commerce, after his death Elenore had received 'VIP' tickets annually for the ball. This to Elenore was more than faintly ridiculous. There was nothing VIP about the ball. It was just a group of local business people, friends really, meeting for a catch-up. She'd explained this to Donnacha the previous year — that it wasn't the great networking event he envisaged it to be. In the end, though, she couldn't persuade him out of it. He was adamant that it was of the upmost importance to go, that it would be his opportunity to get talking to lots of very important business contacts. In the end she agreed to go and take him as her plus-one. He had been over the moon at the prospect and even went to Brown Thomas and bought a new tuxedo. Elenore had laughed at that. She didn't see the point of spending a fortune on a dress that she would never wear again so she was going to pull out an old dress from her wardrobe. The dress was from Coast. She'd bought it for the wedding of a friend she'd been at university with, as she'd known a lot of her former classmates would be there and had wanted to look her best.

She remembered the evening well, how she had spent ages getting ready. She'd even gone down to the village and had her hair blow-dried, which was something she almost never did. The dress was strapless with a geometric pattern and with her long, blonde, wavy hair pinned to one side and a flash of red lipstick, she was happy with how she looked.

Donnacha had arrived in his most recent purchase, a Porsche 911, to collect her at Cavendish. Elenore had pulled back her bedroom curtain and grinned down at him as he pulled up outside the house and bounded out of the car. She was faintly amused at the sight of such a tall man in such a low car. She ran out onto the main landing and down the stairs to greet him.

She saw his face fall as he took her in.

She stopped on the stairs. 'What's the matter, Donnacha!' She hadn't known him all that long at that stage and so wasn't sure what was on his mind.

He looked her up and down. 'Is that what you're wearing? Who's it by?'

For a moment, she didn't understand the question. 'Who is what by?'

'The dress, who designed your dress?'

'It's from Coast. I got it for a wedding a while back – do you like it?' She hadn't realised he cared so much about fashion.

He continued to look up at her, a puzzled expression on this face. 'Yes, it's lovely. I thought, I just thought, you'd go for something a bit more high-end. A bit less high street, you know?' He grinned at his own joke but, as he saw Elenore's face fall, he quickly tried to turn it around.

'You look gorgeous, very sexy, and sure what do I know about fashion anyway? I'm only a man.'

'Obviously a lot more than I do, I suppose. I don't have anything else, Donnacha. I don't want to go to this bloody thing in the first place. I'd much prefer to stay in, make a nice dinner and just relax, the two of us.'

For some bizarre reason, she had felt herself welling up. She must be hormonal, she had thought.

He'd bounded up the stairs and embraced her. 'Forget about it. I'm just being silly. You'll be the most beautiful woman in the room, just because you are. You could wear a plastic sack and you'd still look better than any of the rest of them.'

This had made her laugh and the mood had lightened but still it had cast a shadow over the evening. It was the early days of their relationship and things had been going so well between them. Since she'd met Donnacha she'd felt normal for the first time since losing her parents. He had provided her with a feeling of security that she hadn't even known she was missing. She wanted him to be proud of her when they went out together.

Arriving at the ball, they were greeted with glasses of Dom

Perignon and Donnacha had been right. The women here, none of whom she recognised, were all wearing dresses that looked to her like they cost a small fortune. In fact, it wasn't long before they all began talking about just how much the dresses cost and dropping designer names like Vivienne Westwood and Dolce and Gabbana. One woman was thoroughly enjoying telling the story to anyone who would listen of how she couldn't find the perfect pair of shoes to match her dress, so she'd flown to New York to pick up a pair of Christian Louboutin stilettos.

The ball was different in every way from what it had once been – it wasn't only the people. The room was divided into sections with different types of 'entertainment' in each. A casino dominated one area with women dressed as Las Vegas show girls, wearing tall feathered head-pieces and flesh-toned bejewelled leotards. Another area housed a celebrity chef from TV, giving cookery lessons to the guests. The raffle which had been the high point of the ball of old was replaced by an auction, with ridiculous amounts of money being offered for a weekend in Monte Carlo and the chance to have the celebrity chef come to your house and cook dinner just for you.

Elenore hated every minute of it and was surprised to see that Donnacha was in his element. She had heard the expression 'working a room', but she'd never actually seen it in real life. It was exactly what Donnacha had done that night. He went from one Cork business leader to another, introducing himself, not as Donnacha O'Callaghan, but 'Donnacha O'Callaghan, partner of Elenore Stack'. He followed this up by telling them of the plans they had for Cavendish Hall.

Huddled in the Porche on the way home, Elenore had taken him up on it. Why was he telling people about their plans? They hadn't agreed on anything and at that stage they were only talking about what they might do, nothing had been agreed. Donnacha had brushed aside her concerns, telling her not to worry, and by the end of the conversation she had agreed with him. She didn't need to worry. He knew what he was doing. He needed these people to know who he was. He wasn't just one of the many property developers who had sprung up all over Cork in recent times. He was connected. He was dating the daughter of one of the most respected businessmen Cork had ever known, the founder of a shop that had once been an institution in the city.

That was a year ago. Now here in the kitchen he was doing it again, calming her down, telling her not to worry.

He hugged her tight. 'The ball tonight will be great – remember how much fun we had last year?'

Elenore nodded. The truth was she had totally forgotten about the stupid ball. Even though he had helped her, over the last year, to replenish her wardrobe for the many black-tie events which now seemed to be part of their lives, she had nothing new to wear. Donnacha wouldn't have it said by anyone that his partner appeared in the same dress twice.

He smiled down at her. 'You forgot all about it, didn't you? I know you so well. Don't worry, I left a little something for you on the bed upstairs.'

'Ah, Donnacha, you didn't? Why did you do that? I know you'll have spent a ridiculous amount on it,' she berated him, but knew it was pointless. Appearance meant a lot to him and he wanted her to be happy. Any normal woman would love her partner buying her a dress, especially a designer one. It wasn't Donnacha's fault that she just wasn't one of those women.

Kissing him on the cheek, she walked out of the kitchen and upstairs to see what designer delight awaited her – hoping she would fit into it and worrying that she wouldn't let Donnacha down by not having the right shoes to match.

CHAPTER 2

Donnacha liked to give himself plenty of time to prepare for an event like tonight's ball. Elenore might laugh at him for what she termed his obsession with his appearance, but she didn't realise how important looking the part was. Surveying himself in the mirror, he was happy with the results of the effort he had put in. He was looking forward to seeing Elenore in the dress he had bought her and hoped she would like it. Of course, she wouldn't know by looking at the label just how much it had cost. It was by an up-and-coming British designer who was making quite a name for himself. Models and celebrities were now regularly featuring in the glossy magazines wearing his designs — at least that's what the girl in the shop had told him when he was buying it.

Donnacha's ambition had once been to fit in with his business peers in Cork but now he wanted to set himself apart. Shopping in Brown Thomas was run-of-the-mill — all the men at the ball tonight would have tuxedos with designer names on them but they would all be off-the-shelf. Donnacha was now in a league where he could go a step further in a bid to set himself apart. They had accepted him as one of their own but now they needed to look up to him. He and Elenore needed to set the standard as to what was fashionable in Cork City. The trends they set would be followed and would clearly show the value of the wealth he had amassed.

A recent trip to London had been a great opportunity to kick-start this ambition. At home, he was already working on getting Cavendish Hall in order and, once that was completed, he would have the home needed to match the persona he wished to create. Elenore had no idea of what an asset the house was. Of course, it would have been great to be able to keep it as some sort of guest house, as she had originally wanted, but this just wasn't practical. The house, not to mention all the land surrounding it, was nothing less than a goldmine and Donnacha wasn't going to stand by and let this go to waste. The fine line he had to tread was being able to have a family home at the house while also running it as a real money-earner. What was the point in having a house like Cavendish if you couldn't claim to live there and be Lord of the Manor? But that wasn't something he needed to worry about now and he turned his attention back to his reflection in the mirror.

The Saville Row tailor who created the tuxedo for him had turned out to be worth every penny. He would stand out from all the other men tonight, not to mention the jealousy that would be created amongst the women when they got a look at Elenore, bedecked in the stunning creation he had payed thousands of euros for.

He had better go check on her, to see how she was getting on. He left the bathroom and walked down the corridor to her bedroom. He hated that the house didn't have en-suite bathrooms. He looked forward to a time when he could start knocking some of the walls here on the first floor. No guest in their right mind would be happy to pay the price they were going to charge to have to leave the warmth of their bedroom and walk down a corridor

to use the toilet. By the time he got that work done, though, he and Elenore would have moved out into the east wing of the house which would become the amazing family home that she so desperately craved. She wasn't aware of any of these plans just yet but by the time he got that work under way his divorce would be through. He and Elenore would be married and he would make sure that Elenore understood that his bigger plans were the right ones for the house. Those plans would ensure she would never have to worry about losing it. It would remain in their family for generations to come.

Walking into the bedroom, he found Elenore standing in front of the full-length mirror, shoulders hunched and a frown on her face.

'I'm not sure about this, Donnacha – do you not think it's a bit too revealing?'

Donnacha stood back to look at her. She was right. The dress was revealing and even the flashiest of the women at the ball tonight probably wouldn't dare to wear it. But it didn't look right on Elenore. If she would just stand tall and be more confident it would make all the difference. She was tall and long-limbed, and her body was toned from all the time she spent riding. The dress, floral-patterned, with wide chiffon shoulder-straps, continued down to a deep V at her waist, barely covering her small breasts. A band of chiffon highlighted her slender waist, holding the straps in place and was decorated with a diamond brooch, with the skirt falling in diaphanous folds to the floor.

'Em, yes, there's something not right,' he said. 'What do you think it is?'

Elenore's fair hair tumbled across one of her shoulders and her pale skin was almost translucent in the evening light. She was without doubt beautiful, but it was a different kind of beauty than what was fashionable, and she did as little as possible to enhance it. She had the tall figure of a model, but she was so pale and her breasts were so tiny. Donnacha wished she would invest in some fake tan and was considering suggesting she might like breast implants and a few highlights in her hair to brighten it up. It would do wonders for her. If he could get her to make those few small changes to her appearance, then it might have the desired effect on how she carried herself. Elenore Stack was tall, striking and beautiful. She grew up in a stately home where she had led a privileged life, her every need met by a loving and wealthy family. Donnacha didn't understand why she carried herself with such a lack of confidence but then, unlike him, she didn't need to present herself in a certain way to the outside world. She'd never had to fight to get what she wanted or needed. It had all been handed directly to her. That was why now, when for the first time in her life there was a chance she might lose something that was of real importance to her, she needed help and she needed guidance.

Donnacha was providing this for her but he knew he would need to spend some time working on Elenore herself – building her confidence, letting her light shine so to speak. She was going to be his wife and Cavendish Hall would be theirs. Donnacha's plan was for them to become one of the leading business families in Ireland – to create a dynasty.

'You just need to stand tall, love. A dress like that needs to be worn with confidence. Look at yourself, you're gorgeous. Every woman in the room tonight will be mad with jealousy when they get a load of you in that. You can tell a mile off it's a designer piece – nobody there will have anything like it.'

Elenore smiled at him, a half smile that told him she clearly wasn't convinced.

'Do you think I should put a wrap or something over it? Maybe something that would cover me up a bit?'

'Jesus, Elenore, don't be daft. What's the point in having a dress like that if you're going to cover it up? It's a black-tie event. The whole point of it is dressing to impress.'

Her face dropped, and she gave him that sad, wounded look that always annoyed him. He had to do something quickly to change the mood. He moved over beside her so that she could see both of their reflections in the mirror.

'Look at us, we have it all. Have you ever seen such a good-looking couple?' He tickled her gently and, putting his arms around her, kissed her on the forehead. 'I know you don't buy into all this material stuff but it's part and parcel of our lives now. If we want to be taken seriously, we must look the part – that's just how the world works these days. It's not like how it was for your parents – they were accepted because they came from wealth and nobody ever questioned your father's business acumen. It hasn't been like that for me. I've had to claw my way up to get to where I am today. I want everyone to know I – no, not I, but *we*, as a couple, are a force to be reckoned with.'

Elenore looked at him quizzically, and he knew he had probably overstepped the mark.

In fairness, Elenore's mother came from old money in Cork but her father had not been born into great wealth. He had started out as a shop boy, worked his way up to owning a small haberdashery and from there had built the great Stacks Department Store. For decades after, it had been the go-to place for shopping for the well-heeled of Cork City. Elenore had often told him how her father's marriage to her mother had been quite the scandal. Violet's family had strongly disapproved of the match at the time.

Donnacha had once heard Elenore tell a friend of hers that one of the reasons she loved him was because he reminded her of her father. He supposed there were some comparisons to be made but, while they were both astute businessmen who had started out with nothing, that was where the comparison ended. Jonathan Stack had not grown up in a home where love and affection were replaced by abuse and anger, where you feared for your safety every day and everything you did was criticised and ridiculed. That had been Donnacha's life until he escaped from his family home all those years ago. So, while Jonathan was to be commended for what he had achieved, their stories were hardly comparable, and he himself had overcome much greater odds to achieve his success.

Elenore was still looking troubled. Luckily, he had something to distract her.

Going over to the dressing table, he opened a drawer and pulled out a pale-blue box with a distinctive white ribbon.

'Here, I saw this in London and couldn't help myself,' he said with a grin, handing it to Elenore.

It was a Tiffany's box.

'Oh my God, Donnacha, what is this?' Her eyes were wide in surprise.

'Open it and see.' He watched as she pulled the ribbon loose and opened the box.

Inside was a sparkling diamond choker.

'Donnacha!' she said, shocked. 'What is this for? You shouldn't have – it must have cost a fortune.'

'Never mind the money, Elenore – we have plenty of it and the means to make plenty more. You deserve it.'

He took the choker from the box and placed it around her neck, then turned her back so she could see the full effect in the mirror. He was certain that no one would be under any illusion that it had taken anything less than tens of thousands of euros to put Elenore together for the evening.

'Think of it as an heirloom, love. The first of many to come. You won't accept an engagement ring from me until I'm divorced so I wanted to give you something to show how much you mean to me. Let this be the first gift I give you that you'll pass on to our daughter, God willing, and she'll pass it on to her daughter. It will be like Cavendish – something that will be in our family for generations.'

He was relieved to see that this approach was working. A real smile broke out on her face as he had hoped it would.

'Thank you so very much, my darling. I'm sorry for being a bit cross. You're right. I have to stop worrying so much. I know you know what you're doing and from now on I'm going to trust that.' Sliding her arms around his neck, she gave him a long and lingering kiss.

'Hold off there, lady! If you carry on with that behaviour we'll have to forget about the ball and retire to bed right now.' He unwrapped her arms from around his neck. 'Right, you finish your hair and make-up – I'll go downstairs to fix myself a drink while I wait.'

Downstairs in the drawing room, Donnacha poured himself a stiff whiskey. Glad that he had managed to turn the mood around, he felt he deserved a strong drink while Elenore finished getting ready. Taking a sip, he surveyed the room in which he stood. He supposed it was only natural that Elenore viewed life differently when she had been born into this. Perhaps it had given her a quieter type of confidence. Growing up here, secure in the knowledge that all this belonged to her and her family, meant she didn't feel the need to show off. It sometimes seemed to him that this house was like another member of her family, she spoke of it with such love and affection. She even referred to it as having a soul, as if it were an actual person.

He didn't think Cavendish had a soul, but he had to admit there was something about it, a good feeling when you walked through the front door. Here in the drawing room, even without any heating on or fires roaring in the two large fireplaces, there was a feeling of warmth and calm, as the last of the evening sunlight poured into it. It was as if the house could protect you from the outside world and keep you safe.

Taking a seat on one of the sofas placed around the room, he took it all in. The drawing room at Cavendish ran the full length of the back of the house. There were four ceiling-height windows with white wooden shutters along the back wall which gave uninterrupted views out onto the formal gardens. Intricate cornicing decorated the high ceilings from which hung two impressive Waterford crystal chandeliers. Two deep bay windows, with window seats set in the alcoves, stood at either end of the room, ensuring that sunlight poured in and added to the feeling of warmth and peace, no matter what the time of day. The Bechstein piano, so beloved of Elenore, stood beside one of the windows. The room was divided up into different parts by arrangements of soft furnishings. Three large and imposing sofas surrounded each of the two fireplaces, covered in mismatched and worn floral and striped patterns. A writing desk stood in one of the bay windows. A more formal seating area with gilt chairs covered in gold brocade, two mahogany sideboards and a drinks cabinet completed the array of furniture. Well-worn Turkish rugs adorned the parquet flooring, further adding to the charming effect of this grand old room.

Taking a mouthful of his drink, Donnacha's mind began to wander, away from the safe and secure drawing room at Cavendish and back to the home where he had grown up in north inner-city Dublin. There had been no drawing room in 71 Battersea Row, the two-bed terraced home he had shared with his parents and two older brothers. He had never talked to Elenore, or anyone aside from his ex, Karen, about what his childhood had been like. He had left both his childhood and his family behind when he walked out the front door for the last time all those years ago. If anyone asked him now, he said he was an only child and his parents were dead. For all he knew this could be the case. He assumed his older brothers were still inhabiting some dodgy pub in the city, living off the dole or perhaps caught up in the drugs scene that was now so prevalent in that part of Dublin. If his parents had died at some point since he'd left, nobody had bothered to tell him. Sometimes he desperately missed his mother and chastised himself for his inability to protect her from his drunken father, but that was a life he never wished to revisit.

His father hadn't just been a drunk. Brian O'Callaghan had been a mean drunk. His earliest memories where of sitting on his mother's knee in front of the stove in the kitchen in Battersea Row while she read him bedtime stories. Those were some of the few happy times, but even those memories were invariably marred by sounds of a crash coming from outside – his father cursing whatever had 'got in his way', causing him to trip up. Donnacha's mother would then hurriedly usher him upstairs to the bedroom where he shared one of the two single beds with his brother Declan, and demand that he 'keep quiet and not come down the stairs, no matter what'.

He usually spent those nights shivering with fear while his brother snored beside him, oblivious to what was going on downstairs. At first, he would hear his father shouting at his mother. He could never make out what the actual words were, but his mother always responded and Donnacha would lie there, silently pleading with her in his head. *Just don't answer him, Ma.* Hoping that if his mother stayed quiet his father's anger would disappear.

That never happened and, as Donnacha grew older, he would recognise the tone of his mother's voice changing. Annie would start out speaking calmly, obviously hoping, despite the same scenario playing out far too often, that she had it within her means to calm her husband down. Calmness seemed to have the opposite effect on Brian and worked to make him even more angry. Annie's tone would then turn to one of panic, her voice becoming more high-pitched until Donnacha would hear a bang or a crash or the sound of a stinging slap being delivered across his mother's face.

The bangs and the crashes had somehow seemed better to

Donnacha, especially as a small child – he was able to tell himself they might not be anything to do with his mother. It might just be his father falling over something yet again. The slaps were the worst, even though they usually caused less damage than having her head bashed against a wall. That sound of flesh meeting flesh still haunted Donnacha to this day.

After these episodes, his mother would have blue-and-purple bruises on her face for a few days and she would keep Donnacha home from school. She would send him down to the shop with a list of groceries or ask him to help her around the house, when doing housework caused her to wince in pain.

As the days home from school became more and more frequent and Donnacha began to fall further and further behind, he became used to getting in trouble with the teachers. But he wasn't afraid of them. They might hit him to keep him quiet in the classroom, but it was nowhere near as bad as the punishments meted out by his father for absolutely no reason at all.

He remembered well the first time his father's anger had turned full force upon him. He had been about seven at the time and, although he was used to getting a belt around the ear for answering back, Brian's full fury only came to light at night and was solely focused on his mother. That was until the night – unable to sleep and sick with worry that he would awake in the morning to find his mother dead and gone to heaven, without a chance to say goodbye – he decided to go downstairs and make his father stop.

He walked down the stairs slowly, careful not to make a noise, and coming into the kitchen he found his mother curled up in a ball on the floor. A tuft of her hair was gone from her head and was lying on the floor beside her. His father, with his back to him, stood over her, the poker from the fireplace raised over his head, preparing himself to bring it full force down on her.

Donnacha remembered the strange sensation of trying to talk

but his voice not working. He felt a warm spray running down his leg as fear made him lose control of his bladder and he thought that his ma was going to kill him in the morning because he was big now and big boys didn't wet themselves.

'Stop it, Da, leave her alone.'

He wasn't sure if he had only thought the words in his head or had managed to say them out loud.

'Stop it, Da, leave her alone.'

He must have managed to make some noise this time as his father, instead of landing the poker on Annie, stopped and turned around to face him.

'*What the fuck do you want? Get back up to that fucking bed!*'

His father was walking towards him.

His mother, whimpering, managed to mumble, 'Leave him alone, Brian – he's only a child.'

Whether his father heard her or not Donnacha wasn't sure but, if he had, her plea didn't work. Grabbing him roughly by the arm, he pulled Donnacha across in front of the stove and, opening the door, shoved his hand in and pushed it down on the embers. Donnacha screamed in pain as his mother pulled herself to her feet.

Brian turned back to her and knocked her down again. '*Fuck you, you stupid cunt, and that little pansy!*' he roared.

And then he stood there, breathing heavily, before walking out and up the stairs.

As Donnacha later came to recognise, there was always a moment his father's temper reached its crescendo and, just as quickly as it had rained terror down on the house, disappeared. His attention turned to something else – more alcohol, sleeping – or the worst, when he dragged Annie upstairs and Donnacha could hear the bed creaking through the thin walls and his mother's sobs – as his father did whatever he did to her in the bedroom that made her so sad.

That was how Donnacha's life had been for his entire childhood. He went through phases of willingly doing things to annoy his father, just so he would turn his anger on him and away from Annie. Other times he lay in bed and just listened to what was going on downstairs, usually too tired, cold or hungry to go down and help her.

As he grew up, he saw that his brothers Declan and Jason were going to be exactly like his father. Every penny they earned on the building sites of Dublin, little as it was, was spent on drink and, the drunker they got, the angrier they got. His brothers never raised a hand to his mother but to them she was a skivvy – someone to wash their clothes and put their dinner on the table. Not once did they feel the need to come to her aid when his father battered her, even though they were fully grown men by the time Donnacha reached his teens.

They'd slap Donnacha around too but nothing compared to the beatings inflicted on him by his father. When Brian was drunk, he beat either Donnacha or Annie. When he was sober, he dealt out a litany of criticism and belittlement to them both.

Donnacha had dropped out of school as soon as he could but he was determined not to go onto the building sites and down the same weary-trodden path as his father and brothers. It was 1976 and Ireland's economy was finally picking up. Donnacha spent his days wandering the streets across the Liffey, in the south of the city, listening to the accents of the inhabitants which sounded very different from the harsher tones of him and his north-side neighbours. He practised the accent quietly to himself, attempting to mimic them.

The more he practised, the more this new accent became second nature to him and with that came the birth of the new Donnacha O'Callaghan. It wasn't his fault he'd been born in the crappy house on the wrong side of the Liffey. He wished he had been born just a couple of miles further south and then his life might have been very different.

Donnacha realised that he needed a job to go with this new life he imagined for himself. He had the accent, but he didn't look the part. No one in their right mind would give a decent job to someone like him. It was then that he committed what he considered the one and only true criminal act he ever would: he stole a suit from Clerys. He walked in, saw what he wanted and, casually slipping it off the rail, put it under his arm and confidently strolled out of the department store. It was a miracle that nobody followed him and that he wasn't caught for the theft. As he often thought after, having that suit changed the course of his life forever. Wearing it made him feel different. He didn't feel like the old Donnacha, crippled with fear and living in terror of an abusive father. Instead, he felt confident. Wearing the suit made him feel like the world was his for the taking.

It was that confidence that allowed him to walk into Lawlor's Estate Agents on Baggot Street that autumn after leaving school. The sign in the window had simply read, '**Help Needed**'. He strode in, smiled and was charming to the elderly woman at the typewriter inside the door, explaining that he had come to talk to someone about the job.

The new confident Donnacha clearly had the power to charm the ladies, even older ones, as he was told to come back the next day at twelve to speak with Mr. Lawlor. Back he came and that was how he got his first job, as an errand boy in Lawlor's, one of the most successful estate agent's in Dublin. Donnacha gave it everything he had: he was always on time, he never missed a day and did everything he was asked to do, without question. Old Mr. Lawlor began to trust him and within a few years he had been promoted to an office job. By the time he was twenty he had worked his way up to an agent's role. It was there he discovered his love for property. He spent his days showing potential clients around some of the grandest houses in Dublin and it quickly became apparent that he was a born salesman. In his first year he sold more houses than any of the other agents but, what set him aside and made him really stand out in the eyes of Mr. Lawlor, was the work he did outside of that he had been assigned to do.

Donnacha began looking at property in a whole new way and noticing properties, usually a bit rundown but with great potential, which he felt could make a lot of money for Lawlor's. He began to put in work, in his spare time, carrying out research to find out who owned them. He tracked down the owners and persuaded them that selling their property was the right thing to do. Lawlor's could provide them with the support they needed to sell a property that wasn't in top-notch condition.

More and more clients started to come to Lawlor's as a result of Donnacha's hard work and after his first year as an agent Mr. Lawlor handed him a bonus which equalled what his father earned in a year. That was the day he moved out of home. He pleaded with his mother to come with him, but she refused. She was afraid that his father would fall apart without her – who would look after him and what would Declan and Jason do?

He suspected she would not live for much longer if she stayed there. She was never more than one beating away from her own death. He couldn't understand it. He was offering her a chance to escape, to be safe, to no longer have to worry about money. She no longer needed to be cold and hungry or cower on the floor as someone beat the living daylights out of her. But no remained her answer and in that moment his love for his mother changed. Of course, he still loved her but now he also felt a pity that was close to contempt for her – for not having the strength to take the opportunity to save herself.

From that day on, pity was Donnacha's least favourite emotion and the one that made him most uncomfortable. He pitied people who were weak, who didn't grasp opportunities and make the most of what they had. The thought that anyone should see him as weak was his greatest fear because weakness was simply not in his

DNA. He had been strong enough to see there was life beyond the house in Battersea Row and the pathetic lives lived by his father and brothers. He had walked out that day and never turned back and ever since then it was vital to his very existence that those around him saw him as being strong and a winner in life. Any time he felt in danger of being weak himself, he would look down at the scars on his hand that had never healed after being burned in the fire They reminded him of where he had come from.

Aside from Karen, nobody knew of his upbringing. He never shared it with anyone. He associated being poor with being weak. Elenore knew he hadn't had a very privileged upbringing but had no idea that it had been one of poverty and abuse. Donnacha painted a picture of a working-class background minus the beatings and the hunger. He'd left Battersea Row and never looked back. He fought anyone who threatened him or his success in any way. No one was ever going to take away anything he had worked so hard for or get in the way of his ongoing success.

Glancing around the drawing room, he thought about what work could be done there. It was, in fact, one of the few rooms that needed very little work. The worn sofas could be re-upholstered and the old green velvet curtains adorning the window alcoves replaced. Aside from that, the room's grandeur spoke for itself and once the new heating system was in the house it would be warm all year round.

Scanning the room, his eyes fell on a book sitting on one of the sideboards. There was an envelope propped up against a candlestick behind it. He went over to it. The book was clearly old, with an ornate hardback cover. There was a note scribbled on the envelope: *Found this in the tunnel today, Ronan.*

Ronan was the foreman looking after the renovation work for him. The tunnel he was referring to was something Elenore had mentioned to him recently. She had heard her father talking about it when she was a child, but she had never been in it. From what she remembered, her father had said it ran from the basement of Cavendish to the farmyard. It probably would have been used back in the day to bring supplies from the farmyard up to the house. Apparently Jonathan had it sealed off for safety reasons many years ago. The idea of it intrigued Donnacha and he thought it might have the potential to be used in one of those murder-mystery-weekend things that seemed so popular now. He had instructed the builders to find access to it, which they had done from the farmyard end. But they still hadn't figured out where it emerged into the basement. There was a maze of tiny rooms and corridors connected to the kitchen with lots of old furniture piled up in them for storage over the years. They'd had to put up scaffolding at a few points where the curved concrete roof of the tunnel was damaged. They'd now made it safe and tomorrow they hoped to be able to walk to the end and establish where exactly the tunnel reached the house. He hadn't told Elenore about this work. He knew she would criticise the move as spending money unnecessarily. He hoped that by tomorrow evening they would be breaking into the house from the basement and he would unveil it to Elenore as a big surprise.

He liked what he had seen so far but thought getting insurance to use it for hotel guests might be a bit tricky. It could prove to be a great place for storage though. His office in the city was overflowing with files, many of them containing information that he felt was too sensitive to leave unattended when he went overseas. If the building was broken into or worse still, if he was audited, who knew what might happen? The tunnel might prove an ideal place to store them.

Opening the book, he saw that it was handwritten and looked like a diary. He had hoped it might be a first edition of something that would prove to be of value. He cast it aside as Elenore walked into the room, looking considerably happier than she had earlier. The revealing dress still did not sit on her with ease, but at least now she was smiling and standing a little taller which made her look better.

'What are you looking at there, love?' she asked him.

'Oh, nothing important – Ronan found it somewhere and left it for me – looks like an old journal or something. Anyway, come on, if we don't hurry up we're going to be late for the ball.'

'You sound like my Fairy Godmother,' Elenore laughed, as she linked her arm in his and they walked out of the drawing room and towards the front door together.

CHAPTER 3

The Royal Hotel on the banks of the River Lee was lit up like a Christmas tree for the ball. A red carpet was rolled out through the front door and a string quartet was playing upbeat music beside a champagne bar as they walked into the foyer. Donnacha immediately spotted his business partner, Jerry Reynolds, sipping a glass of champagne while cornering a blonde woman in a gold-lamé backless dress. His wife, Jennifer, was nowhere to be seen.

Donnacha began twirling Elenore around to the strains of the Argentinian tango which the string quartet was playing, in an effort to stop her clapping eyes on Jerry with the blonde. As he twirled, he caught Jerry's eye and Jerry hastily excused himself from the woman and made his way across the foyer. He winked at Donnacha who silently patted himself on the back. If Elenore had spotted Jerry with the blonde she would have gone off on a tirade and spent the night questioning him on what he thought Jerry was really like. She already had her strong suspicions that half the time he wasn't faithful to Jennifer. There was no love lost between her

and Jennifer, but at the same time she thought no woman deserved
to be cheated on and regularly told Donnacha that if he ever had
any evidence of Jerry's infidelity he was morally obliged to make
Jennifer aware of it.

'Donnacha, Elenore, how are you? Don't you look a treat this
evening!' Jerry took Elenore's hand and, dropping into a low bow,
planted an exaggerated kiss on it.

Donnacha knew the over-the-top action would annoy Elenore
immensely.

'Don't the two of you look dapper!'

Donnacha knew by the way Jerry was slurring his words and
using old-style language like 'dapper' that he was the worse for
wear already.

'How are things, Jerry? The place is looking well this evening.
Let's get a drink and go find our table. I assume they've put us
beside someone worth talking to?'

Jerry might see the night as a chance to get drunk and chat up
women but Donnacha wasn't going to waste it in the same way.
He was here to meet people. It was likely there would be a couple
of the local politicians here tonight. If the night went as planned
and he could get the ear of one or two of them, he might be able
to get some assistance with a particular problem he had with
planning permission for his latest development.

They entered the ballroom which was lit by giant chandeliers,
with walls covered in white chiffon dazzling with fairy lights.
There were about thirty round tables, covered in crisp white linen
tablecloths, silver cutlery and tealights and surrounded by chairs
bedecked in white covers with white satin bows. In the middle of
each table was a vase out of which poured at least twenty white
hydrangea blooms.

Donnacha was delighted to see that one of the politicians he
hoped to talk to, Tim Collins, and his wife Moira were already
seated at the table where he, Elenore, Jerry and Jennifer would sit.

The evening passed quickly for Donnacha. Some of the men there made time to take their partners out dancing when the big band took to the stage, and he knew Elenore would moan later on about him ignoring her. She had to understand, though, that tonight was a chance to further his plans and he couldn't miss out on that.

Course after delicious course of fine food was served up to them. Dublin Bay prawns, caramelised fois gras, Dover sole meunière and 8-ounce fillets of Irish beef, washed down with Bollinger, Sancerre and Châteauneuf-du-Pape.

The highlight of the evening was the auction which was compèred by a well-known TV3 presenter. The rumour going around the city was that she was the girlfriend of a local radio-show host, who sat in the audience beside his stony-faced wife.

For the auction, even Donnacha was prepared to break away from his conversation with Tim Collins to splash some of his hard-earned cash in front of his peers. The first few items of the auction didn't hold any interest for him. An all-expenses-paid weekend shopping-trip to New York was hardly worth raising his hand for when most of the audience already travelled regularly to the Big Apple to top up their wardrobes. A year's supply of Bollinger seemed a bit too crass.

A number of other items went up for auction, causing great revelry amongst the audience as friends tried to outbid each other whilst all the while showing off how much money they had. Finally, the last item for auction was rolled out onto the stage.

It was a painting by a West Cork artist who had caused quite a stir a few months previously. He had held an exhibition in the community hall of the village where he came from. The controversy that arose from the exhibition was due to the fact that the majority of his paintings were of blood-soaked sanitary products. Elenore had commented to Donnacha at the time that it looked like a big publicity stunt for the artist, who called himself

Zee. Aside from the subject matter, she had thought the paintings were garish at best and the standard of the painting was on a par with that of a five-year-old. Even so, the exhibition had received coverage in all the national newspapers.

Now the painting was standing on a plinth on the stage, in a large gilt frame. The subject appeared to be a tampon dripping in blood although that was open to interpretation. It was surrounded by childish blocks of primary colours against a white background. Donnacha wasn't quite sure what something like that would be worth. He'd read all about Zee in the papers but there had been no mention of how much his paintings were selling for. But bidding on art was classy and Donnacha was sure that when the other guests saw him bid on this they would view him as someone who knew that there were more highbrow ways to invest than building apartment blocks.

The bidding started at five hundred euros. A world-renowned horse-trainer from the same village as the artist quickly jumped in with a bid of one thousand. With the fast jump in bids everyone in the room was suddenly alert. This was followed by a counter-bid from the owner of a hotel chain for five thousand. Sensing competition, Jerry threw his hat in the ring with a bid of eight thousand, although Donnacha was certain that Jerry didn't even know what he was bidding on, given the amount of champagne he had consumed.

Donnacha decided it was time to really show them what he was all about. Until now Elenore had been sitting quietly beside him with a faintly amused look on her face but, as he raised his hand and shouted out a bid for ten thousand euros, he heard her gasp beside him. A swift kick was delivered to his shin from under the table.

Elenore was not the only one who was stunned. The entire room was now buzzing as if it had been injected with a shot of electricity. This was the most exciting thing that had happened at a social event in months. Jerry caught the glare Elenore gave Donnacha and, never one to shy away from causing trouble, added a bid for twelve thousand, drawing gasps from the crowd.

Donnacha could feel Elenore's nails digging into his forearm by way of warning, but decided to pay no heed and, grinning over at Jerry, shouted out: 'Fifteen thousand euros!'

This time the crowd was silent. Even for the well-heeled in the audience, this was beyond their usual excesses. Donnacha knew there would be hell to pay from Elenore, not to mention the fact he was throwing away fifteen thousand on something that probably wasn't worth even a tenth of that. But it was worth it. The looks on the faces of the audience made it worth every penny. Donnacha O'Callaghan was a man of substance and every single person in the room tonight knew it.

The woman on the stage announced that the painting was sold and Donnacha jumped out of his seat and ran onto the stage. He grabbed the microphone from the bewildered MC and declared, 'I am delighted that tonight has been such a success and I am particularly delighted with the outcome of the auction.' He now looked towards Elenore. 'I've bought this painting for my beautiful partner Elenore Stack. Let's just say it's a late birthday present – so Happy Birthday, darling!'

Sitting in the audience, Elenore was overcome with mortification. She would kill Donnacha – not only for the ridiculous waste of money but for making a show of her like this. Besides, her birthday was almost a month ago and he'd already bought her an expensive present – what was he talking about? Why was he making such an over-the-top gesture? There was absolutely no need.

Blushing with embarrassment, she looked at the ridiculous painting. If he thought she was going to hang a picture of a used tampon on the walls of Cavendish he had another think coming.

CHAPTER 4

1922

Cavendish Hall
25th September 1922

Dear Diary

Sometimes I hate living here more than anything in the world. Today Mama forbade me to go out to walk in the woods alone. She said it has become dangerous and if I want to go walking I have to ask her permission. If she is not here, I must await her return. Mama can be very stupid. She does not understand that I am not a child any more and it is 1922. Why can she not understand that it is no longer like it was when she was young? Some women can even vote now, and our lives no longer revolve around finding a suitable husband.

That is, of course, another problem for her. She desperately wants me to get married but cannot think where she is going to find someone who lives up to the massive expectations of Papa and her. There is a definite lack of eligible gentlemen here in County Cork.

Annabel Carbery's mother is planning to take her to London after Christmas for the Season, in the hope of finding a suitable husband to marry her off to. I overheard Lady Carbery tell Mama that Annabel would settle for nothing less than an earl. If Mama could take me to London for the Season she would jump at the chance, but Papa says it is not possible. I cannot understand why. I always thought I would go, and Mama always talked to me about it when I was a child. That was before, and things have changed now. Instead I am stuck here with no excitement or parties to attend. All we can do is visit our neighbours and even those visits are becoming less frequent. Papa says there is a civil war going on in this 'godforsaken country' and travelling the roads is no longer safe.

That is why he gave me this diary. He says writing in it will give me something to do and keep me occupied. I cannot imagine what I am going to write here. I have never heard of anyone starting a diary in September. Why he did not give it to me as a Christmas present last year I do not understand.

I am left with no one but Mildred and Taffy for company and, even though I love them more than anything, a dog and a horse don't allow for excellent conversation.

However, Mama might have said I cannot go walking in the woods, but she never said anything about taking Taffy out for a ride! There is, of course, the problem of not always having someone to tack her up for me. We still have one stable boy, but he works on the farm also now. There are only two horses left in the stables now, apart from Taffy, so there's not much work for him to do there. Papa says his farm work is more important than tacking up Taffy so that I can ride out. If Tadgh, the stable boy, is busy I must wait until Papa is in the mood to help me and Papa's moods are getting worse and worse all the time. I will just have to learn how to do it myself. It cannot be that difficult after all.

Sometimes I think back to what it used to be like here at Cavendish. When all the servants were here and there were always guests coming and going from the house. Now there is only Mrs. Carey and May who work in the house and they do not even live here. When I was a little girl there were more servants than I could count and there seemed to be a ball every month: a Summer Ball, a Hunt Ball, a New Year's Eve ball. There was always something to plan and look forward to and I couldn't wait to grow up so that I could be part of it all instead of being shepherded to bed by Nanny when the fun was just beginning. Now I am finally the age I always wanted to be and, instead of having a lovely exciting life, I am stuck here with not even one person my own age to talk to. Life is very unfair.

I wonder where Nanny is now? I know I am too old to have a nanny but, even so, I could always talk to her. She is probably looking after another little girl somewhere. I do miss her, but I certainly do not miss my old governess. I am glad she is no longer here and that my formal education is finally over. I remember how she used to rap me on the knuckles if I did not say my French verbs correctly. I feel sorry for whatever poor young lady she is teaching now.

I do hope this war ends soon. Papa says he does not know what is going to happen. He cannot understand why they (I assume when he says 'they' he means the Catholic Irish) were not happy with what they got. He says that in time they will realise what a stupid mistake they have made. Sometimes I listen to what he and Mama talk about at dinner but other times I make up stories in my head. I listened for a little while at dinner yesterday. Papa said they made a mistake even trying to establish a republic and they should have learned their lesson and been happy with the Treaty. He said he was willing to go along with that for the sake of peace, as long as the country remained part of the Empire, but this situation of fighting against each other in ditches is ridiculous. What sort of a country was it where they all turned on each other? It was clear that his suspicions that they were nothing more than a pack of barbarians had been true all along, he said.

Mama just nodded like she always does. I think most of the time she doesn't even understand what he is talking about. I think Papa can be very unfair sometimes. I don't think the people that live in the village are barbarians. Look at Mrs. Carey who works in the kitchen. She is very kind and gives me the best apple dumplings without telling Mama.

I saw her son Tadgh, our stable boy, last week in the woods. Despite Mama forbidding me from walking out on my own I sneaked out anyway and she never knew. I told Mama and Papa that I was going to the library to read and I knew they would play cards for hours after dinner. I took a candle with me, went down the back stairs and out through the long dark tunnel to the farmyard, which is easy to do now as there are so few servants to run into. There I met Mildred and we escaped into the woods. I was only walking for five minutes or so when I saw him ahead of me. I would have ignored him, but Mildred started barking and he heard her and turned around. When he saw me, he tipped his cap and said, 'Hello, m'lady.'

That was the height of excitement in my life this week. I wonder what he was doing walking in the woods? I don't think he should be in the woods. He should go straight home as soon as he is finished his work. I did not say anything to Papa though as I did not want to get Tadgh into trouble. He is probably just bored like me. I wonder what he does when he is not working? Perhaps he helps Mrs. Carey in their own house.

I do not usually pay him any attention, but I did notice he suddenly looks a lot taller and although I would never say this to anyone, only my diary, he has become quite handsome. I never noticed that before. I am sixteen now though, so it must be natural to notice these things. Mama would be very shocked if she ever heard me say that!

I might go down to the stables now and see if he can tack up Taffy for me. It might be fun to go for a ride though Mama would be very annoyed if she were to find out. It is strange as you get older that your parents no longer know everything about you, but I suppose that is life.

I will write again soon.

TRHLEC xxx

CHAPTER 5

Karen turned over in her bed, her head throbbing from the pain of the headache that accompanied the flu she couldn't appear to shake. A scream erupted from the bathroom, where her eleven-year-old son, Aaron, had gone moments earlier to take a shower.

Dripping in water, Aaron came into her bedroom, a towel wrapped around his waist. 'The hot water is gone, Mum.'

'Oh, love, were you frozen? I'll organise someone to take a look at it. You go on and get dressed. You don't need a shower now. Aren't you going to play football anyway?'

Aaron nodded at her and left the room. He had started to show full-on teenage traits in the last few months even though he was still only eleven – showering and putting gel in his freshly washed hair was becoming a daily occurrence. He'd also shot up in height and was becoming more handsome by the day.

The water had been causing trouble for a few days now and Karen feared there was something wrong with the boiler. She'd have to contact the landlord to come fix it. The apartment block she lived in was relatively new and in an extremely upmarket area of Cork City. It had been built by the property-development company owned by her ex-husband. It always amazed Karen that so many things could go wrong in such a new development. There were constant issues with the heating and the plumbing. Any time she mentioned this to Donnacha he told her she was being ridiculous. He claimed the building was state-of-the-art and the man who bought it and who was now Karen's landlord wouldn't have paid top-dollar for anything second-rate.

All Karen wanted to do was bury her head under the pillow. Her landlord was not an easy man to deal with. She knew it would take him ages to get someone out to look at it. She could always ask Donnacha for the money and tell the landlord she would hold the amount it cost back from next month's rent. But that would involve calling her ex-husband and with her head groggy from the flu she just couldn't face that right now.

Donnacha paid the rent on the apartment along with all the utility bills. He also paid for the fees at the private school which he insisted on Aaron attending. To the outside world it appeared that Donnacha was beyond generous and he certainly couldn't be accused of shirking on his responsibilities. But the problem was the mind games he played with Karen that nobody knew about. The agreed amount of money to cover the rent and the bills was handed over every month but not before Donnacha made her sit down and go through the cost of every bill from the previous month. He insisted on being provided with proof of payment. As if she was going to use the money for the ESB bill to head off on a shopping spree!

If she called him and asked him to organise someone to fix the boiler, he would use the opportunity to remind her of how much she depended on him. He would belittle her for being unable to support herself. She knew in the end he would give her the money, but she wondered was it worth the psychological warfare that would be waged on her before she got it.

The truth of it was she would love to be able to work full-time and earn enough money to at least be able to pay half the rent. But she couldn't. Her own mother, Gretta, had been diagnosed with dementia a few years back and could not be left on her own in the house. Luckily Karen had the support of her next-door neighbour Maggie who kept an eye on Gretta, allowing Karen to go to work three days a week. She didn't know what she would do without Maggie. It wasn't that she was particularly career-driven but going out to work for those few days did keep her sanity intact.

Another issue with Donnacha was his insistence on sending Aaron to that damn school. If she could turn back time she would have insisted that he go to one of the local public schools. In her opinion the school was nothing but a breeding ground for entitled little brats and its whole ethos appeared to be based on rewarding the wealthy. Morals and manners didn't appear to be part of the teaching curriculum and, although she was happy with the top-notch education Aaron was receiving, she found herself having to chide him far too often – for speaking in a silly accent or acting like a spoilt brat.

Donnacha paid the school fees without question every year and made sure that Aaron had all the required kit so that he wouldn't stand out amongst the other students. That was typical of Donnacha, of course – he'd pay the fees because if he didn't it wouldn't be long before all the other parents would know about it. Donnacha wouldn't have anyone call him a cheapskate. That was him all over. She'd never met anyone so caught up in what other people thought.

Pulling herself out of the bed, she walked into the room next door to check on her mother. Gretta was sleeping peacefully, even though it was after nine o'clock. Guilt overtook her once again. If she was a good daughter, she would stay at home full-time and take care of her mother. It would be repayment for all those years

Gretta had stayed at home, looking after her and her brother, sacrificing her freedom to be the typical Irish mammy. But Karen couldn't do it. She needed that time out of the house. She needed to feel like she was earning something of her own, small as it was, and not depending entirely on Donnacha to support her.

Karen thought back to when she and Donnacha had first met. He had money back then, but nothing compared to what he had now. Donnacha had amassed his real wealth over the last ten years. He hadn't been the cocky businessman when they'd first met either. Like Donnacha, Karen had grown up in inner-city Dublin. She was in her final year at school when she first caught the attention of the very handsome Donnacha O'Callaghan. Donnacha was still working in Lawlor's Estate Agents in Baggott Street and living in a flat in Rathmines, which at the time had seemed like the height of sophistication to Karen. She had met him in a nightclub in town – he'd come to her rescue, after a barman refused to serve her, rightly guessing that she was yet to turn eighteen.

They immediately embarked on a passionate courtship. Karen had been swept off her feet by this man who had so much ambition and was very different from anyone she had gone out with before. His youthful good looks meant it was a while before Karen realised the age-gap and that Donnacha, at thirty years old, was almost thirteen years older than her. At the time the age-difference seemed massive, but he had treated her in a way she was unused to and he had money. He could take her places that were beyond the realms of possibility for any of her previous boyfriends.

Karen was the only one who knew about Donnacha's past. He still talked about it back then. There had still been some innocence about him and he didn't have the chip on his shoulder that appeared to weigh him down in later years.

Within six months she was pregnant and had dropped out of

school without completing her Leaving Cert. He had stood by her which was more than she could say for some of the boyfriends of her classmates who had succumbed to the same fate. He had organised a flat for them to move into. It was still no palace but a step up from the one he was sharing with his friends. Karen's mother, after the initial shock of the pregnancy, had been thrilled.

Karen had never excelled academically but Gretta had always said that wasn't important. She was pretty, and she was street-wise. Her mother had always had faith that when an opportunity presented itself Karen would not be one to miss it. As far as Gretta was concerned, Donnacha was exactly the opportunity Karen needed. This sharply dressed man was clearly on the up and all Karen needed to do was be a good wife and reap the benefits of what Gretta was convinced would be Donnacha's very successful life.

They were married before Aaron was born and Karen remembered the excitement with which she had looked forward to their lives together. Donnacha was working on some project which he assured her was going to be their golden ticket. He was still working in Lawlor's at the time but had already set up the business with Jerry on the side. Together, he and Jerry had persuaded old Mr. Lawlor to come in with them on the purchase of a massive piece of farmland in South County Dublin. Donnacha and Jerry's new business venture would be responsible for developing the land. The project had been a huge success and it was at that time that Donnacha had left his job at Lawlor's and they had moved to Cork – the second city would be the headquarters of his and Jerry's business.

It was a couple of years after Aaron's birth that things began to change and, as time went by, they continued to get worse. Even though she long suspected that Donnacha was being unfaithful to her, it was not until Aaron was about seven that she knew for certain. Or maybe she had known for certain from the start but just didn't want to admit it to herself.

The signs became less and less subtle over the years and, in the end, she waited outside the office one night, hidden in the shadows. She had hoped against hope she was wrong. He had called her earlier in the day to say he had to work late as it was coming towards the end of the financial year and he was chained to his desk. By six he had walked out the front door and into a nearby pub.

She watched from the front window of the pub as he walked the length of the bar to a discreet corner down the back where he seated himself beside a woman. The woman had wrapped her arms around Donnacha's neck and he had pulled her close to him as they shared a passionate kiss.

Karen had wanted to run into the pub, pull the two of them apart, and slap Donnacha across the face – but, not wanting to fit the stereotype of every scorned woman, she managed to keep her dignity intact.

The real fighting only started after they split up. She had settled in the apartment and had been eager to get on with her life. But soon after the split her mother had become ill and, even though she could not deny that Donnacha kept a roof over her head, having to constantly justify what she was doing with every penny he gave her was driving her insane.

She was concerned about the future and how she was going to look after her mother. Gretta's health was declining rapidly. Karen feared that the day would come when she would no longer be able to take care of her and would need professional help. That would mean either putting her mother in a home or paying someone to help take care of her full-time. Unless she had some kind of nest-egg, both of these options were beyond her reach.

Now she was facing the uphill battle that would be their divorce settlement. Donnacha had employed a team of slick lawyers while Karen had to make do with what she could afford. This stretched to cover the costs of a solicitor in whom she didn't have much faith. It wasn't the solicitor's fault – no one stood a chance against Donnacha's legal team.

Initially she had hoped the divorce would be relatively straightforward. She never had to chase Donnacha for the money to cover the rent, bills or Aaron's school fees. She had assumed he would be willing to pay a lump sum to ensure her financial future was secured, in addition to the maintenance. He was a very wealthy man, after all.

She and Donnacha had never owned a home so there would be no proceeds from the sale of a family home to divide between them. That left his business. This was now proving to be a grey area as he had set it up just before he and Karen got married. In addition, what Donnacha had presented to her solicitor as a valuation of the business was laughable. She would need money behind her to fight against what Donnacha was proposing. She hadn't taken into consideration that she would need money for things like getting her own independent valuation of his business. It looked like it was going to be a costly and complicated divorce.

She did have one advantage though that Donnacha had no idea about. She knew about his past but, even better, she knew what had happened with that first piece of farmland in South Dublin. She knew he had been involved in the payment of money to a high-profile politician to ensure the land was rezoned, allowing him to build on it. Today you couldn't open a paper without reading about that kind of thing. There was a big tribunal in progress in Dublin about similar things that had been happening with property developers and politicians.

Karen not only knew about it, but she had details. She knew dates when Donnacha had met with certain people and, even worse for him, she knew of one politician who had resisted his attempts at bribery. All it would take would be one phone call to the newspapers. With verification from that politician of what Donnacha had attempted to do, his career would be over.

Donnacha wasn't as smart as he liked to think. She knew he was convinced that he was the master of deception and she as his innocent little wife hadn't noticed what he was up to – too busy painting her nails to listen in on his many indiscreet telephone conversations.

Thinking back on it all made her more and more agitated. How dare he? And now, by all accounts, he was up to his old tricks. She had heard rumours circulating that he was carrying on behind that poor girl's back with anyone he could find who was stupid enough to fall into bed with him. Karen had never met Elenore but felt only sympathy for her. Aaron had nice things to say about her – how kind and quiet she was, how she listened to all Donnacha's crap – and how he feared that Elenore really wasn't that sure about all the work that was going on in her lovely old house.

Of course, the big old house must have a lot to do with Elenore's appeal for Donnacha. Karen had seen pictures of Elenore and, although she really was beautiful, she knew she wasn't Donnacha's type. She wasn't glamorous enough.

Karen really wanted a break. She was sick worrying about her future and sick of Donnacha and the manipulation he got away with over and over again. She'd had enough. She was going to do something about it. But now – at least until her mother woke up – all she could do was get back into bed and pull the duvet over her head.

CHAPTER 6

The week after the ball Donnacha travelled to Poland with Jerry on business. They were looking at the possibility of investing in a new development of apartments there. Elenore didn't usually like it when Donnacha went away on work trips, as she missed his presence in the house, but the atmosphere between them had soured considerably since the night of the ball. She felt like it was a good time for them to have a break from each other.

Donnacha's behaviour on the night had annoyed her greatly. It was bad enough that he had spent that much money on the awful painting, but his jumping on the stage and naming her had been beyond embarrassing. He had then spent the evening in the ear of Tim Collins the politician, and completely ignored her, failing to take her out on the dance floor even once.

It hadn't helped that the seating plan had placed her with Donnacha on one side and Jerry Reynold's wife Jennifer on the other. She found Jennifer difficult company and was never quite sure what to talk to her about. Jennifer's main interest appeared to be what married man was sleeping with someone else's wife. Elenore didn't find this type of gossip in the least bit interesting and what puzzled her most was that she strongly suspected Jerry was not faithful to his wife. She wondered if Jennifer had the same suspicions of her husband and chose to turn a blind eye, or if she trusted Jerry completely and was simply not worried by his incessant flirting with other women. Donnacha was always telling her tales of Jerry going for nights out on the town and not returning home until the next morning, with no explanation as to his whereabouts. Elenore didn't understand how a relationship could operate like that. As she had listened to Jennifer talk on and on about all the various affairs that were taking place, involving the very people in the room that night, she began to think that maybe solid, stable marriages weren't all that usual any more.

Elenore had come from a secure and loving home, where she had been protected by the care of her parents. When she was growing up, even though there were only the three of them – in addition to the array of family dogs that had made the house a home over the years – Cavendish had always been filled with love and laughter. Violet and Jonathan doted on each other and were always holding hands and sneaking kisses when they thought no one was looking. When she was a teenager, Elenore remembered finding this affection between them embarrassing. In later years, when she looked back on it and the security that the love between them had created for her, she knew that she wanted to find a man with whom she could have a relationship similar to that of her parents.

That was why, when Donnacha O'Callaghan had come into her life, she had been certain he was the one with whom she could create that longed-for stable relationship. Donnacha had come from a similar background to her father and had worked hard to create a secure future for himself. He was more outgoing than her father, as Jonathan, like his daughter, was not one who liked to be the centre of attention. But he made Elenore laugh and he saw things in a way that she didn't. He saw the potential of Cavendish and he wouldn't rest until he persuaded her that his vision was the right one for the house and for their future.

Elenore's father had bought Cavendish in the early 1960s. He had only been in his thirties at the time but had already made Stacks Department Store a hugely successful business. With his career looked after, he set about creating a family home for himself and his new wife. A new roof had to be put on and insulation put in. A new heating system that was state of the art for the 1960s was installed, ensuring the water coming from the new plumbing system could be warmed at the drop of a hat. The basic electricity system had been completely overhauled. Her parents had lovingly sourced furniture and dressings for the house from auctions and antique dealers up and down the country. Jonathan had also placed huge importance on preserving what remained of the existing original furniture.

Elenore remembered her father walking her around the house when she was a young child, pointing out all the improvements he had made – not that she took in much of all that technical detail at the time, but she loved the intimacy of the time spent with her father. Cavendish was a labour of love, her father said, and no house deserved care and attention more than it did. It had been sold by its original owners in the late 1920s after which time it was run as a convent. The nuns moved out to a more modern building in Cork City in the early 1950s and for almost a decade the house had lain idle, allowed to go to rack and ruin. Elenore knew now that what she had thought were chats with her father were in fact history lessons. Jonathan would tell her how many houses similar to Cavendish had been burned by Irish rebels as they didn't want the Anglo-Irish classes owning the vast land that surrounded them. He painted stories with his words, of how the house would have been when the original owners lived in it. He described great balls and hunting parties and carriages sweeping up the driveway, pouring out ladies dressed in silk ballgowns. Elenore, as a child, always wished she had been part of that family – imagining how she would travel everywhere in a carriage and wear long dresses and bonnets.

Jonathan would then put on a sad voice, telling her about the nuns who had taken over when the great family had left. There had been no more parties or hunting then until one day the nuns got very bored and decided they needed to move to the city and have some fun. But they loved the city so very much that they forgot about Cavendish. They even forgot to close the front door and grass began to grow up the steps and into the hall. A family of foxes moved into the drawing room and when finally the windows began to fall off, birds flew in and built their nests in Elenore's bedroom. Elenore had imagined them spending many happy hours flying all around the house. She had liked the idea of the animals and birds living there but she knew by her father's voice that the house must have been sad. She would feel bad for it because it didn't deserve to be forgotten like that. She would tug on her father's sleeve, prompting him to get back to the happy part of the story.

'That's when you found it, Daddy, didn't you?'

Jonathan would smile down at her and say, 'Yes, love, that's when I found it. I was out for a drive with your mother one day and we parked the car at the front gates. We had no idea what was inside the gates, but it was a lovely sunny day, so I said to your mother, "Let's take a walk and see what's in there".'

The young Elenore knew this part of the story by heart. 'And Mammy fell in love with it, didn't she?'

'She certainly did,' her father would answer. 'We climbed over the gate and walked the whole way up the avenue and I remember we were laughing and laughing. To this day I don't know what we were laughing about, but we came around the last bend and there was Cavendish in front of us. She stopped and looked at the house and, when she turned towards me, I saw the most beautiful vision: your mother, framed by Cavendish, with the sun beaming down on her lovely golden hair and a smile lighting up her face – and I knew then that this was our home. I knew if I fixed it and we moved in, I would be able to keep a smile like that on her face all her life – and sure isn't she still smiling to this day?'

Remembering this story and all the other many stories her father told her as a child often brought a tear to Elenore's eye. She missed her parents every day. Her father's protective presence in her life and her mother's wit and wisdom. The home that they had created really was their legacy and it fell on Elenore's shoulders to ensure that legacy continued.

She thought back to the 'great family' her father had referred to. They had been minor aristocracy and had built the house in the early part of the nineteenth century. As was the case with many houses like it which had survived the Irish War of Independence, followed by the Civil War, they had presumably sold it when the political situation meant that living off the estate and the hard work of its tenant farmers was no longer a viable option.

Elenore thought it strange that she didn't know a huge amount about the Cavendish family. It had occurred to her, when she was making her plans to run the house as an exclusive guest house, that being able to outline the history of the house would be of real interest to the guests who would come and stay in it. She knew there were estate records in existence, possibly in the National Library in Dublin. Donnacha said the idea of boring people with the history of the house wasn't something they needed to put too much effort into. She had never followed up with her plan to find the records, but it was still something she was determined to do when she finally had some spare time.

Thoughts of the history of the house drew her eye over to the diary on the kitchen worktop which Donnacha had mentioned to her the night they were getting ready for the ball. She hadn't thought about it again until she saw one of the builders making his way towards a skip with it the following day. She had stopped him from throwing it away and, when she took it out of his hand, she had felt how fragile it was, as if handled it too roughly it could very easily disintegrate. The builder informed her Donnacha had told him to dump any rubbish they found and had specifically pointed to the book when giving the order.

She had brought it into the kitchen, placed it gently on the kitchen table and, after making herself a cup of coffee, sat down to examine it. Intrigued to find it was indeed a diary, she had skimmed over it but the noise of the builders banging away upstairs meant she hadn't been able to concentrate for very long.

Her mind had wandered to thoughts of who it was had written it. It was from 1922 so it was likely to be a member of the Cavendish family. The entry she managed to get through was written by a young girl who seemed even younger than her years with her childish references to her 'Mama' and her clear boredom at being imprisoned, as she seemed to view it, at Cavendish.

With the more loud bangs coming from upstairs, her thoughts moved on to what would have happened to the diary if she hadn't happened across the builder about to deliver it into a skip, never to be seen again. Suddenly she was very angry. This was her third time to be angry in as many days, but this anger was worse than what she had felt when she saw a builder sawing wood on her piano or when Donnacha had bought that wretched painting. This was teetering on rage and that rage was brewing into a fast-moving storm pointed straight in the direction of Donnacha.

How dare he, she thought. Here was something, over eighty years old, appearing to be a handwritten account of life at Cavendish, and Donnacha had directed one of his workers to throw it on the scrapheap?

'How could he?' she asked aloud and Alfie lifted his head from his basket beside the fire and cocked it to one side, looking quizzically at her.

She began to wonder just how much Donnacha really understood the house or cared about maintaining its integrity. The only answer she could come up with was that he obviously *didn't* care if he could so carelessly discard something that could shine a light on what life had been like in the house all those years ago. It had been her greatest wish to bring the house back to what it had been in its heyday. A place where guests were welcomed as part of the family. Donnacha had persuaded her that this wasn't such a good idea and, if she wanted Cavendish to remain in their family for future generations, she would have to think bigger than that. She had thought bigger and was going along with his plans wholeheartedly – but, if he had so little respect for the history of the house, then she had bought into those plans under false assumptions.

She calmed herself down over the next day and decided she needed to sit down and have a serious talk with Donnacha on his return from Poland, but that wasn't for another three days. At a loose end and eager to share her anger with someone, she decided to invite her oldest friend, Leslie, over for dinner.

Elenore and Leslie had met on the first day of primary school and had been inseparable until universities at opposite ends of the country had separated them thirteen years later. They had remained close over the years. Leslie had moved to London, got married and divorced. Eventually she had come home and settled down with the boy, now a very handsome man, who had been her first love in her school days. Leslie often joked about all the time she would have saved, not to mention the money spent on a costly divorce, if she had just married Ben straight out of school.

The two friends delighted in the fact that they now lived back in such proximity to each other, just like their schooldays. They had both valued the friendship they had, whereby they could go for months without seeing each other and with one phone call pick up exactly where they had left off. Now they could see each other again as often as they wished.

Always eager to catch up on the latest happenings at Cavendish, Leslie immediately accepted Elenore's invite to dinner and added, 'I suppose, seeing as you have a free house, what with Donnacha being in Poland, I had better stay the night with you. I can't bear the thought of you wandering around in that big empty house all alone.'

Elenore loved the way Leslie referred to her being home alone as 'having a free house' as if they were seventeen years old and not in their thirties. She knew that Leslie staying over would mean a large amount of wine would be consumed and they would have great fun reminiscing about old times.

She spent the evening cooking up a storm in the kitchen, with Alfie following her every move as the delicious smells grew stronger and stronger. Elenore loved to cook but her dishes were always simple and hearty. She had four or five dishes that she stuck to and all had been her favourite things cooked by her mother when she was a child. For dinner she was cooking roast lamb with all the trimmings and had stocked up on a few bottles of Malbec to accompany it. Donnacha had once described Elenore's cooking as being just like her personality: straightforward and honest.

Initially she had thought that they should eat in the dining room but on reflection decided that it was far too formal for a catch-up between old friends. Not to mention the fact that the problems with the heating meant they would probably freeze to death. Instead, she turned off the main light in the kitchen and lit the room with lamps and an array of candles.

When the doorbell rang promptly at eight o'clock, greeted by an outburst of barking from Alfie, she surveyed the room and found she was delighted with the atmosphere the soft lighting created. The basement kitchen was large, but the warmth of the

Aga worked wonders in heating it up. It was the perfect setting for an evening of wine and laughter.

Running up the back stairs to the main hall, she opened the front door to find Leslie, armed with a bunch of lilies and two bottles of wine. Ben waved at her from his car as he turned in the drive.

'Is Ben not going to join us for a drink?' she asked her friend.

'Join us for a drink? Highly unlikely – he's so excited by the prospect of a night without me, sitting in front of the television with a can, watching the soccer without any interruptions, I'm surprised he had time to stop the car to let me out.'

Sure enough, Ben was speeding down the avenue.

Elenore smiled at Leslie, loving the easy way they fell so comfortably into each other's company. She knew Leslie's exasperation with Ben's plans for the evening was fake as it was clear the two remained firmly besotted with each other after five years of marriage.

Elenore directed Leslie into the house and down towards the kitchen where she relieved her of her bounty and, placing the flowers in an old jug, gave them pride of place in the centre of the kitchen table.

'Right, the dinner won't be ready for another fifteen minutes so pull up a pew there by the fire. I'll pour us a glass of red and I want to hear all your news.'

Taking out two of her crystal wineglasses, she poured them a glass each as Leslie made herself comfortable. Elenore was delighted to see her friend had finally put on some weight. She thought back to the time when Leslie's first marriage fell apart and she had rushed to London one cold November weekend to provide her with some much-needed support. Shock had hit her at the sight of Leslie when she had answered the door to the grotty flat in Hackney. Her friend, who had always been brimming with good health and happiness, had been reduced to little more than skin and bone. Her previously lustrous auburn hair, which had always been her crowning glory, was hanging lankly and her eyes appeared to be sunken into her face and were surrounded by dark circles.

Elenore had spent the weekend with her and together they had come up with a plan of how Leslie would get out of the awful situation she had found herself in. She had admitted that marrying Gary, who she had known for only six months, had been a stupid decision. Gary, the up-and-coming artist, turned out to be capable of drawing little more than the Dole. What little money he did have, he spent on a mix of alcohol and cocaine. He had shown his true colours only days after the wedding. Leslie was working in Selfridges and knew she was only days away from being fired. The entire situation was grim.

What had finally driven her to get some help had been coming home to the flat one evening to find Gary had cleared out all the clothes she had got at a severely discounted rate from the high-end department store – presumably to sell. It was part of her contract that she had to wear the clothes sold in the store and without them or any money to buy more, discounted or not, she was going to be fired from the job. With that came the prospect of no way to pay the rent and being cast out onto the streets of London. All Gary's cool arty friends, who had welcomed her so warmly when they had first become a couple, had disappeared. As if this had not been enough to take on board, Gary was getting more and more aggressive with each passing day and she feared it was only a matter of time until his shouting turned to more violent behaviour.

Elenore had barely given her the time to tell the awful truth of her situation before calling her father and getting him to book them into a hotel for the weekend using his credit card. Jonathan didn't have to be asked twice: he had known Leslie since she was a child and he viewed her as a second daughter. They hadn't taken anything from the flat except Leslie's handbag and passport. By the Sunday evening, they were on a flight back to Cork.

Leslie had spent the next few weeks resting at Cavendish, ashamed to let her parents know she was home. Jonathan and Violet had looked after her until she had felt strong enough to face the fallout from her ill-fated marriage.

It turned out leaving Gary had been easier than actually divorcing him and it had taken several years before Leslie managed to free herself of her status as his wife. He had no interest in being married to her but his frequent disappearances into the underbelly of London, missing appointments and court dates, had meant the divorce process had dragged out for a long time.

The Leslie who sat in front of the fire in Elenore's kitchen this evening was very different from the girl who had returned from London. She had gone home to her parents, who in the end had been incredibly supportive. After a while she went back to college to do a diploma in public relations and eventually set up her own highly successful PR firm in Cork City.

A couple of years after reuniting with Ben, her first love, she had downsized the PR firm, with the plan being for them to start a family soon after they were married. Five years on and there was still no sign of any children. Elenore knew a child would make Leslie happy beyond her wildest dreams but Leslie was wise enough to appreciate that she had a man who she loved dearly and a pretty nice life. As she said herself, they'd keep trying – they hadn't run out of time just yet. Elenore wondered for a minute as she walked over to hand the glass of wine to Leslie if her weight-gain meant there was some news on the baby-front but quickly realised she wouldn't be waiting so eagerly for a glass of wine if she had just found out she was pregnant.

The two friends settled in for their cosy chat, catching up on all the news from the village: who was getting married, who was pregnant and who was building a new house. Unlike the gossip

Elenore had often listened to from Jennifer, Jerry's wife, the two women relished sharing good news about their old school friends. If either of them had been made aware of any bad news they felt genuine sympathy for whatever former classmate had had a trauma come to their door. Both Elenore and Leslie had been visited by pain and sadness in one way or another over the years and never found satisfaction in someone else being affected by misfortune.

They soon moved on to dinner and laughed their way through it. They remembered old stories from school, wondering what had become of former teachers and recalling the misery they had inflicted on them when they were children.

Two bottles of wine later the mood turned sombre when Leslie revealed that she had better enjoy her last night of drinking as she and Ben were due to embark on their third round of IVF the following week.

'I know we have a lovely life and I know I am so lucky to have found him again but sometimes our house is so quiet. We constantly make plans for holidays and weekends away catching up with old friends. Don't get me wrong, I know there are so many people with real problems – we are the lucky ones. But I sometimes catch Ben looking at a woman pushing a pram and he gets this sad look on this face. I know he wants a child more than anything. I am afraid of what might happen to us if I can't give him that. I am afraid of what might happen to me.'

Elenore reassured her friend that Ben was a good, kind man who loved her more than anything and, baby or not, she knew that that was never going to change.

'You will have a baby. I know it. You are still young and healthy – just give it some more time.'

Leslie nodded in agreement. 'Yes, you're right. I do have a good one in him. I shouldn't doubt him and if it's meant to be, it's meant to be, right? Now, never mind me and my sad story, feeling all sorry for myself — you haven't told me anything about you. What's going on with you and Donnacha? Will we hear the pitter-patter of tiny feet from you two any time soon?'

Elenore was surprised at Leslie's thinking that she and Donnacha were at the stage of planning a family. She sometimes suspected that Leslie didn't have a lot of time for Donnacha. She had never come straight out and said she didn't like him, but her friend often questioned her about how he was treating her and if he was perhaps being given too much power when it came to the remodelling plans at Cavendish.

'Oh no, we're not even thinking that way just now. Maybe after the divorce and once we have all the work finished here, we can start making those kinds of plans.'

Elenore hesitated and Leslie immediately picked up on it.

'Spit it out there, girl — what is it you want to say?'

'Look, I am going to tell you something that is annoying me. But I don't want you to hold it against Donnacha when it's all sorted, and I am not annoyed any more. Promise me?'

Leslie nodded and Elenore then proceeded to tell her about the night at the ball. She told of the ridiculous amount of money spent on the painting, the way Donnacha had behaved, how he had ignored her for most of the night and had been much more interested in who he could network with. Could she be with someone who would spend such an extravagant amount of money on a painting? And a horrible distasteful painting at that which had possibly been bought just in order to draw attention to himself?

She then went on to tell Leslie about the diary and how finding out that Donnacha had been happy to dispose of it, which might seem like a small thing, had really got to her. It made her question if he understood her connection to Cavendish and the importance of the house to her.

Elenore's story came out fast as if she couldn't wait to get the words out. 'I know I'm being silly but why wouldn't something like that matter to him? If a piece of Cavendish's history doesn't matter to him, it makes me wonder what else doesn't matter to him that I haven't thought about.'

'Listen here, that is a completely legitimate concern,' said Leslie. 'This is your home – it's your history. I know how much it means to you and how much love you have for it. Not to mention the fact that you have been living on a building site for the last few weeks. It's perfectly natural to have doubts but, Elenore, it is your house. You have the right to call a halt to all of this work at any time, maybe even just to take a breather. Would that be an option? Donnacha is obviously flush with cash if he can blow that kind of money on a stupid painting. If Cavendish isn't paying its way in the timeframe he has in mind, would that be a huge deal? You two aren't exactly going to starve, now are you?'

Elenore reflected on what Leslie had said for a moment and then nodded. 'Yes, you're right. I hadn't thought about it that way. Actually, I suppose I'm the one putting the pressure on. After Dad died I gave myself a window of time to turn the house into something commercial. But, as you say, what's the hurry?' She paused. 'Mind you, if I had stuck to my original plan, the work that I had wanted to do would be long completed by now.'

As the words came out, she wondered if this was true. She thought back to what her original plans had been. Before her father died, he had done his best to ensure the house was structurally sound, but a lot more needed to be done. The windows needed to be treated. The heating system had been constantly on the verge of collapse until Donnacha had it removed and began to replace it. She also had other plans: remodelling of the bedrooms in the attic, which had originally been the servants' quarters – she'd wanted to make them suitable for guests. And improvements in the kitchen would be necessary to allow her to cater for larger numbers than the house was used to feeding in modern times.

Then there were the stables. She would need to make them

suitable to house more horses. And, indeed, buy more horses to use for hacking. That wouldn't happen now. Donnacha maintained that people didn't want to be outside on horses when they could be inside in luxury.

There was also a barn on the estate that she had envisaged would make a fantastic coffee shop if group bookings slowed at any time. She would be able to fall back on the business of opening the gardens for people on day trips to wander around and stop off for a refreshing cup of coffee or snack. Donnacha had immediately dismissed this as far too provincial, saying that the guests who stayed at the house wouldn't want to see locals wandering around, interrupting their expensive holiday. Elenore had disagreed with this and felt strongly that both enterprises could run happily side by side. But, again she had gone with Donnacha, persuading herself that he had done this kind of thing before. Never with a guest house or a hotel but property development was property development and he was the expert not her.

'Penny for your thoughts?' said Leslie, raising an eyebrow. 'Or maybe another glass of wine for them?' She waggled the bottle.

Elenore sighed and held out her glass. 'You know, thinking about it, I suppose my original plans were unrealistic. I mean, they were modest compared to Donnacha's but too ambitious and costly without his management and financing. I need to remind myself that it is Donnacha's money that has been spent making the changes so far – and his energy. I should just relax and let him get on with it.'

Leslie grimaced. 'If you can live with that.'

'It's just that I feel I have very little control – that it's all been taken away from me. I can't even imagine what the house is going to look like when it's finished. I heard him on the phone the other day talking to someone about buying bathroom fittings in bulk.'

'In bulk? What did he mean by that? You have three bathrooms on the first floor and one on the second? Is four bulk? Maybe it is?'

Elenore shook her head. 'I don't think four is bulk and, when I queried him on it, he said he was just doing some research. In case we ever decided to do more with the house. What more could he want to do? It's not going to be the kind of place where every room has an en-suite bathroom – imagine the work that would involve – knocking walls, basically redesigning whole floors – and then where would *we* be? Sleeping in one of the outbuildings so our paying guests can avail of my home?'

The two women laughed at the idea but then caught each other's eye and wondered if such an idea was really beyond the realms of Donnacha's far-reaching ambitions.

'Okay, we seem to keep coming back to not very pleasant topics of conversation tonight,' said Leslie, 'between me and my infertility problems and you and this big old house. I thought we were here to catch up and have some fun. Let me see this diary!'

Elenore went to the kitchen dresser and gently took the diary down and the two friends spent some time poring over it, dipping into it here and there.

'This is amazing – wow!' said Leslie. 'Imagine this has been in the house all these years and no one ever came across it before! I wonder did your parents know it was here?'

'I don't think so. I'm sure Dad would have told me about it if he knew of its existence. He used to talk about the Cavendish family alright – about a fire here in the 1920s and that the family sold up soon after that. He knew there was a Lord and Lady Cavendish but he never mentioned a daughter. In fact, once when I was little I got upset at the thought that they had to leave Cavendish so he comforted me by saying that they didn't mind – because they had no children and they were going back to London to have grand old time! But, of course, that may not have been true …' She sighed. 'I know so little about the history of the house. The estate papers are not here. I've been meaning to take a trip to the National Library one day to have a good look at them.

I can't believe it's something I've never done. You'll have to come with me.'

Leslie agreed. 'Yes, of course. I'd love to. We can fit in a bit of shopping too. But where did the builders find the diary?'

'Well, that's the other exciting bit of news. Did I ever tell you what Dad used to say about there being a tunnel from here down to the farmyard?'

Leslie nodded. 'Oh, yes, I vaguely remember something about that. Remind me.'

'So, Dad used to talk about this tunnel that ran from the farmyard up to the house. I think it was probably used back in the day to bring supplies from the farm up to the kitchen. Anyway, when I was a child, he had it sealed off because he felt it wasn't safe. I hadn't thought about it in years and then for some reason, about a month ago, it came into my head and I mentioned it to Donnacha. Then, before he went to Poland, he said he had some news for me. He said he hadn't been able to get the idea of the tunnel out of his head and thought it would make a great addition to the house when we have guests coming here. He thinks it would have great potential to be used as part of those murder-mystery-weekends people love so much now. He wanted to see if it could be accessed before mentioning it to me as he didn't want me to be disappointed if it couldn't. So – the builders found the entrance to it down at the farmyard and have been working their way up through it. They couldn't figure out where it ended here in the house and were stuck for a while as seemingly part of it was unsafe – they were afraid the ceiling might fall in, so they put up scaffolding to take care of that and eventually they got to the end of it.'

Leslie jumped in. 'Oh my God – that's so exciting! Have you been in it yet?'

Elenore shook her head. 'No. The entrance from here is in one of the storerooms off the corridor that leads from the boot room.

They've managed to cut a hole in the wall where Dad had the original door sealed up. There was an old dresser in front of it that Dad must have put there for storage. You know how he never threw anything out even when it would never be used again. I've gone and had a good look at the entrance alright. The reason I haven't explored any farther is because things have been so frosty between Donnacha and me since the ball – I wouldn't give him the pleasure of asking him to walk down it with me. It's pitch dark. You can't see a thing – in the old days they must have used lamps of some kind. That's where the builder found the diary. It was somewhere at the farmyard end. He was clearing it out and he just came across it. Imagine!'

Elenore looked at Leslie and saw that she had that familiar look of what could only be described as devilment on her face.

'I think we should go have a look. I'm here with you now and we have Alfie. He'll keep us safe.'

Elenore looked at the little dog, not sure what assistance he would provide if the tunnel collapsed in on them.

'It's safe enough, isn't it? If the builders have walked through it and put up scaffolding in it, it must be okay, right? Where's your torch?'

Elenore knew there was no stopping her friend now. Her desire for having fun combined with too many glasses of wine was too much to call a halt to her plans.

'Okay, come on then. Isn't it amazing the bravery a few glasses of this stuff gives you?' Elenore clinked her glass against Leslie's and they both drank, then pulled their chairs out from the table and headed towards the entrance to the boot room that lay behind the kitchen. Elenore grabbed a torch off the dresser as she passed it and called on Alfie to follow them. Leaving the heat of the kitchen, they went out into the boot room. From the back of the room a door led to a corridor with a low ceiling and a concrete floor. There were numerous small doors off it.

'I remember playing hide and seek in here as a child and Mam used to go mad. She said it wasn't safe. Do you remember?'

Leslie nodded. 'When was the last time you were in here?'

'I honestly can't remember. We never use this part of the house at all. It's been left to its own devices for years.'

The light from the boot room dimmed as they moved forward and Elenore turned on the torch, revealing the massive spiderwebs that hung from the low ceiling.

'I hope you're not still afraid of spiders?' she said.

Leslie giggled nervously.

Coming to the end of the corridor Elenore stopped and opened one of the doors, revealing a small room full of junk, such as a couple of lopsided three-legged chairs, broken picture frames and old milk crates. A dresser stood in the centre of the floor having been moved from its previous position against the wall. The large hole that the builders had knocked out in the wall was big enough for a person to pass through. It gaped eerily with nothing but pitch blackness beyond it.

Elenore shone the torch down the dark tunnel. Looking at Leslie, she said, 'I'm terrified. This is bloody creepy – how stupid are we?'

Alfie ran ahead of them down the length of the tunnel.

'Look, Alfie certainly isn't sensing anything out of the ordinary,' said Leslie, 'and he might come across as brave but personally I think he's afraid of his own shadow.'

This made them laugh as in the torchlight they watched the confident little dog run into the darkness.

'Let's go back,' said Elenore. 'We've seen it! The rest of it is just the same.'

Leslie laughed. 'I suppose.'

Walking into the tunnel Elenore whistled for Alfie and called his name but he didn't return. They stood for a few minutes, continuing to call him, but still he didn't come back.

'I'll murder that little fecker! He's probably after getting the scent of a mouse or something. He'll never come back to us now.'

She shone the torch in Leslie's direction to see if her friend had any suggestions on how to summon Alfie.

'He's your dog. You really should learn to control him better. Leave him, I say.'

Elenore knew Leslie was teasing her and that she adored Alfie. 'You're right. I really should have taken your advice and spent the money on those obedience classes. Come on – we're going to have to follow him. It's freezing down here. The sooner we get him the sooner we can get back to the heat of the kitchen.'

They walked on. The tunnel's ceiling curved low over their heads. It was barely wide enough for the two of them to walk side by side which gave it a claustrophobic feel.

'I hope that battery lasts,' said Leslie.

'Don't say that.'

'I can see what Donnacha meant about it being used for murder-mystery tours. It certainly fits the bill.'

They finally came across Alfie. He had discovered a wooden door in the wall of the tunnel and was scraping at it furiously.

He stopped scraping and wagged his tail in welcome as they arrived.

'There you are, Alfie. What are you up to?' Elenore bent down and patted him on the head, relieved to find him.

'What has he found here?'

Elenore shone the torch at the door. There had been no doors off the tunnel until now.

'He's probably chased a mouse in there! If not a rat! *Ugh!*'

Using her full force, Elenore tried to push the door open but it wouldn't budge. Then Leslie put her weight against the door too, and between the two of them they managed to push it open.

Inside was a tiny room not much more than a couple of metres square. It was filled floor to ceiling with filing cabinets piled one on top of the other. On the floor lay an open foil wrapper containing a half-eaten mouldy sausage sandwich.

'Disgusting! Well, at least now we know what Alfie was so excited about.' Leslie picked up the tinfoil package with a tissue and moved it off the floor onto a cabinet. 'But what the hell are all these? These cabinets look fairly modern – they hardly belonged to your father?'

Elenore shook her head. 'No, definitely not. Dad had this place sealed off, remember? Did Donnacha put them here? But there's acres of space for storage in the house. Why would he be putting stuff in here?'

'Temporarily maybe? Before moving them into the house?'

'Doesn't make sense.' She shone the torch over them.

'Are they empty?'

Bending down, Elenore pulled open the drawer of the cabinet closest to her. It was full of filed papers. Taking one out and unfolding it, having to stretch her arms wide to open it fully, she saw that it was an architectural drawing from one of the first developments Donnacha had worked on in Cork.

'Well, this seems fairly old,' she said. 'He must be using this as a place to store paperwork from projects he has finished working on. I supposed you do need to keep all this stuff, probably for legal reasons or something, in case there are any problems in the future.'

Leslie pulled out another cabinet and riffled through the papers inside. They were drawings, solicitors' letters and information relating to planning applications.

'Oh, come on – let's get back to the kitchen,' Elenore said as Leslie pulled open another cabinet. 'I'd murder a cup of tea. Nothing exciting here. Look at us, pretending to be amateur Nancy Drews!'

'Hey! What's this?' Leslie said, startled. 'This one has Cavendish scribbled on the back of it.' She pulled a folded paper out and opened it, while Elenore shone the torch towards it.

It was an architectural drawing of Cavendish.

Elenore took out another sheet of paper from the same cabinet and it too was a drawing of her house. She checked out the other contents of the cabinet. They were all architectural plans of Cavendish Hall. There were over ten of them, all detailing plans for the house and the land around it. At a glance, none of them bore any resemblance to the plans she and Donnacha had discussed between them.

'What are these?' she said, bewildered.

Leslie quickly took control. 'Come on, let's get out of here, it's absolutely freezing. Take those with you – we'll take them up to the kitchen and take a proper look.'

Helping Elenore gather up the drawings, Leslie checked that Alfie was still beside them and they left the room.

They made their way back to the kitchen – glad to re-enter its warmth but anxious about what they were about to discover.

CHAPTER 7

Cavendish Hall,
5ᵗʰ October 1922

I am so very sorry, dear Diary, that I have ignored you for a while but finally something of excitement has happened to me. I am in love. Yes, I am in love. I cannot believe that I am writing this. It never occurred to me that something of such huge significance could happen to me and in such a short space of time. The last time I wrote I was very bored and no longer happy with my life here at Cavendish but in an instant all that has changed. I have read about love in some of the novels I found in the library. Mama would be shocked if she knew I was reading such books, but I have been able to read them in secret and now I truly understand what those heroines were talking about when they described the handsome gentlemen that they had fallen in love with.

I'm in love with Tadgh! I cannot think about anything but him. I think about him from the moment I awake in the morning until my eyes close last thing at night. I spend my days planning how and where we can meet safely. I imagine what it would be like if he were to kiss me. I wonder does he feel the same way about me. He must feel the same way about me. It is simply impossible that only one person could feel this way about another and that the other person does not reciprocate!

I wonder how I will know for certain that he does love me too. I wonder if he will try to kiss me. I imagine how I will tell Mama and Papa about our love. When Tadgh finally professes his undying love to me, we will have to make plans for our future together. I do not think he would be happy living here in Cavendish and I doubt Mama and Papa would want that. I think it would be better if we, after we get married, ask Papa if we can have one of the small cottages on the estate. Mrs. Carey will teach me to cook and bake and Taffy and Mildred can come live with us. We will be blissfully happy.

But of course, I have not told you how this all happened and, indeed, there are very many more things that must happen before we can be married. What if Tadgh does not wish to get married? Of course, I cannot think like that. I know he loves me. It is becoming clearer and clearer with every passing day.

After the last time I wrote to you, I was bored and frustrated with being stuck here in the house all the time. I went to the stables the very next day. By a stroke of divine luck or perhaps it was fate, Tadgh was there and not working on the farm. He got Taffy ready for me and I happily stood by and watched him as he did this. He is very manly. I dream of him taking me in his arms and kissing me.

When Taffy was ready, I stood up on the mounting block and Tadgh held her reins while I mounted her. I was almost about to leave him and be on my way when he spoke to me. He's never said a word to me before in my life except for 'Good morning, m'lady' and 'Good evening, m'lady'. But this time he said, 'I am sorry for bothering you, m'lady, but it is likely not very safe for you to be riding out in the woods alone.'

At first I didn't know how to respond to him. I was shocked that he had spoken to me. But thankfully I gathered myself together and said, 'Well, perhaps, Tadgh, you should accompany me — to keep me safe.'

He smiled up at me and my heart almost melted. 'That would be lovely, m'lady, but I have to work. I tell you what, I am going to start my work down on the farm now. Why don't I walk with you as far as there?'

It was the best thing I had ever heard. It's only a short trot down to the farm. I knew I would only be with him for a few more minutes but I was so happy at the thought of spending even a little more time in his company.

We left the stable yard together, me on Taffy and Tadgh walking along beside me. At first there was silence between us and I was unsure of whether to break it or not. But I thought I might never get a chance like this again and I must seize the opportunity.

I started by saying 'Do tell me, Tadgh, what do you do to ward off the boredom when you are not working? I do find it terribly boring here.'

I was outraged by his response as he laughed at me. No one had ever laughed at me before and I was not happy that he thought it was appropriate to do so.

'Have I said something to amuse you, Tadgh?' I asked him.

Again, he grinned and said, 'Nothing at all, miss. I apologise for laughing. I did not mean any harm at all.'

That might have been the end of our conversation. Tadgh didn't appear as if he was going to share what he does to keep himself occupied. But just then, and again I can only imagine that it was fate, something happened that I now understand would change my life forever. There was a loud bang, not too far away — a gunshot. Then Taffy reared up, throwing me from the saddle.

I got such a fright and felt very ashamed that I had not been able to control my animal in front of Tadgh, but it really was fate as Taffy was quite used to hearing gunshots — whether from poachers or the gamekeepers we used to have before.

Tadgh rushed straight over to me and taking both my hands helped me up off the ground.

'Are you alright, m'lady?' he asked.

I said I was and held on to his hands for a moment to catch my breath. They felt so warm and strong.

Then he said, 'It is because of that you shouldn't be riding out into the woods alone. It's not safe for you. Does the Master know you are here alone?'

I told him that indeed no, Papa did not know but that if I didn't have some way to escape from the house there was a strong probability that I would become insane. I told him that if he told anyone or tried to stop me from going out into the woods again, I would ensure he got into very real trouble.

Again, he laughed at me but this time I told him it was not funny at all. Papa would be even more angry if he found out Tadgh knew I was going to the woods alone and so he had absolutely no reason to laugh.

He agreed that I was probably right, and he certainly did not want to get in trouble with the Master and I then said the boldest thing I have ever said in my life.

'Well, what are we going to do about it, Mr. Carey? I need to get away from Cavendish and you are now my accomplice — therefore how are you going to help me?'

He suddenly became very serious. 'All I am going to do is to tell you it's dangerous. Have you any idea what is going on around here?'

I told him I knew there was a civil war going on but, war or no war, I was going to continue riding out and he could either help me or not.

Shaking his head, he finally agreed, although I am assuming he knew he must. If I told Papa that Tadgh was aware that I was riding in the woods, neither of us knew exactly how much trouble he might be in.

'Very well, m'lady, you've left me with no choice. I don't know what it is you expect me to do but, whatever it is, I suppose I am agreeing to do it.'

So, we made a plan that he would meet me twice a week for no more than twenty minutes — that was how long he could risk his absence from the stables or the farm going unnoticed.

We made our arrangements to meet at the stables, two days later, and with that he picked up Taffy's reins, brought her over to me and putting his hands around my waist hoisted me into the saddle.

'You have some cheek, m'lady, but I admire a bit of spirit in a girl. Now get on home and don't go out to those woods alone. There's plenty of parkland for you to ride on at the front of the house. Now, listen, when I see you again, if we meet anyone between the stables and the woods you must say you are having trouble with your saddle and I am walking beside you until you are sure it is alright. Once we get out into the woods it will be easy enough for us to go our separate ways if we hear anyone coming near us. But I am warning you. If we are ever in the woods and I tell you that you have to leave — don't ask me any questions. You have to promise me you will turn Taffy and ride straight back to the house just as fast as you can.'

I have no idea why he was being so dramatic, but I agreed to what he asked. With that he walked off towards the farm.

I thought I might die of excitement while I waited for our next meeting. But I didn't die and now I have met Tadgh three times and each time we are sharing more and more about ourselves.

Yesterday, we walked down to the stream together. When we walk, he leads Taffy. He said it is best if we stay away from certain parts of the woods, where he knows people meet. He didn't say who these people are, but I am beginning to think they may be some of the rebels. We heard gunshots two more times and each time Tadgh said it was nothing to worry about. I asked him how he knew that, and he said he just knew.

He is worried about Ireland — he started talking about the political situation on our second meeting but stopped as soon as he remembered who I was.

'I really shouldn't be talking to you about these things,' he said. 'You are the enemy, m'lady.'

He laughed when he said this, and I did too. It seemed so silly that we are supposed to be enemies. I told him not to worry, he could say whatever he wanted to me, I really didn't mind, and despite what Papa says I understand why people like him might not want our kind around. They were here, and this was their land long before it was ours.

'I bet your Papa is in favour of the Free State though, isn't he?'

I couldn't tell him that Papa thought all the actions from 1916 onwards had been ridiculous and well enough should have been left alone. Instead I said, 'Yes, he does agree with it. Papa feels a complete break from the Empire would not be helpful for any of the people of Ireland. It's just they don't all understand that yet.'

That made Tadgh angry. 'But that's the whole problem. They think we can't rule by ourselves, that we are not capable of it. They think the whole country will fall apart without them. I tell you, they are wrong, and they will see they are wrong. This country will be back on its feet in a few years once we are finally rid of them and it will not be something anyone will ever regret.' He stopped talking for a while and then he apologised to me. 'I am sorry, m'lady. You may be one of them, but I wouldn't want you to leave. I found myself looking forward to meeting you today. You certainly are a breath of fresh air in my life. It is very mundane aside from these few meetings I've had with you.'

I told him my life was exactly the same, mundane and boring, and I had really enjoyed our meetings so far. I even said I hoped that they would continue for as long as possible.

He smiled at me. I knew what I was saying was making him embarrassed and I felt shy to say it, but it was at that moment I knew I had fallen in love with him.

We were standing very close to each other and I was sure he was going to kiss me then but something spooked Taffy and she moved her big head in between the two of us and the moment was gone.

Tadgh said it was time he got back to work. He put his hands on my waist but this time he hesitated a moment before lifting me into the saddle.

'See you in a couple of days, m'lady,' he said then.

Looking down into his beautiful face, I could not bear him calling me 'm'lady' a moment longer.

'Tadgh, don't you think if we are going to be friends that perhaps you should call me by my first name?'

'I don't know about that, m'lady. Are we friends now?'

'Yes, we most certainly are and the next time I see you I want you to call me Edith.'

I must go now. It is almost dinner time. I will see him again in two days. I fear I won't be able to sleep with the anticipation between now and then.

TRHLEC

CHAPTER 8

The light pouring through the gap in the curtains had been annoying Donnacha for the last half-hour, but he was too hung-over to get up and close the curtains properly. Stretching his hand out, he felt on the bedside locker for his phone to check the time. Even that small movement caused his head to throb. He needed painkillers and he needed them urgently. Locating his phone and blinking his eyes to focus on the screen, he saw the time read 10.05. This was his and Jerry's last day in Warsaw and he didn't intend on wasting it. Hung-over or not, he had better get his act together – get up, showered and get moving.

He had managed to plan this trip far better than the previous one. The last time he and Jerry had travelled to Poland together had been the first time for them both and they had failed to factor in time in their schedule to sample the real delights of the country's capital – in addition to taking advantage of the numerous development opportunities that were on offer.

Donnacha was used to travelling and regularly availed of the delights of the local women, whenever and wherever he had the chance, but his and Jerry's eyes had been opened on arriving in Warsaw. It appeared the reputation Polish women had of being amongst the most beautiful in the world was well-deserved and, not only that, Donnacha and Jerry were treated as if they were gods. It was only at the end of that first trip that they had a small amount of time to discover what was on offer in the city when you were willing to pay for it. The prostitutes here were unlike anything Donnacha had ever witnessed elsewhere in the world. High-end massage parlours catering for all tastes and escort services were available in all the nightclubs.

Donnacha and Jerry were determined not to make the same mistake this time and, as well as fitting in meetings relating to three projects, two of which looked like they had the potential to be extremely lucrative, they decided they would allow themselves two nights and a day at the end of the trip to fully sample what they had missed out on their first trip.

Thinking back to last night, Donnacha was happy that they had fulfilled their ambition. He had spent a very happy hour in a massage parlour, followed by dinner with Jerry and three blonde stunners. He and Jerry had parted ways not long after dinner and Donnacha and his new friend Anna had gone to a nightclub, while Jerry departed to an unknown destination with his two companions. On returning to the hotel last night with Anna, Donnacha had a vague recollection of seeing Jerry from across the lobby, getting into the lift with two women. Not the same women he had been at dinner with but equally beautiful.

He grinned to himself. Warsaw was the future – he intended on spending as much time as possible here from now on. If the projects discussed in the meetings came to fruition, and Donnacha was quite certain they would, there would be no shortage of excuses for many more return trips.

Pulling himself into a sitting position in the bed, he scanned the room. It was a mess, but of course that wasn't his problem. The evidence of last night's debauchery was scattered everywhere, his clothes flung in every corner and condom wrappers littering the floor. For a moment an unexpected image of Elenore flashed through his mind. He wasn't sure where it came from. He usually didn't think too much about her when he was away for work. He supposed it was his hung-over state and the stark comparison between the wild sex he had indulged in last night, where anything and everything was on the cards, and the safe, boring sex he was used to at home with Elenore.

Their bedroom in Cavendish certainly never resembled anything like the scene laid out before him. 'Made love' – those very words made him smirk. They were the words Elenore used. He wouldn't refer to what he and Anna had done last night as 'making love' in a million years.

He couldn't imagine Elenore shaking off her inhibitions – not to mention that the thought of her lying in bed afterwards and smoking a joint made him laugh.

There were definitely benefits to their relationship though. Elenore was relaxed – she never nagged like his ex-wife used to but was happy to let him take the lead on most things. She also brought Cavendish with her. With his wealth, good looks and charm he supposed he brought more to the relationship than Elenore currently did, but he knew that eventually it would balance out. Elenore would learn to be more glamorous as she grew into herself. As for Cavendish, it was currently only a shadow of what it would one day become. Her provision of the stately home and its potential as a business enterprise would eventually lend them status as a couple that money simply could not buy.

Stretching his arms over his head, he decided it was definitely time to get moving. Picking up the receiver of the hotel phone, he dialled Jerry's room. The phone rang a few times and Donnacha was about to hang up when he heard Jerry's muffled voice croak a hello.

'Good morning, Jer. I take it the tone of your voice signals a very good night was had by all?'

Jerry's attempt at a laugh came out as a further croak. 'Fuck! I can barely talk – yes, a good night certainly was had by all. I am definitely dealing with the consequences this morning though. I need food urgently – have you been down for breakfast yet?'

They agreed to meet in hotel reception in half an hour in the hope that a hearty breakfast would set them up for the blow-out that would be their final day and night in Warsaw – for now.

It was close to eleven when the two men arrived in the hotel reception. Realising they were too late to avail of the breakfast included in their room rate, they decided to head out in search of breakfast elsewhere. Conveniently located in the centre of the city, the location of their hotel couldn't have been better. Walking out into the morning sunshine, Donnacha felt almost as if he were on holidays. If he hadn't been feeling the effects of last night's overindulgence, he would have been open to going to a more traditional eatery. Instead, he and Jerry made their way past the Palace of Culture and straight to an American-style café. There they knew they would be served up just the right type of food to soak up last night's alcohol and set them up for the day.

Having found a seat in a corner of the café, which afforded some amount of quiet, the men placed their orders. They included two Bloody Marys, reasoning hair of the dog was the only way to cure how they were both feeling. Soon the waitress appeared with steaming plates of eggs and bacon, the smell of which made them feel better immediately.

For a while they chatted about the business meetings they had held. Jerry expressed his concern at the amount of money they would need to invest in one of the projects – the development of a shopping centre, not far from where they were now. The scale of this enterprise was huge, and the men mused on how issues such as planning permission didn't seem to pose a problem here in Poland. You just needed enough money to throw at the situation.

They discussed the merits of the other two potential projects, but both agreed that while one, a development of apartments, had the potential to make a serious profit they didn't want to bite off more than they could chew. Having discussed it at length, they decided that the shopping-centre development would be their focus here in Warsaw and began to sketch out a business proposal to present to the bank when they got home. All going well, this would raise the required funds needed to buy into the project.

The Bloody Marys went down nicely, so much so that Jerry put in an order for a second round.

After the waitress delivered the drinks to their table, he raised his glass.

'*Here's to us!*'

Donnacha clinked his glass. 'Cheers, Jer! Look at us, who'd have thought we'd end up here?'

The two men grinned at each other.

'I'm serious, Jerry, I never thought that I could end up somewhere like this.'

'What? You mean a crappy fake American diner in the middle of a former communist country?'

'Don't be such a smart-arse, Jer. I mean here, making property deals in a foreign country. I never thought I'd end up here when I was working as an errand boy in Lawlor's or even less so when I was growing up.'

As with everyone, with the exception of Karen, Donnacha had never shared the full details of his childhood with Jerry. He had over the years made references to it, indicating it hadn't been idyllic.

'We've all come a long way, Donnacha. Of course, you made the right move and got out of your first marriage and moved on to something better.'

Donnacha nodded. 'I certainly did, although after spending a few days here it'll be hard to go back to the humdrum of domestic bliss with Elenore. This monogamy thing is not all it's cracked up to be.'

Jerry laughed. 'Ah here, I don't think either of us can claim to be monogamous! I mean, I know you don't pay for it at home, but you still get your fair share of action aside from Elenore.'

'Yeah, I know, you're right and I get what you're saying. Thank God I got away from Karen when I did – at least I got a change. What about you, would you ever think of leaving Jennifer and finding someone younger and fresher?'

'I don't think so, mate. Jennifer knows too much about me. She's been with me since the beginning and, unlike Karen and Elenore, she's been part of every deal I ever made. If I was ever caught for some of the things I've done and got sent down, Jen would go down with me – guilty by association, I suppose.'

'Yeah, you're unlucky in that respect. Jen really does know everything about your past but, on the other hand, she seems fairly relaxed about you playing away from home?'

'She's okay about it now and playing a little herself, but there was a time when things were very different. I remember the first time she found out I had cheated on her. She went mad. Over time though, she's mellowed and of course we have the kids to think of now. Jennifer knows which side her bread is buttered on and she knows I always go back to her, no matter what.'

'Well, here's to Jennifer then! Good for her!' Donnacha raised his glass again.

'It's not all a picnic, you know. I still have my fair share of crap to put up with. I know Jen has had at least two affairs in the last few years, but we have a don't-ask, don't-tell policy. It's a bit hard to stomach sometimes, especially when she first meets these blokes and I can see she's going around all starry-eyed for someone else. That disappears after a while though and she comes to her senses.'

'I can't imagine Karen would ever have been that understanding but then she wasn't thinking long-term. The first time she found out I cheated on her, all she could think about was the betrayal. I bet, if she had her time back again, she would be more understanding – tried a bit harder. Her life would be a lot easier now if she'd had the intelligence to stick by me. Sometimes I wonder what she would have done if she'd known about some of the deals I was doing – thank God she doesn't know a thing. She never paid attention to my business dealings the way your Jen does.'

'And what about Elenore?' Jerry asked.

'Oh, Elenore is a different kettle of fish altogether – all she cares about is bloody Cavendish. I'm just hoping I can get my divorce over and done with as soon as possible, so I can marry her. I haven't broached it with her yet, but I know there'll be no problem getting the house signed into both our names once we're hitched. She's easy-going like that and she trusts me completely. Besides, she will benefit from all the changes I've planned for Cavendish as much as I will.'

Jerry looked at his friend in surprise. 'What the fuck, Donnacha? You mean to tell me you've already put money into Cavendish, you've approached people about getting help to have most of the land rezoned and your name still isn't on the deeds?'

'Calm down. Jer, it's grand. I haven't put too much money into it. The rest of the stuff I'm doing is just putting out feelers. You know, so I know what sort of potential I'm looking at. Nothing bad is going to happen. I didn't get where I am today without taking some risks. The only way to deal with Elenore is to keep feeding her the fantasy of this amazing family life we're going to have at Cavendish. That's why I had to get some of the work started before getting my name on the deeds. That way she'll view it as some kind of joint venture. That way she feels I'm really committed to our future. Which, of course, I am. Elenore is going to make a great wife.'

Jerry shook his head in disbelief. 'I'm telling you, you're playing with fire, Donnacha. I wouldn't part with a penny if I were you. Not until it's all a sure thing.'

'And I'm telling you, calm down. It's a done deal. There's not a thing in the world to worry about with Elenore. All I need to worry about is Karen and making sure she doesn't take me for all I'm worth, but I think I'm covered there too. Sending Aaron to that school was the best thing I ever did. Paying out a fortune in school fees along with the rent and the bills is viewed as paying maintenance. Any judge will conclude that I am paying more than my fair share. I've also managed to hide most of the money in my bank accounts, so I'm covered. By the time Cavendish starts raking in money, Elenore will be Mrs. O'Callaghan the Second, every unit in this new shopping centre will be sold and, with the help of Tim Collins, we'll have planning permission for the most luxurious apartment block ever to be built in Cork!'

Jerry smiled at his friend. 'I have to say, I admire your optimism. You are the golden boy. You imagine great things for yourself and, lucky bastard that you are, they happen.'

'It's nothing to do with luck, Jer, absolutely nothing. Now where's that map? There's a casino down the street here that I am sure we haven't been to yet. Let's go spend some of our hard-earned cash and make the most of our last day here. We've a lot of work to do when we get home.'

CHAPTER 9

Cavendish Hall,
15th November 1922

Dear Diary,

It has been so very long since I wrote to you and so many things have happened. Just after I wrote my last entry the most amazing thing in the whole world happened to me. Tadgh kissed me for the first time and he has kissed me many, many times since. I have been meeting him almost every day. We would meet every hour if only for Mama and Papa. They have not even noticed yet how often I am missing from Cavendish, but I fear it will not be long until they do. But now there's another cause for concern, so Tadgh and I might not be able to see each other as often any more.

Before I tell you about that, I must tell about the joy I feel knowing for certain that Tadgh has the same feelings for me as I have for him. He loves me, and I love him. I wish I could write down every detail of our every encounter, but I find myself so very tired after I meet him. All I want to do is lie down on my bed and daydream about our next meeting.

Now I must tell you what the cause of my concern is. It is the reason that I make sure to hide you so well, dear Diary. I think May Ryan, our servant girl from the village, is beginning to suspect there is something between Tadgh and me.

She is the girl who comes to help Mrs. Carey with the house. May seems to spend all her time watching me and asking questions. Papa said the other day that he wished he could return to the old days when servants knew their place. Mama said he was lucky that we have any servants left at all. He told Mama that May had come to him recently and asked for more money. Papa laughed. He thinks it is silly that servants should have what he called 'ideas above their station'.

I was in the library just this morning, pretending to read but really dreaming about my future with Tadgh, and May was there cleaning the fireplace. Out of nowhere, she started talking to me. That has never happened before, as Papa is adamant that servants should be invisible.

'Lady Edith,' she said, 'there is something you should know.'

She has never spoken to me before, aside from answering me when I ask her for something. I got such a shock that she was addressing me in that manner that I did not know what to say, aside from, 'What is it, May?'

'Well, m'lady, you know there are some people around here who wish that you and your family didn't live at Cavendish?'

'I am aware of that, May, but I do not think that is something you or I need worry about,' I responded. 'Now I think it best if you finish your cleaning here and return to Mrs. Carey in the kitchen.'

To my utter surprise she did not leave it at that and instead continued. 'All I am saying, m'lady, is that people you might think are your friends might not be friends of yours at all. You should keep to your own kind, m'lady.'

With that I lost my temper. 'That's enough, May! Get back to the kitchen immediately. If you do not get on with your work, I am going to tell Mama that you have been chattering here instead of doing what you are paid to do.'

She then had the cheek to get up from in front of the fire, look me straight in the eye and say, 'I'll go back to the kitchen alright, m'lady, but I am telling you that you need to be careful.'

With that, she picked up her cloths and brushes and walked to the door, as if she had all the time in the world.

I contemplated telling Mama but thought better of it. I do not want Mama becoming suspicious or asking questions that I do not want to answer.

I am most alarmed at what May said. Nobody must know about Tadgh and me. We certainly need to keep our relationship a secret. I am sure we have been very careful and have even stopped meeting at the stables. He tacks up Taffy for me to collect later and then goes and waits for me in the woods. May, who never leaves the house during the day, could not have seen us, I'm sure — but perhaps someone else did and told her?

Later I rushed down to the woods to meet Tadgh as arranged. He took me in his arms, murmuring how much he had missed me, and kissed me over and over again.

I have never before felt the way I do when I am with Tadgh. It is a feeling of excitement and butterflies in my stomach and light-headedness. I sometimes feel that my heart is bursting with love. I love talking with him and sharing with him my dreams for the future. And I love hearing his thoughts on all that is happening in Ireland at the moment.

But before he could get a chance to start talking about politics and the war, I had to tell him about May. I told him of the conversation I had with her when she started warning me about keeping 'to my own kind' as she said. I could see from his face that he was worried. He said we might have to stop seeing each other so often, for a little while at least.

I told him I wouldn't be able to bear that. We talked about how it could be that May might suspect something. There is no one else working at the stables only Tadgh. The only way he would be missed from there is if Papa suddenly wanted to take the carriage out and Papa never goes anywhere these days. If he had gone looking for Tadgh in the stables and found that he wasn't there, he would assume he was working on the farm and ride down to fetch him. And, if Tadgh was nowhere to be found, I definitely would have heard him angrily reporting it to Mama at dinner. But, even if May overheard him complaining about Tadgh's absence, why on earth would she connect that with me? There are the other workers on the farm, of course – only a few of them and they are usually out in the fields. We wondered if perhaps one of them saw us in the distance and told May. Tadgh seemed to be brooding a little after that and I couldn't help but wonder if there was something he was keeping from me.

I told him we can continue to meet every day but only after darkness falls. He said this could absolutely not happen as it was too dangerous to go into the woods after dark and that we would definitely be caught. I asked him what he meant but all he said was that the war is happening all around us and that he wouldn't allow me to go to the woods after dark. He said he didn't want to talk about it any more after that.

I knew that he was annoyed and that he was trying to figure out in his head how May might have found out about us. I thought it was best to change the subject and bring him back to his favourite topic of conversation which is all that is happening in Ireland.

We moved deeper into the woods to talk. Tadgh said it was best, if we do continue to meet, to make sure not to go to the same part of the woods each time. We walked for a while and finally found a spot that he was happy with and sat down. Then Tadgh began to talk. He told me how he does not have any issue with my family in particular, but we need to understand that times are changing and the sooner we accept that, the better it will be for everybody.

I asked him where he expects us to go and he said we should go back to England to the vast estates we have there and to farm our own land — not expecting tenant farmers to do all the work for us so that we can live such privileged lives. I told him I had never thought about it like that but that he was wrong. Papa does not own any other lands in England. He does have a townhouse in London, but he cannot live off that. Families like Lord Carbery's have estates in England and Scotland as well as estates in Ireland, but not Papa. If Papa had to sell Cavendish I do not know how we would survive.

I told Tadgh how, in my family, we do not talk about money. It is not something that has ever concerned us and, besides, it is considered poor manners to talk about such things.

Tadgh said I was very lucky and that was another privilege of my class. It was easy never to have to talk about money when you have plenty of it. He said when you constantly had to worry about where your next meal was coming from, or that the rent on your house was going to increase and you would not be able to pay it and you might be thrown out on the road, then thoughts of money occupied your mind all the time.

I argued with him that he was not being fair to Papa, as he was not guilty of all that Tadgh was accusing him, and his peers, of. Papa had already been forced to sell large parts of the estate to some of his tenants. He only had a small number of tenants still on the estate and I was sure he did not raise the rent to a level that they could not afford.

'I am afraid you do not know what you are talking about, Edith,' Tadgh said.

I feel butterflies in my stomach every time he calls me Edith. I am still not fully accustomed to it. I don't think I ever will be, even when we are an old couple.

'Since my father passed away ten years ago, we live month to month, not knowing if we are going to be able to keep the house. If

we lost it, me and my older brother might have some chance to work as labourers — but what about Ma? Where would she live? She'd end up in a workhouse.'

'Papa would never let that happen to Mrs. Carey and you know that.' I could not let Tadgh say that Papa would be capable of such a terrible thing.

'Well, it doesn't matter any more. I am leaving. There are a few things I have to take care of but very soon I'll go to America. My brother Jimmy is going to work our little bit of land and look after Ma. And soon I'll be able to send them money from America.'

'Your mother will always have a job at Cavendish,' I told Tadgh, but my mind was racing and my heart suddenly thumping. America, I thought. He is going to America?

'She wouldn't have a job at Cavendish if there was no Cavendish,' he said. 'I know you love that house, but sometimes the things you love are not the things you need.'

I had no idea what he was talking about, but I didn't ask because suddenly my mind was filled with fear. If Tadgh left for America, I would never see him again.

Seeing the fear on my face, he said, 'Don't worry, Edith, it won't be long now, and then I will be able to leave. I am going to America and I want you to come with me.'

Relief flooded through my body when he said that. I am not sure if he is serious about it and how soon he means to go. He said he has some things to take care of. I think he might mean he needs to put some money away before he goes. If so, that could take a long time. I didn't want to make him feel bad by asking him about money.

Of course, I said yes to him straight away. I told him I would love more than anything in the whole world to go to America with him. We had to part ways then as we had spent far more time together than we should have. We decided not to meet tomorrow. I do not know if I will be able to survive more than a day without seeing him. *I wonder if he really is serious when he talks about going to America? Thinking about it fills me with more excitement than I have ever thought possible. But I will have to wait. I will have to wait, dear Diary, and see what is to come.*

TRHLEC xx

CHAPTER 10

Two days after Leslie's visit to Cavendish and their discovery of the architects' drawings in the tunnel, Elenore was beginning to feel slight cabin fever and needed to get out of the house. She knew if she stayed home a moment longer she was going to drive herself insane. She'd had one conversation with Donnacha on the phone since the discovery that night, but that had been just a check-in call – with Donnacha letting her know that all was well with him and the meetings in Warsaw were going well.

It had taken all the willpower Elenore had to keep quiet about what she and Leslie had found. She knew it was for the best not to have the conversation over the phone. If she gave Donnacha even a hint that she was aware of what he was doing, that would give him ample time to come up with an excuse. She wanted to surprise him, convincing herself that she would know by his reaction if these drawings were just drawings or were in fact plans for Cavendish that he was preparing without her knowledge.

She hadn't thought so far ahead as to consider what she was

going to do after she confronted him. When she imagined the
conversation in her head, she could picture Donnacha saying,
'Don't worry, sweetheart, obviously I would never think of
undertaking anything like that at Cavendish. It was just the
architect running away with ideas the way architects do.'

She felt comforted when she imagined him giving this
explanation but, every time she pictured it, there was a voice in
the back of her head saying: *Just because he tells you something like
that doesn't necessarily mean it's the truth.*

She did her best to ignore the voice. She couldn't bear to think
about what it meant if Donnacha did have these ridiculous far-
fetched plans for the house – or worse, if he not only had the plans
but tried to fob her off with lies. She would be forced to think
about what that meant for their relationship, her future, the life
she had planned with him. It was at that point that her thoughts
would spiral completely out of control and she would feel like
picking up the phone and screaming at him to provide her with the
answers she needed. But she refrained and when she was yet again
about to reach breaking point, she would pick up the phone to
Leslie and they would talk over what exactly their find possibly
meant. They'd had the same conversation at least five times at this
stage.

Elenore had to admit to herself that her memories of the night
were a bit hazy, with all the wine she and her friend had
consumed. But the presence of the drawings, which she had not
removed from the kitchen table, were a constant reminder that
not long ago she had been stressed and frazzled due to the building
work that was taking place. Now she was stressed, frazzled and
unsure of her relationship. She had been confident that she and
Donnacha were very much in this together – now she was no
longer sure. Could it be a simple misunderstanding? Surely he
wouldn't dream of planning something like this? Weren't they a
team, a partnership, like her parents had been? She had never

before had reason to distrust him, so why now? Why did this one thing, that might yet prove to be nothing, leave her questioning the very core of her relationship with him? She'd give anything to go back to just being stressed and frazzled about the building work.

Her eyes were drawn yet again to the blueprints strewn across the table. When Leslie had told her in no uncertain terms that she was to take what she had found and bring them back to the kitchen, Elenore willingly obeyed her. She hadn't even been sure of what it was she was carrying in her arms but something inside her said it wasn't good.

The two women had returned to the kitchen from the tunnel and spread the drawings across the table. The first thing Elenore looked at was the name on the drawings. In the bottom right-hand corner, it read, *JP. Clarke and Sons, Architectural Design and Engineering*, followed by an address in Cork. The name was familiar to Elenore, as it was the firm Donnacha used for all his projects and she had frequently heard him dropping the firm's name into conversation.

Sitting down at the table they had begun to go through them. Page after page revealed horror after horror. The destruction of much of the woodland on the demesne for the inclusion of a golf course with a massive club house and accompanying car park. A two-storey extension at the back of Cavendish housing a swimming pool, leisure centre and spa. All the outbuildings converted and extended to allow for twenty extra housing units with access to the original house. The east wing of the house, which had lain derelict for years, converted into one large housing unit. A further fifteen houses dotted around the new golf course and a whole twenty acres of land on the furthest corner of the estate turned into what looked like a housing estate with a new road running across the demesne, splitting it in two and connecting the new housing estate to the village.

Leslie had looked over at Elenore and, seeing the paleness that had descended over her friend's face, feared she was about to faint. She immediately tried to take the situation in hand.

'Don't jump to conclusions, Elenore. I know it looks bad but there could be a really simple explanation.'

Elenore tried to respond but she was unable and only managed to shake her head. She picked up Elenore's wineglass and handed it to her. 'Here, take a sip of this. It'll take the edge off the shock.'

Elenore downed half the glass before regaining her ability to speak.

'A simple explanation? I really don't think so, Leslie. What is this? Why? Who would do this? This is Cavendish, chopped up, knocked down, rebuilt and destroyed, and that's just all the new additions. Look at the drawings of the inside of the house. Look at them, Leslie! Look at them! He's knocking down walls, he's splitting bedrooms in two, he's putting in en-suite bathrooms, he's put a bar in the bloody kitchen – here in my mother's kitchen! If this bloody-well happens, we won't be sitting here pouring our own drinks, we'll be calling over a bloody barman to do it for us!'

Leslie smiled at Elenore but knew it wasn't really a joke. This was Cavendish, her friend's beloved home. Her history and life's memories were encased in this house. Now it looked as if the one person she should be able to trust the most had taken that home and those memories and ripped them apart.

Standing up, Leslie went over to Elenore and wrapped her arms around her.

'Okay, you're right. I promise I'm going to stop trying to put a positive spin on this. From now on, all I'm going to do is help you get to the bottom of what is actually going on here.'

At that moment a mixture of anger, adrenaline and fear were pumping through Elenore's body, but for a split second she felt nothing but love and gratitude for her oldest friend. Leslie had always known exactly the right thing to do, and say, in her time of need.

'Thanks, Leslie, thank you. Whatever this is, I have a feeling I'm going to badly need your help. I don't know what I'm thinking at this stage. I can't believe Donnacha can be serious about this and yet it is there in black and white. Maybe that's just a format they use, do you think? Maybe he and his architect friend were just messing around?'

Even as the words came out of her mouth, Elenore knew they couldn't be true. Many hours of work and research had gone into crafting these drawings. They weren't the product of someone just playing around to see what could be done in their dreams. Donnacha and his architects were hardly the type of people to play around with things anyway – they were serious business people.

Leslie shook her head. 'Look, here's what we need to do. We need to arm ourselves with the facts. One step at a time and no looking too far ahead. Looking too far ahead only makes you panic. Right now, we concentrate on getting all the information we can. First things first, he can't have actually submitted this for planning permission, can he? Not when he doesn't own the land?'

Elenore shook her head. 'I don't know. I don't know anything about planning permission. Jesus Christ, why don't I listen to him? He drones on about these things often enough. I should pay more attention.'

'You pay enough attention and why would you be bothering yourself with planning-permission issues? You were only dealing with improvements to the interior of the house – you didn't have to get planning permission for them, did you?'

Elenore shook her head. 'No, Cavendish is listed alright, but as long as we weren't making any changes to the exterior and no structural changes on the inside, there were no planning-permission requirements. The work I am aware of is fairly limited – fixing the roof, upgrading the heating, replacing carpets, that sort of thing. None of it would need planning permission.'

'And what about money? I mean, I know Donnacha is loaded, but is he really in this league – to undertake all of this?' Laura gestured to the architects' plans. 'I'm no builder but I'm guessing this level of work would run well into the millions.'

'Of course it would – I'm guessing ten million at a minimum. Fuck, does Donnacha have that sort of money? Although if he can drop fifteen thousand on a bloody painting, maybe he does.'

'Right, back to my limited knowledge of planning permission – don't people put deposits on land and buy it – subject to planning permission?'

'Yes, I think so. People usually put a deposit on a site and then seek planning permission. That means if they are refused the permission, they haven't bought the land outright and so it's not a waste of money.'

'Okay. But this is different, this is commercial, not a one-off house. If someone is seeking planning permission in their name, for land they don't own, surely the person who owns the land has to be made aware? You can't just go off and start looking for planning permission to build on someone else's land presumably.'

'No, I'm sure you can't. But I really don't know. So that leads us back to square one, and we're none the wiser. Maybe Donnacha and the architect were just fooling around. Imagining what could be but not actually serious about it.'

The women sat up late into the night, going around in circles but still not able to come up with a plausible reason that made the existence of the drawings okay.

When they finally went to bed, Elenore tossed and turned all night, continuing her pattern of getting no sleep, this time for very different reasons.

Now, here she was, with Donnacha soon to return, and she had got no more sleep and all her questions remained unanswered. The only thing that had given her any moments of respite had been thinking about the diary. She had devoured it, losing herself in this world of Cavendish in 1922, allowing herself just a few moments of respite from her worries.

She thought some more now about the girl, Edith, who had written the diary. Had she escaped, Elenore wondered, and if she had, had she ever come back?

Forcing herself back into the present, she decided it was time to get out of the house and focus on getting answers to some of her more pressing dilemmas. She had decided to go to the library and see what she could find out about planning laws. On a whim she gently picked up the diary and placed it in her handbag, reluctant to be parted from it.

Driving down the avenue of the house, the horror of what she had found struck her once more. According to the plans, the avenue would no longer exist. There would be a new entrance to the demesne – closer to the village. Elenore asked herself for the hundredth time, what the hell could he be thinking and was it possible that the man she loved and was planning her future with, was actually planning all these terrible changes behind her back? She also couldn't fathom what his reasons might be for leaving the drawings in the tunnel. They had been well hidden. There was no question about that. Donnacha would have been certain that she wouldn't have done anything more than peek into the entrance of the tunnel, unless he was accompanying her. He would have thought the cold, dark and fear of encountering rats would have been more than enough to put her off. He hadn't banked on Leslie coming over and the courage provided by a few glasses of wine.

Coming to the end of the avenue, she turned right and drove the five kilometres that brought her into the village. Ballycastle had indeed been a village when Elenore was a child but its close proximity to Cork City, within commuting distance, meant that the village had grown into quite a substantial town. Numerous housing estates had sprung up on its edges over the last number of years. The town itself was booming and bore no resemblance to what it had been like when Elenore had gone to school there. An array of new shops lined the wide main street – boutiques, supermarkets, cafés and restaurants. The town had been by-passed by an extension of the Dublin to Cork motorway a few years previously. At the time the bypass had caused great concern for many of the local business owners, but their fears had been unfounded as the population of the town continued to grow. During the summer season, tourists still took a detour off the motorway to visit the charming town, stopping at the cafés and restaurants before resuming their journey to the city.

Parking her car beside the library, Elenore gathered her belongings and made her way towards the building. Being an avid reader from childhood, she had spent many a happy Saturday morning in the library with her mother browsing, always finding it difficult to limit her selection to the two books she was allowed take out as a junior member. She remembered how she usually ended up coming out with three or more books. Her mother would take the additional books Elenore wanted out, as part of her five-book limit. On returning home her father would joke that they wouldn't see her for at least a week now, as she curled up in her room, lost in the magical world that reading opened up to her.

Unlike the rest of the town, the library hadn't changed all that much from when she was a child. She had renewed her membership on returning to Cavendish after university and, while she didn't get to visit it as often as she wished, she came to the library whenever she got a chance.

Opening the door, the comforting smell of books hit her. Back in time, there had been nothing only books in the building but now there was a row of computers where local people wishing to improve their computer skills could take classes. Some of the rows of books had been replaced by DVDs to rent. Still the atmosphere on walking in the door was the same as it had always been and for that Elenore was glad. Comfort and peace were what she craved now and walking into the building gave a sense of just that.

Needing an escape from the problems that were confronting her, she decided to allow herself some time to browse. Picking out various books, she read the blurbs on their backs with pleasure – but most of all she enjoyed the feel of the solid hardbacks in her hands. Lost in a world of historical romance, stories of people leaving the rat race to pursue lives in exotic locations and others who had overcome terrible childhoods to thrive later in life, Elenore soon lost track of time. When she eventually lifted her head to look at the clock on the library wall, she was shocked to see that an hour had passed.

Chiding herself for wasting so much time, she pulled herself away from the rows of books and went to the counter, where a young woman sat. Elenore recognised her as Alison Evans. She had gone to school with her older sister, Linda. Elenore didn't recall having ever seen her in the library on her previous visits.

'Hi, Alison, I'm not sure if you remember me? I'm Elenore Stack – I went to school with Linda?'

The girl smiled back at Elenore, but the vague look in her eyes told Elenore she had no recollection of her. Nonetheless, she played along with the routine, which Elenore assumed was a requirement of a librarian in such a small community as Ballycastle.

'Yes, of course I remember you,' she replied, letting out a giggle at which Elenore raised her eyebrows. 'Oh, sorry, I didn't mean to laugh. It's just, I only started this job last week. I'm back in the village less than a month and it's as if nothing has changed since I left.'

Elenore smiled, not particularly wanting to engage in small talk. 'Well, welcome back. Where have you been all these years?'

Alison chatted on, something about going to UCC and living in Australia and now she was back here, because what was the point of being in Australia when things were so good at home? Elenore wondered how she was going to steer Alison back to doing her job. The girl rambled on, explaining that working in the library was only a stopgap and she would be taking up employment in a much better-paid job, probably in Cork City, just as soon as she could.

'Well, best of luck with that and tell your sister I was asking for her – but I wonder could you help me? I'm looking for some information on planning permission.'

As Elenore said the words she immediately regretted them, remembering that both Alison and her older sister were notorious gossips. No doubt, by the time the library closed this evening, it would be all around the village that Elenore Stack was applying for planning permission to do some major work on Cavendish.

Putting that thought to the back of her mind, she continued. 'I was wondering if there's a section here with books that might explain the whole process. I'm thinking of doing a course on the whole area of planning and I thought I'd get a head start by doing some prep work here.'

In for a penny, in for a pound, as her mother had always said. Now, by this evening, the village would be talking about how Elenore Stack had ideas above her station and was planning to become a professor in UCC!

She watched as Alison took in what she was saying and saw that she was not going to be of any help.

With a blank look on her face, Alison said, 'I don't think there's a planning section but let me have a look on the computer here.' She fumbled around on the computer for what seemed like an eternity, and finally said, 'Try the shelves over there by the back wall – I think there might be something there.'

It was probably the least helpful information that Elenore could have hoped for, but eager to get away from Alison and begin her research, she moved in the direction of the back wall.

Twenty minutes later, she was overcome with frustration. The back wall was full of books in relation to house building, books on historical houses and coffee-table tomes on how to best lay out your garden. Planning permission issues were not being dealt with on the back wall. Having gone through each row, trying to find something of use, she let out an aggravated sigh, and was immediately embarrassed as the man standing beside her threw her a glowering look.

She dropped her head in order to avoid his attention, pretending to be engrossed in a book at knee level, but out of the corner of her eye and much to her mortification, she saw that he was still looking at her.

Before she could turn and remove herself, he leaned in towards her and in a loud whisper said, 'You know sighing is forbidden in the library – it's clearly outlined in the member's handbook.'

If it had been another day, Elenore would have laughed at his stupidity and imagined recounting the story of the ridiculously grumpy man in the library to Donnacha. Today, however, was not that day. The events of the last seventy-two hours finally caught up with her.

'How dare you, how dare you tell me I can't sigh in the library! The last I checked you weren't meant to talk here either – I don't see that stopping you! Who are you, the bloody library police?'

Shocked by her own outburst and picturing the embarrassment that she knew would follow, she took a step back and looked up into the man's face, only to find him laughing at her.

This had the result of making her angry again, and momentarily she lost her senses and let rip. 'Oh, I'm sorry, are you laughing at me? Am I funny to you? Well, I'm glad I'm of amusement to someone! What the hell is your problem?'

The effect was perhaps not what Elenore was looking for. She realised her whisper-shouting had turned to actual shouting, and the man's laughter had turned to a look of real concern.

'I'm really sorry – I was joking – are you okay?'

A look of kindness crossed his face and it took Elenore all her strength not to cry – simply because someone was being nice to her.

'Oh God, I'm mortified. I'm really sorry, of course you were joking, obviously. Honestly, I'm fine. I'm just having a really tough day and I came here looking for something and I can't seem to find it.'

He was nodding in agreement now. 'That happens to me all the time – you should hear some of the sighs that have come out of me in here – the librarian has asked me to leave on at least three occasions.'

Elenore felt herself warm to his gentle humour.

'Can I help you with anything? I am a bit of a historian, so I do spend a lot of time here. I know this place like the back of my hand.'

Elenore looked at him quizzically. 'I don't think you're going to be any use to me then. I'm looking for information on planning permission and as a historian you probably won't be able to help me with that.'

What was wrong with her? Her thoughts and her words didn't seem to be matching up today. What was she doing here? Like some amateur Miss Marples, trying to find out information so that she could figure out just how much of a liar her partner really was. All of a sudden, she felt lightheaded and queasy. Elenore had never fainted in her life but was afraid she was about to.

She swayed slightly, and the strange man put a hand out to steady her. 'Are you alright?' He asked. 'You look very pale all of a sudden.'

Elenore took a deep breath. 'I don't feel very well to be honest. I'm a bit dizzy. I think I need a drink of water.'

His face was full of concern now, 'Oh my God, I am a complete idiot. Here am I giving out to you for sighing and now I've gone and made you feel sick. Right, I think I've talked enough crap for one day. Hold on a second. I'll get the librarian to get you a glass of water and then I am taking you for a good, strong cup of tea.'

He hurried over to the desk where Elenore could see Alison filing her nails. After a short exchange Alison disappeared, returning a minute later with a glass of water. The man brought it back to Elenore and she gulped it down. She then found herself being led towards the door and, before she could utter another word, he was marching her up the street towards a café.

When they arrived, he found them a table and went to make their order at the counter. Sitting down, Elenore felt marginally better and she watched him as he joined the queue. He was exceptionally tall – definitely well over six feet. He was dressed in blue jeans and a woolly jumper that looked as though his mother might have knit it. His red hair was cropped tight to his head. He was very slim and Elenore thought the jumper would have looked absolutely ridiculous on most people but the combination of broad shoulders and the openness and warmth that emanated from him meant that somehow he managed to carry it off.

An hour later, Elenore found herself drinking her third cup of tea and listening intently – well, almost – to this very, very talkative man. His name was Seán, and he was a history and PE teacher in a secondary school in the city. He had recently moved to Ballycastle, where he had bought a house in one of the new estates. He didn't know anyone in the village yet, but he'd heard of Cavendish and was dying to get a look around it.

Now he was talking to her about his job and how difficult and spoilt most of the kids he taught were. He'd thought, having given up teaching years ago to move to America, that he would never go back to it. But here he was, home again. Well, not quite home – West Cork was home but Ballycastle would have to do for the time being.

Although she was enjoying listening to him, and grateful to him for not asking her any questions given her strange behaviour in the library, Elenore wondered, not for the first time, at the capacity of men to talk endlessly about themselves. She let that thought slip away, enjoying not having to think about Donnacha and his plans for Cavendish, and instead focusing on Seán, who it seemed loved to talk about himself more than anything else in the world. Although now he was talking about his family. His smile widened, and his green eyes lit up as he talked about his parents in West Cork.

Another half an hour slipped by and, looking at her watch, Elenore reminded herself that she should get going. She needed time to think. She needed the quiet of Cavendish to plan her next move. Today had been a total loss. She had achieved nothing and knew just as much about planning now as she had when she set out.

'So why planning? Are you looking to do something with that big house of yours?'

Seán's abrupt change of conversation brought her back to reality.

'Planning? Oh no, I'm not building anything. I suppose I just want to get a handle on what the whole process entails – it's always fascinated me.' She couldn't believe how quickly that lie had come out of her mouth and how stupid it made her sound. Who in the history of the world had ever been fascinated by planning-permission laws?

'Really? Well, I won't deny it's an unusual fascination but to each their own. I love local history – of course, that's no surprise given my chosen profession.'

It crossed Elenore's mind for a moment to take the diary out of her handbag and show it to him. If he was interested in local history, he might be the very person to shed some light on the diary's author – but now was not the time. She had too much to think about and to do. She needed to forget about the diary and remain firmly planted in the present day. Standing up to leave, she made her excuses.

'Well, it's been really lovely to meet you, Seán – thank you for looking after me and thank you for not asking any questions. I'm sorry again for shouting at you in the library.'

Then she reached into her handbag to take out some money. She knew he'd paid for the tea at the counter and she wanted to give him her share. Searching with difficulty for her purse in the depths of her vast handbag, she took out the diary, her make-up bag, one of Alfie's leads, and some other items and laid them on the table to make it easier, while Sean looked on bemused. Embarrassed, she at last located the purse, took it out and placed a couple of euros on the table in front of Seán.

He was having none of it. 'Will you stop, Elenore! I'm not taking any money off you. It was only a few cups of tea.' He picked up the money and forced her to take it back.

'Oh, well, thank you, Seán.'

He then began to help her gather up the other items but paused as he picked up the diary. 'What's this? It looks very old.'

Elenore took it from him. 'It is very old. It was found by one of the builders at the house. It was nearly thrown out, but I rescued it. It's fascinating. It belonged to a girl who lived in Cavendish in 1922.'

'Wow! Found by a builder?'

Elenore quickly told him about how it had come to light, glossing over the fact that her soon-to-be husband had deemed it appropriate to consign the diary to the scrap heap. She added that it seemed to have been written by a daughter of the Cavendish family.

Seán nodded in agreement. 'That sounds about right. Keeping diaries was very fashionable for young ladies back then.'

'I'm puzzled about how it ended up in the tunnel – just discarded, when it was obviously precious to her.'

'Yes, that's strange certainly. Who knows what might have happened to it and to her?'

Elenore hesitated, feeling she had imposed on the man enough for one day, but then said, 'Would you like to take a look at it, Seán? I found it only a few days ago and I wouldn't mind getting the opinion of someone who actually knows something about history – and has an interest in local history, what's more. Bizarre as it sounds, I know very little about the history of Cavendish. To my shame, I've never got around to doing any research on it. I only know the bits and pieces my father told me about it.'

Looking like all his Christmases had come at once, Seán took possession of the diary and began to gently turn the pages.

Realising she wasn't going to be able to leave right now, Elenore sat back down opposite him. Watching Seán avidly scanning pages, Donnacha popped into her head. Donnacha hadn't given more than a moment's attention to the diary, and then ordered to have it thrown out. Seán, on the other hand, was enthralled by it.

'Have you read the whole thing?' he asked at last. 'What have you learned so far?'

She filled him in on the broad outlines of the story recounted in the diary.

'Not just any diary then,' he said. 'A very dramatic one from a very dramatic moment in Irish history.'

'Yes, you're right. It's extraordinary.'

'Amazing, Elenore – what a lucky find – brilliant for you, a primary source of history hidden in your house all these years – just brilliant.'

'It is. The one thing that puzzles me is that I have a memory from my childhood of my father telling me the Cavendishes had no children. They left sometime in the late 1920's and, when he told me that, I got upset at the thought of someone having to leave my beloved Cavendish. So he said they probably didn't mind – because they didn't have children and they would be less lonely in London as they had friends there.'

'Maybe your father said that just to make you feel better –
maybe he was just making it up?' Seán ventured.

'Maybe. But don't you think he would be more likely to
comfort me by saying that they didn't mind leaving because they
had their daughter with them? Rather than lying outright? No, I'm
inclined to think he just didn't know about her. Which is odd.'

'And now, Elenore Stack, you are intrigued – who is this girl
that lived in your house and walked the same hallways that you
walk and who evidently never existed? Maybe it's a ghost diary,
maybe we're just imagining its very existence.'

'You really don't stay serious for very long, Seán, do you?'

He grinned over at Elenore and she couldn't help but think
what easy company he was, aside from the constant talking, but
maybe he was just doing that to give her some breathing space,
given how upset she had been in the library.

'I can be serious, but today I thought – this woman needs
cheering up and I am the one to do it! But now, Elenore, I have to
go. I am due to give a history grind to a delightful fifteen-year-old
and I need to get a move on.' He smiled warmly at her. 'It was
lovely meeting you, Elenore. I know something is wrong. I don't
want to know what it is but, whatever it is, I hope you get it
sorted.'

Elenore watched him bound out of the coffee shop, off to sell
his peculiar brand of humour to some unsuspecting fifteen-year-
old. Diving into her handbag, she went in search of her car keys.
She really had to clean the bloody bag out. She was unable to find
anything in it.

Her nail caught on something in the depths of the bag and she
felt it break. 'Oh, for God's sake!'

Looking up from her bag, she saw Seán standing by the table
again.

'I thought you were gone?'

'Yes, I was, but now I'm back. I want your phone number. Not in some weird, creepy, stalker kind of way. I want a proper look at that diary and, seeing as you live in Cavendish Hall and I am keen to get a look at it, I am not letting this opportunity pass me by. As I am a teacher, I do have Garda clearance, so it is all perfectly legitimate.'

Feeling her face break into a grin, the first proper grin in many days, Elenore couldn't help but agree to Seán's requests. Aside from the fact she found him charming, he might actually help her to find out more about the diary.

'Okay, Seán, you're on. Find me a piece of paper there and I'll give you my number.'

For a brief moment she felt something approaching normal, until she was alone again, and the unanswered questions in her life surrounded her like a fog, causing a dull and heavy pain in her heart.

CHAPTER 11

Cavendish Hall
21st November 1922

Dear Diary,

Today we met but the last week has been torturous. I hardly saw Tadgh and I felt absolutely dreadful. I thought today would never come. The only thing that has kept me going was that Tadgh said he was working on a plan for our escape and that the next time we met we would be able to talk about it properly.

There has been some communication between us. We agreed that if we needed to tell each other anything we would leave notes for each other. We picked one of the empty loose boxes in the stables and agreed to leave notes hidden under a small rock that Tadgh placed in it.

Also, I have gone to the stables every day. I pretend to Mama and Papa that I am going to say hello to Taffy and give her a treat. Mrs. Carey gives me some carrots and Taffy is always happy to see me.

Tadgh has been there sometimes, but we are very formal with each other. I say hello to him and he tips his cap to me. I think it is silly to behave like that. There is no one around and May is back at the house. But even though there is no one around, Tadgh thinks it is important to be this careful. Each day he has left me a note, telling me how much he misses me and that he cannot wait to be with me again.

Finally, today came and I followed the usual routine as I do on the days we have agreed to meet in the woods. I went to the stables and Tadgh had left Taffy tacked up for me. I set off, knowing he was waiting for me in the woods. My heart was beating with excitement at the thought of being in his arms again.

When I got to the place we had agreed on I dismounted and soon he was beside me. He took me in his arms and kissed me passionately. We found the perfect spot, under a large oak tree by the stream. Tadgh sat down and pulled me down beside him. Sitting there with his arms wrapped around me felt like the safest place in the world. When we finally stopped kissing, Tadgh asked if May had said anything more to me. I told him she hadn't. He then said he wanted to tell me his plan of how we would escape. I rested my head on his chest and listened to him talk of how, after Christmas, we'd leave for Queenstown. He said he had some money he had managed to save, and his uncle had given him a certain amount. He asked if I have any money. I told him that I do have some — a small amount that Papa gave me recently. I have never before had any money of my own, but Papa said it was important that I had enough money to get back to our townhouse in London, just in case anything happened. I said I thought Papa was being silly, as what could possibly happen that I would need to get to London in such a hurry? Tadgh said Papa was probably right.

We totted up the various sums of money and Tadgh said it was more than enough to get us safely to America. We will spend a few years there, while Jimmy looks after Mrs. Carey and then, in time, when things have settled down and Ireland is a republic, we will be in a perfect position to return home and have our own house. Tadgh said we will never be able to have a house as grand as Cavendish but, by the time we return, no one would be living in houses like Cavendish. Maybe we will buy a farm and Mrs. Carey can come live with us and look after our babies.

I giggled when Tadgh mentioned babies. 'Babies! Just how many babies do you think we are going to have?'

Tadgh tickled me under my ribs. 'I do believe you are blushing at the mention of babies, Lady Edith! Now it's time you went home — I have work to do.'

He promised me that by the next time we meet he will have worked out the details of how we are going to make our escape. I do not know how I will get to Queenstown but Tadgh said I should not worry, that he will think of something.

Before we parted, he kissed me tenderly and I missed him already, even before he walked away. But Christmas is only a month away and after that we will leave for America and start our new lives together.

Now all I must do is wait and be very careful not to arouse the suspicions of Mama and Papa. May Ryan had better keep quiet too. I do not know why she is so interested in what I do — it is none of her business.

Now, dear Diary, I must say goodbye. I will write again soon, when I know more of our plans.

TRHLEC

CHAPTER 12

Karen's instinct was to drive her car as fast as it would go, but fear made her stay within the speed limit. If there was a speed van on the road to Cavendish and she was clocked breaking the limit, she would die of shame.

Her heart was racing as she pulled into the avenue of the house. Her anger with Donnacha and his manipulative ways had not abated. She'd had to wait until she was off work and Maggie, her neighbour, was free to look after her mother and Aaron. She'd spent her time imagining what she was going to say to him, but she still wasn't sure. She really hadn't thought this through very well and, as always, had acted on a gut feeling. Acting on gut feelings always seemed to land her in trouble. Trying to calm herself, she planned again how exactly she was going to play this. She didn't want to make a show of herself in front of Donnacha's partner and she didn't want to give him any reason to badmouth her to their son.

She hoped Elenore would be there. It might work in her favour if she was there to witness the conversation. Surely another woman would see the merit in what she had to say? She might be able to persuade Donnacha that she was right.

She was going to be as cool and collected as possible. She would calmly explain her situation. She had been a good wife. She wouldn't mention in front of Elenore how she had turned a blind eye for so long to his infidelities but Donnacha would know what she meant.

She would say she deserved more than him paying only maintenance after they divorced – especially when that maintenance covered fees for a ridiculous school that Aaron didn't even need to be in. He had the ability to secure her future. She needed more than a roof over her head – she needed to know she would be able to look after her mother no matter what happened. It was the least he could do after all he had put her through. He also needed to stop interfering in her life and demanding proof of how she spent every penny he provided to her.

That was her case and she felt it was reasonable and sound.

The avenue to the house seemed to stretch out in front of her for miles. She had heard how grand it was, but she was still not prepared for the scale of it when she finally turned the last bend and saw the massive house in front of her.

Expecting to see Donnacha's ridiculous Porche parked in the drive, she wasn't sure whether to be relieved or further angered by finding the parking area in front of the house empty. What was she thinking? She should have just called Donnacha and had it out with him over the phone, but she knew how that scenario would unfold as she had attempted it many times before. Donnacha would simply hang up, accusing her of being hysterical. He would then ignore any further attempts she made to call him back for at least a week. By the time she saw him again she would have calmed down to some extent. Besides, Donnacha would ensure that he was not alone with her and that Aaron was always there – making it impossible to talk about her financial situation.

Parking her car, she jumped out of it and sprinted up the steps to the front door. Pressing her finger on the doorbell, she waited. What seemed like an eternity passed and somewhere from within the depths of the house she could hear a dog barking. She waited for a few more seconds and rang the bell again. She hadn't considered that there might be nobody at home and her journey would be a complete waste of time.

The thought of the petrol she had wasted, driving the whole way out here, fired up her anger again and she began banging the door knocker, knowing there was nobody there to hear her – but somehow hoping if she released some rage at the house, it might transfer to Donnacha.

She continued to knock on the door until her wrist hurt and, deciding that Donnacha was in no way worth a wrist sprain, she finally admitted defeat and turned around to go back to her car. As she turned, she spotted a car coming up the avenue. It wasn't Donnacha's Porche which left the likelihood that it was Elenore's car, probably returning her back home after an expensive shopping spree or spa treatment. She hadn't bargained for this. Meeting Elenore in the presence of Donnacha was one thing, encountering the woman alone was an entirely different matter.

Unsure of what to do, Karen found that she was rooted to the spot, unable to move. As the car came closer, she could see Elenore peering through the windscreen at her, obviously unsure of who she was. When Elenore emerged from the car, Karen was surprised. She had seen a few pictures of Elenore and had to admit she was beautiful, although it had occurred to Karen that she was not the type of glamorous women she would have expected Donnacha to trade her in for. Looking at her now, there was no denying that Elenore was indeed beautiful. She was tall and striking, but it was the way she carried herself that shocked Karen the most. She was almost hunched over, as if she was carrying a massive weight on her shoulders. Karen supposed that's what life with Donnacha did to a woman. Despite her differences with Donnacha since the break-down of their marriage, she had found herself walking tall. It was as if no longer being with Donnacha had given her back something she had lost during the marriage.

Not only was Elenore hunched over, but she looked tired. Karen had never before seen her in person but the heavy dark circles under her eyes and the lank way her thick hair fell around her shoulders were giveaway signs. Her clothes surprised Karen too. Instead of designer jeans – perhaps a white silk shirt and a cashmere sweater which was meant to look casual, thrown over her shoulders – Elenore was dressed in leggings that were thinning and a long cardigan that had clearly seen better days.

Pulling herself into the moment and chiding herself for what was a nasty critique of a complete stranger, Karen waited for Elenore to address her, which she was now about to do.

'Hello there, can I help you?'

Elenore looked at her, and Karen knew that she was trying to figure out exactly who she was.

'Hi, I am really sorry to bother you and to call without warning. I'm Karen, Donnacha's ex-wife. I was looking to speak with him, but I'm guessing he is not home?'

'Is everything alright? Is Aaron OK?'

Karen was touched that Elenore's first concern was for her son and now felt even worse for the way she had pre-judged her.

'Yes, Aaron is absolutely fine. It's nothing bad, don't worry, and again I am really sorry for calling and ruining your day. I just need to talk to Donnacha – it's only in relation to our arrangement. I would have phoned him, but he never seems to have the time to talk about it over the phone.'

'Well, thank God Aaron is alright. I don't think I could handle anything else bad happening.'

Karen was shocked to see that there were tears in the other

woman's eyes.

'Oh, I really am sorry. I have obviously called at a bad time. I'll get going – will you just tell Donnacha I need to talk to him when he comes back?'

As she nodded her head, the tears were no longer welling up in Elenore's eyes but instead running unchecked down her cheeks.

'Are you okay? What's wrong? Oh God, I can't go and leave you here like this. When will Donnacha be home?'

Elenore was shaking her head. 'He won't be. He's in Poland.'

She was beginning to sob now, and Karen had never been more uncomfortable in her life.

'Is there anything I can do to help? Can I call someone?'

Elenore shook her head and there was silence for a moment as she tried to compose herself.

'Sorry about that, let me start over.'

With what looked like great effort to compose herself, Elenore said, 'Hi, I'm Elenore. Nice to meet you, Karen. Is there any chance you'd like to come in for a cup of tea?'

Unsure how to respond to this, but with no other choice than to agree to the offer, Karen nodded her head. 'Yes, okay. I really don't want to be bothering you, but a cup of tea would be lovely.'

Elenore walked up the steps and, putting her key in the door, pushed it open and invited Karen inside.

Standing in the hall, Elenore took in a deep breath and then let out a shout: '*Alfie, be quiet!*'

The cacophony of barks abated. Aaron often mentioned Alfie, the terrier.

The house was beautiful. Karen was ushered into a porch with double glass doors leading into a double-height-ceiling hallway. Karen laughed to herself – hallway was hardly the right word. Karen's entire apartment would have fit neatly into the space. Dark wooden floors were decorated with old and worn Turkish rugs, chandeliers hung from the ceiling which was adorned with intricate cornicing, and a massive timber staircase filled the centre of the hall, breaking into two on a landing and curling up either side to the next floor. The hall was filled with beautiful mahogany furniture, sideboards and tables, along with a couple of massive mirrors and even a stag's head mounted on one of the walls.

Despite the formality of the hall, it somehow felt warm and inviting – an atmosphere aided by the warm colours on the walls and the bright sunshine streaming in through the front door and the massive window on the landing. It felt lived in and Karen immediately liked it.

'You'll have to excuse the state of the house – we're having work done at the moment – the stairs carpet is being replaced and we are meant to be starting to paint next week.'

Despite Elenore's apology, the place didn't look like it was in a state at all. The only giveaway sign that any work was taking place was a large paint-splattered white sheet in one of the corners on which stood some paint tins.

'Don't apologise to me, you should see the state of my place.'

Karen continued to follow Elenore, trying to get a peek behind the many doors that led off the hall. If the circumstances had been different, she would have asked to see the rooms that lay behind the heavy wooden doors. She tried to imagine what it must be like to live in a house of this size – how difficult it would be to clean it. But then, she remembered, she was imagining a life like her own, living in this house where she would be doing all the cleaning. Elenore must have staff, though she knew they weren't full-time as Aaron had said he hadn't seen any when she had questioned him.

Elenore made her way along the side of the grand staircase, where she turned to her right and through a door, leading Karen away from the warmth and opulence of the hall and into a much colder corridor, from which led a concrete staircase. Behind this doorway they encountered the source of the barking – a jolly fluffy white terrier greeted Elenore as if she had been gone for days – jumping up on her legs, wagging his tail and generally acting like today was the best day of his life.

'Get down, Alfie!' Elenore said to the dog, but the gentle tone she used had no impact on Alfie and, when he spotted Karen, he greeted her with the same enthusiasm as he had his mistress.

'Sorry about Alfie, he gets a bit excitable when he's been left alone for too long.'

Karen didn't mind, she loved dogs, and this little bundle of fluff was particularly endearing. 'Don't worry about it. I've heard Aaron mention him. I'd keep a good eye on him if I were you – it wouldn't surprise me if Aaron tried to steal him. He'd love a dog of his own but unfortunately we don't have the room.'

Karen felt like she had said the wrong thing – she was making comparisons between her own life and Elenore's but that wasn't very fair. Conversation with the partner of your ex-husband was fraught with difficulties – someone should write a handbook on what not to say.

As Elenore began to descend the concrete stairs she cautioned Karen, 'Be careful on these – they're uneven – a bit tricky to manoeuvre when you aren't used to them.'

Karen took her advice and held onto the bannister as she went down the stairs, arriving at another corridor where Elenore led her through another door. Karen now found herself in a kitchen – warm, inviting and homely. She was surprised that one house could hold so many different atmospheres: the opulence of the main hall upstairs, the coldness of the back corridor and now this country-kitchen homeliness of the kind that featured in interior decorating magazines.

Elenore gathered up a large pile of what looked like blueprints from the table. Struggling to roll them up, she then deposited them on a large dresser. She motioned to Karen to take a seat at the sturdy kitchen table

'Sorry it's a bit cold in here – I've been gone for much longer than I expected and the Aga has probably gone out. Give me a couple of minutes and I'll get it going again.'

Karen smiled at her. 'Will I put the kettle on, while you look after that?'

'Yes, that would be great – just let me go out to get some coal. I'll be back in two seconds.'

As Karen busied herself, filling the kettle and opening press doors, looking for mugs, it dawned on her that Aaron was right – there were no staff here. For the second time she was guilty of judging Elenore. This person who was going out to bring in coal didn't fit the image of the spoilt rich girl she had imagined. She was acting strangely, what with the tears and everything, but she seemed normal and down to earth.

Don't make assessments too quickly, Karen warned herself. You've been in her company for no more than ten minutes, give it some more time before making any final judgements.

She just managed to locate tea bags and a jar of coffee as Elenore came back into the kitchen with a bucket of coal.

'Sorry about that again, the sun might be shining outside, but the fire here needs to be kept going all the time – the walls are so thick there is a permanent chill in the air down here. That's the trouble with having your kitchen in a basement. Obviously, back in the day the people who owned the house probably never set foot down here, but the range would have been on constantly for cooking.'

Karen nodded. 'Do you spend most of your time down here?'

'On a day-to-day basis, yes, but it wasn't always the way. When my parents were alive, we had one sitting room upstairs that we used as a family room, you know, with comfy sofas and the TV. My dad used the morning room as his office. But now that we're getting the work done, the family sitting room will need to be used by guests, so out with the battered sofas and in with more formal furniture – like there is in the rest of the house.'

Karen was taking it all in. Aaron had said there was work going on at the house. They were planning on turning it into a hotel. That would be Donnacha's idea, no doubt.

'That's why I prefer to be down here,' Elenore went on. 'Don't get me wrong, I love the more formal rooms upstairs and they're great for things like Christmas dinner and parties, but on normal days you need to be comfortable. As things are now, this is the most comfortable room in the house.' As she finished speaking the kettle came to the boil. 'You sit down there, Karen, and I'll make the tea – or would you prefer coffee?'

'Tea, please – no sugar.'

Elenore soon placed a couple of steaming mugs on the table, with a jug of milk. Then she added a plate of chocolate biscuits. 'Help yourself there and I'll get this sorted.'

Karen watched as she opened the top of the Aga and, using a poker, riddled the fire before shovelling in coal. She then began turning a wheel, which squeaked noisily on the door of the oven, adding oxygen to the fire.

'Now, that will light up in a jiffy. I have an electric heater here. I'll just throw that on while we're waiting for the fire to light up.'

Karen was glad of this – now that she was sitting still at the table, the cold was beginning to make its presence felt. She thought of how she hadn't had to put the heating on or light a fire in her own house for the last two months, due to the time of year and the slightly higher than average temperatures. It would never have occurred to her that a disadvantage of living in a house like this was that you didn't get to save on your heating costs, come the summer months.

Elenore took a seat opposite her at the table, with no more tasks to keep her busy, and an awkward silence fell between the two women which they filled with sipping tea and munching biscuits.

Karen realised she had to jump straight in, but she didn't know how much she wanted to tell Elenore. She had no gripe with

Elenore. She didn't want to involve her in the issues she was having with Donnacha. At the same time, maybe Elenore could be of help and a straightforward conversation hopefully wouldn't cause any harm.

'I suppose you must be wondering why I'm here, Elenore?'

Smiling at the strangeness of the situation she found herself in, Elenore answered, 'Yes, well – the thought had crossed my mind.'

'Look, I don't want to involve you in any of this and, before I go on, I would like to say thanks for the way you look after Aaron when he's here. He only has good things to say about you. I know you care for him.'

'That's no problem at all, Karen. Aaron is a great kid. It's a pleasure to have him here – he has great manners and he never causes any trouble.'

'Well, thanks for saying that. I can't imagine he never causes any trouble – he *is* a kid – but he's a good one. The more people he has in his life, looking out for him, the better it will be for him. I just want you to know I'm grateful.' She took a deep breath before continuing, realising there was no way of avoiding getting into deep waters. 'It's great to finally meet you in person. We really should have met before. I asked Donnacha if I could, a few times after he'd met you and it became clear that you guys were serious. I really did want to meet you before you met Aaron, but Donnacha wouldn't have it, I'm afraid. He never explained why.'

'I know. I wanted to meet you too, Karen. If only to reassure you I wasn't going to be some kind of evil stepmother. I thought it was important to reassure you. You are Aaron's mum after all.'

'So why didn't you? Why didn't you organise for us to meet?' She already knew what Elenore's answer was going to be, but she wanted to hear it directly from her. But Elenore was hesitating. 'Donnacha didn't want it, right? I'm guessing he hasn't painted me in a very flattering light. That's no surprise, that's Donnacha all over.'

'What do you mean?'

Elenore was staring at her and Karen felt she'd said too much. That was her all over. She never thought before she spoke.

'I'm sorry. I've spoken out of turn.'

But Elenore was having none of it. 'No – you know what, you're right. Donnacha doesn't have the greatest things to say about you – but, as I've found out over the last few days, Donnacha seems to do, and say, a lot of things that simply don't add up. Please go on, Karen. Tell me more about why you came here.'

'Well, as I said, I came here to talk about money, Elenore. I need to talk to Donnacha about what he's prepared to offer me as part of the divorce settlement.'

'Well, I know about that situation. Donnacha has filled me in.'

'Oh? And what do you think about it?' Karen asked cautiously.

Elenore hesitated before answering. 'Look, I don't want to delve into your business ...'

'No, go on ... I want to know,' Karen said firmly.

'Well, in fairness to Donnacha I don't think it's his job to bankroll you for the rest of his life. As long as he looks after Aaron properly, I don't think it's fair that he has to share half of everything he has with you.'

Karen sighed. This was going to be difficult. She had been stupid to think Elenore would do her any favours. Elenore hadn't known Donnacha anywhere near as long as she did, and she had no idea of the type of person he was. Of course she would support him. She didn't know whether to continue or not. Elenore might become antagonistic if she chose not to believe what she had to say. She decided to carry on.

'Elenore, I don't want half his money. If he has said that, it is simply not true. What I am saying is that with all his wealth he can afford to be more generous than he's offering to be. I am in a difficult position and Donnacha has it within his power to help me. It pains me to have to ask, but my mother is unwell – her health is declining fast. I can take care of her now, but I need to know that no matter what happens in the future I'll be able to continue taking care of her properly. All the maintenance in the world will be of no use to Aaron if his mother is worried sick all the time because she can't take care of his grandmother. I swear to God, I wish I didn't have to ask for this. As far as I can see, most of the money he has was earned by dubious means. I would prefer not to have anything to do with it, but I have no choice. Most women get maintenance along with some kind of payout. Donnacha is engineering it so that he only has to pay maintenance. We had no joint assets. Apparently, everything he has is tied up in the business – and even with that he doesn't own the business outright. I know his estimation of what the business is worth is a complete fabrication. But I don't have the means to fight him on this.'

Elenore looked like she was going to break down in tears again and Karen was beginning to wonder what exactly was wrong with her. She clearly had more on her mind than the information Karen was telling her. Surely hearing your partner's ex-wife talk about a divorce settlement wasn't enough to make you cry. It seemed there was more going on here than Karen knew about.

'Karen ... what do you mean by "dubious means"?'

'Oh, Elenore, I didn't come here to talk about the past. How Donnacha makes his money is no longer my business. Anything I know about him is from the past. I have no idea what he does now.'

'That's fair enough, but it is my business. Karen, I've found something over the last few days, in relation to Donnacha, that is really worrying me. Now you come here and tell me things about him that I wasn't aware of. He's telling me you're trying to take him for everything he's worth. When you tell me your side, though, it doesn't sound that unreasonable. I am Donnacha's partner, he wants to marry me. I deserve to know the whole truth, so please, if there is anything you know, you really need to tell me.'

Karen knew she had no choice. She had to tell Elenore all she knew. It seemed she had arrived into a situation where Elenore already knew something unsavoury about Donnacha. The conversation they'd just had was not what would normally be expected between an ex-wife and a current partner. It was good that they could be civil to each other – but, having Elenore turn to her, apparently hoping for her to fill in some gaps in her knowledge of Donnacha was not something Karen had expected. She did feel pity for the woman, remembering what it was like to live with Donnacha and constantly being unsure of the truth.

'Okay, it seems I owe you that, after showing up on your doorstep unannounced and throwing all this at you. But before I begin, is there any chance we could have another cuppa? I've run dry.'

Elenore got up from the table, put the kettle back on the hob and rinsed the cups, making small talk about the weather and how lucky they had been with the summer that year. All the time, there was an edge of tension in her voice, as if she was dreading what she was about to hear.

She set two fresh mugs of tea on the table and sat back down. 'Right, please go on and let's get this over and done with.'

Karen wasn't sure how far back to go with the story but promised herself that she was going to keep it to business. It wasn't her place to tell Elenore about all the wrongs Donnacha had done to her personally over the course of their marriage.

She started with how they met, and how he had been unlike any of the other guys she had known. How she was young and naïve and had fallen head over heels in love with him. She wasn't sure how much Elenore knew about his childhood so she didn't mention his troubled past – or the fact that his overcoming it made him all the more alluring.

She went on to tell Elenore about falling pregnant with Aaron and how her love for Donnacha had grown even more then, when he had stood by her without question, insisting that they marry straight away. He was quite a bit older than her and at that stage he was fast progressing his career, so marrying him seemed like the best and smartest option. Not only that but she was crazy for him, so it was a done deal.

Elenore was shaking her head, 'But I don't understand, where did it all go wrong? What happened that you guys didn't make it?'

Unsure of how to work around her question, Karen did the best she could, trying to gloss over the facts of Donnacha's infidelities.

'Donnacha changed. When we met first his ambition was one of the most attractive things about him. He wanted a better life and he wanted to share that life with me. As time went on, his ambition turned to ruthlessness, he wanted to make money at all costs. I used to tell him to relax – we had everything we needed. We had a really nice lifestyle – I could get the kitchen remodelled as often as I liked, we went on two or three foreign holidays every year. I understood he needed to work to maintain what we had but, as time went on, his dealings became murky. He started out finding cheap land or property with real potential, borrowing and working really hard on it to ensure he could sell it at a profit. That was relatively simple and straightforward – a lot of one-off deals, but each one making us money.'

'And how did that change – that's still what he does really, isn't it? Only now he does it on a much larger scale?' Elenore was still seeking some reassurance.

Karen was not going to be able to provide it for her. 'Well, no, Elenore, at least that is not what he was doing when our marriage ended. Donnacha's problem became his inability to understand the word no. I remember the first time it happened. He had seen a piece of land – we were still living in Dublin at the time – and he was convinced this was the ideal location for a housing development. He had that bloody Jerry in his ear, telling him that was what they needed, that it was going to be the project to make them a million. The only problem was, it was farm land and so there was going to be no building on it. It was in an area where there were no similar developments – no largescale housing, no proper roads of the kind that would be needed to service a development of its size.'

'I know what you're talking about,' said Elenore. 'He's spoken to me about that one, about all the hard work it took, to finally be able to build it. He always refers to it as the breakthrough one. He's said that after that it all suddenly became easier. I always thought he meant that by doing whatever work was needed the first time meant they had a template and could use that if they came across any other projects with the same issues. I'm guessing that's not what he meant?'

'It wasn't hard work, Elenore, that was the breakthrough in that project – it was money. Donnacha and Jerry used money to bribe politicians to rezone the land so that they could build on it. That was just one instance. From then on, whenever Donnacha wanted something, he was prepared to bribe whoever he needed to, in order to get it. I just hope for your sake he has changed.'

'And did he tell you all of this? How do you know? Maybe you got it wrong?' Elenore was pleading now.

'I am afraid not. He never told me a word of it but, by the time all that began, my guard was up. To this day, I would imagine if you asked him he would swear he kept it all completely hidden from me. But he wasn't as secretive as he thought. I didn't trust anything about him at that stage and so I listened to every phone call. I even went to his office once, when I knew he wasn't there. I told his secretary I wanted to leave a gift on his desk for him as a surprise so of course she let me in. I went through some files and it was fairly easy to find what I was looking for. The only stupid move I made was not taking copies of everything. If I had those now, I doubt he would be so slow in offering me a payout as part of the divorce.'

Elenore's face was now the colour of snow and the cup she held in her hand was shaking. 'Sorry, Karen, that's a lot for me to take on board, but thank you for being so honest. I don't think many people would be as honest with me as you've just been. But I still have one more question. You said you didn't trust anything he did at that stage – what exactly does that mean? Is there more I should know? He always tells me that you and he just grew apart. What was it that made you so suspicious of him in the first place, if you weren't overly concerned with his business dealings from the outset? Why the sudden change?'

Karen had feared this was coming, but it was one thing letting a woman know that the man she loved was involved in illegal business practices – it was quite another to tell her that he was capable of adultery.

'Are you sure you want to hear this? I have a feeling that there may be no going back. I used to think when I was younger that it was better to always know the full truth, but I am not so sure now. Maybe it's not? When you weigh up the amount of hurt the truth can sometimes cause, maybe sometimes it's better to be oblivious?'

She knew by Elenore that she was not going to be able to avoid this for much longer.

'I need to know everything. As I said, I am supposed to be marrying this man. It now seems he has lied to me about a lot of things – both in his past and regarding some of the things he does right up to the present. You have no idea of the significance of the timing of your visit, Karen. Well, I did mention to you that I found out something about Donnacha a few days ago. It was about plans he has for this house. I won't go into the details now but I was hoping to be able to give him the benefit of the doubt. Now it seems he has a history. Before I tell you any more about that, I need to know – and I am going to ask you straight out – was Donnacha unfaithful to you?'

Karen moved back in her chair. God help her, it looked like she was about to bring this woman's whole world crashing down around her. And it didn't look like she was going to be leaving Elenore's kitchen any time soon.

CHAPTER 13

Cavendish Hall,
23rd December 1922

Dear Diary,

To think this is going to be my last Christmas at Cavendish! I have not met Tadgh as often as I would have liked in recent weeks, but I have so very much to share with you now, dear Diary. Days have dragged by with nothing but boredom but on the few days that I have met Tadgh we have planned so very much. We have only met four times since the last time I wrote to you. That was because Tadgh said we had to be more careful than we have ever been. The few times we did meet, we talked of nothing but our plans for our future.

But now, the day we will leave will soon dawn. I am as excited as I have ever been. Of course, I am playing along with Mama and Papa, pretending that my excitement is because Christmas is almost upon us. I am glad it is this time of the year. At least it doesn't look suspicious to them that I am giddy with joy. They think I am acting as I would have always acted when I was a child. It shows how little they know about me and my life. When I consider that they still view me as a little girl, I know in my heart that I have made the right decision — to leave my childhood behind and start the rest of my life with Tadgh in America.

Tadgh at first wanted me to leave with him before Christmas, but I told him that was simply not possible. However silly Mama and Papa are, I know how much they adore this time of the year. They might not know who I have become but that does not mean that they will not miss me and worry about me. I want to have one last perfect Christmas with them. We now plan to leave Cavendish on New Year's Day and travel to Queenstown. There is boat sailing from there on January 2nd and Tadgh has secured us tickets. I had to give him some of the money Papa gave me, but I still have a good deal left and of course I trust Tadgh without question.

I cannot believe how brilliantly our plan has come together. The Carberys are having a ball on the 1st of January and Mama and Papa have both agreed that I can travel to the ball alone. Papa has asked one of the tenants who helps him on the farm to take me there and deposit me in Castle Carbery. Mama has written to Lady Carbery and it is arranged.

All I need to do now is plan how I am going to get away from Castle Carbery the day after the ball without them noticing and raising the alarm before the boat sets sail. Tadgh says all I need to do is get out of the house by saying I need to go for a walk. I am sure it will be more difficult than that to get away on my own, but somehow I must manage to do so. Castle Carbery is a mile outside Queenstown, so I will walk from there and hope that I do not meet anyone on the road who might raise the alarm.

Papa would be beside himself with anger if he knew. He still maintains that I am not to leave Cavendish without being accompanied by someone. What would he say if he knew I was planning a mile-long walk on my own?

Lady Carbery is under strict instructions from Mama to find me a suitable husband at the ball. It is highly unusual that they are allowing me to go alone and more unusual that Mama is willing to miss the ball herself. There are so few of them these days. Papa says they cannot attend though, as Mr. Barkley, a solicitor from Cork, is coming to visit Papa with some news on January 1st and that he needs Mama there to support him.

I do not know what the news could possibly be, that he would need Mama's support, but whatever it is Papa is getting very apprehensive about it. Mama keeps telling him not to worry, to put it out of his head and enjoy the usual Christmas traditions. I am sure it will be nothing of importance and they will both be sorry they missed the ball in the end.

I asked Mama for a new dress for the occasion. I thought it was the perfect excuse as I will need a new dress for my wedding once we reach America. Unbelievably, she refused! Mama has never refused me a dress before, especially for an occasion such as a ball at Castle Carbery. She said Papa insisted that we could no longer be spending money on such frivolous things. She looked very worried when she told me this news. In fact, she looks worried most of the time now. I noticed the other day how old she has become. I hope Papa looks after her properly when I am gone.

I told Tadgh about their unwillingness to buy me a dress, but he said that was not something I needed to worry about. He said it would be a long time before I had the opportunity to wear a fancy dress again. I was unsure of what he meant by that and asked him to explain. Suddenly he became very serious and said he needed to talk to me. He then went on to tell me that I needed to understand that our lives, once we get to the other side of the Atlantic, will be very different to what I am used to here. He said we would have to work, both of us, and we would have to be careful with every penny we have, little and all as it would be.

He asked me to think very carefully before I made a decision, for certain, to go with him. Of course, I immediately told him I had made up my mind to go with him the very first day he mentioned it to me. Nothing in the world was going to stop me from going now.

He smiled at me then and kissed me and he said that our lives might be difficult for a while, but the opportunities were without limits and, if we both worked hard together, we would be able to make a good life.

Tadgh appears to be very worried though and I do not think it is about our American adventure. He says he has things to take care of before he leaves. He said if only I would agree to leave with him before Christmas, he would not have as many things to look after. I do not know what he means by this and, when I questioned him, he grew silent and left me in a hurry. I never asked him again what he meant by this as our time together is so precious. I suppose this is something I will have to learn. When I am his wife, it will be my job to support him and if he is uncomfortable sharing some things about his life with me, then so be it. I do not think it is the job of a wife to constantly question her husband and so I am trying to master the art of keeping my questions to myself. We had our first fight when I refused to leave before Christmas, but I have to stay true to my belief on this. I must give Mama and Papa one last Christmas.

There is something else I have not asked Tadgh about, but I think for now it is best not to. Early last week, on a day that we had agreed we would not meet, I went out to the woods nonetheless, as I was bored having been housebound all day. May Ryan should have been in the kitchen, helping Mrs. Carey prepare for dinner but to my horror I saw her. I saw her there in the woods, talking to Tadgh. She was talking to my Tadgh. Their heads were close together and it looked as if they were sharing secrets.

I kept my distance so that they would not see me, but I watched as they stood like that for a few minutes, and then Tadgh handed her something. I was unable to see what it was, but she took it and placed it in her pocket. I was not concerned about Tadgh handing her something, or even talking to her. I am sure it must have been a note for Mrs. Carey. It was the look on May's face when she turned around to walk back to the house. It was a look of tenderness. I know that look, I have seen it before. I have seen it in my own reflection in the mirror when I am thinking about Tadgh.

I am sure May is in love with Tadgh. That is why she is suspicious about me and why she is watching my every move. She knows there is something between us and she is jealous. May Ryan's presence at Cavendish makes me want to leave all the more. I cannot wait to be as far away as possible from her, in a place where Tadgh and I do not have to hide our love.

That is not the only problem May is causing. Aside from the absence of something suitable to wear on our wedding day, I am concerned about how I am going to take my clothes with me, and May is not being helpful. Mama asked her to start planning my wardrobe for my visit to the Carberys and May was taking two evening dresses and three day dresses to clean. I told her I would need a larger number of dresses than that. I also told her I want her to wash all my underwear and pack not only my four pairs of shoes, but also my riding boots.

May, yet again, answered me back! She said she could not do that, as, if I wanted to take all my dresses, they would all need to be cleaned and I would have nothing remaining to wear over Christmas. She then fell silent for a minute and I knew there was something on her mind.

'What is it, May?' I asked her.

'Well, m'lady, it is nothing – only that I do not understand why you need so many dresses when you are only going to be with Lord and Lady Carbery for three nights.'

I told her it was absolutely none of her concern and that, if she did not do as I asked, I would tell Mama, and she would be in the most terrible trouble.

May looked at me and said, 'You will not tell Lady Cavendish.

You cannot.'

This took me by surprise, but I managed to answer her. 'Do not underestimate what I am capable of, May. You are in for a very big shock if you do.'

She obviously thought better of what she had said and decided to apologise. 'I am sorry, m'lady, I was speaking out of turn. But please be careful. These are dangerous times and you have to keep safe.'

She was looking at me with an almost tender look on her face. It was not unlike the look she had the day I saw her with Tadgh.

'You may go now, May — and, please, there is no need to worry about me.'

She took my dresses and left the room and I found that my heart was beating uncontrollably. Does she know about my plans to leave with Tadgh? Did Tadgh tell her when he was talking to her in the woods? Does she not want me to leave with Tadgh because she is in love with him too?

I have no idea what she is up to and I have no one to talk to about it. I cannot confide any of this to Tadgh. I know he would be angry if he knew I was out in the woods alone on a day when we were not due to meet. He might think that I was spying on him and that is the last thing I want. I love him with all my heart, I would do anything to keep him happy. I think I am feeling out of sorts because the time for us to be together is getting closer and closer but at the same time passing very slowly. In just over a week we will be together, and I will no longer have to worry about May or anyone else. All I need to do is hold my nerve. The days will pass and then the rest of my life will finally begin.

I will write again soon, dear Diary, and of course I will be taking you with me, to record all the wonderful things I am soon to encounter.

TRHLEC

CHAPTER 14

The day of Donnacha's return to Cavendish had arrived and Elenore was still no clearer about what she was going to say to him or how she was going to handle the situation. Part of her wanted to shout and scream at him, show him the drawings and demand answers – but another part of her wanted to say nothing. That part of her wanted to forget about all the things she had discovered and pretend it had all been just a bad dream.

She had always hated conflict of any sort and, what with losing her parents over the last few years and the ongoing worry of how she'd keep Cavendish, she wasn't sure if she was able for any more dramatic events in her life.

If it turned out that Donnacha was not the person she had believed him to be, which looked more likely with each passing day, she didn't know what that meant for her life and her future. Would they have to break up or was there another way to deal with all of this?

These questions kept going around and around in her head and she felt like they were driving her insane. Donnacha was her security. He had come into her life at a time when she had felt alone. In many ways it had felt like he was the replacement for the family she had lost.

Was it possible that she could have got it so very wrong? She knew from the outside they looked an unlikely match. Donnacha with his flash way of living might seem unsuited to her and her much more understated and quiet ways. But wasn't that what made them such a good match, the attraction of opposites?

And he was kind to her. After all, he was doing all this work to ensure she could keep Cavendish. And he was kind in other ways too. He looked after her, he made sure she made the right decisions. He was always thoughtful, buying her expensive gifts and taking her to exciting places.

And yet, there was a voice in the back of her head which she seemed unable to silence, questioning this kindness and thoughtfulness. What if what Karen said was true and he really was ruthless when it came to his work? How far was he prepared to go to make more money? What if all the work at Cavendish wasn't for them but just for him? With that thought came more unanswered questions. Did his thoughtfulness extend to listening to her opinion and taking her views on board? The more she thought about it, the more he seemed to be coming up short. She thought of how much she had wanted to keep the changes to Cavendish at a small scale and how she had expressed this to him, many times, and how he had seemed to listen. But in the end, it always came back to his experience and his knowledge, and how he knew what was best.

Was it true to say that she had allowed him into her life at a time when she was at a particularly low point? If her parents had still been alive, would their relationship have progressed beyond anything more than a short-term fling?

It was hard enough dealing with all those questions without

having to consider the other things Karen had told her: the lies, how he had cheated on her throughout their marriage and the horrible way he continued to treat her now that they were separated. The picture Karen had painted of Donnacha was not one that bore any resemblance to the man Elenore thought she knew. But how well was that? She had only known him for a short time. Karen had known him since she was a teenager.

And then there was the final devastating piece of information Karen had shared with her. Elenore knew she hadn't wanted to tell her but eventually, after a final prod, she had dropped the bombshell. The reason her marriage had ended was because Donnacha had cheated on her. Then Elenore had asked her: did she think Donnacha had given up his cheating ways after she had finally left him? Karen had done her best to avoid that question too, saying it wasn't for her to say. She didn't have any knowledge of what Donnacha did now, all she was concerned about was getting him to make a fair settlement in the divorce. But Elenore kept on and on, picking at it, like a scab, until finally Karen gave her an answer.

She said she honestly didn't know and had no proof, but she had heard rumours around Cork City. Mutual acquaintances of theirs, people she had known when she was married to Donnacha, had told her things. She tried to soften the blow by saying Cork was a small place where people loved to talk, and gossip became exaggerated as it was passed around.

Elenore wanted the full details and Karen finally gave in. There were rumours about one of the women who worked in the solicitor's firm Donnacha employed. She was married but they were often seen together. The rumour was that she sometimes accompanied him on trips to Dublin.

Now the worst thing about the situation Elenore found herself in was that she had no proof of anything. It was all rumour and hearsay, combined with revealing details of what Donnacha had done in the past. Even that was Karen's side of the story. Could she fully trust Karen? Did she have some hidden agenda Elenore was unaware of?

The one piece of proof Karen did have was from a friend – Charlie Redmond, the former politician. He had resigned from the ruling Government party less than a year before, after raising questions about the granting of certain planning permissions. He had put it out to the media that it was his choice to leave – but it was very much hinted at, in the papers and on the street, that he had been pushed. The truth, according to Karen, was that Charlie had indeed been pushed, but that he was also suffering from cancer. He had decided that, whatever time he had left, he was going to spend it with his family. As it turned out, he had made a full recovery but with that came a new attitude to life that made him stay firmly out of the spotlight, enjoying his retirement with his family in West Cork.

Not long after the breakdown of Karen and Donnacha's marriage, Charlie, a kind, old-school gentleman as Karen described him, had taken her out for lunch. He had confided in her that Donnacha had tried to bribe him. This time it was in relation to fast-tracking a planning application for a small development of holiday homes on the Beara Peninsula. Charlie had refused but wanted to share this with Karen as he believed she was better off out of the marriage. In Charlie's opinion, many shady deals had taken place between developers and politicians in the last few years. It was only a matter of time before the whole house of cards came crashing down. He didn't want Karen to still be married to Donnacha when this happened.

The thoughts kept swirling round and round in Elenore's head. Donnacha would drive up the avenue in less than three hours, and she still had no clue of how she was going to deal with him. She had shared her findings of the architect's drawings with Karen, who hadn't seemed at all surprised. She said it sounded exactly like something Donnacha would do and that Elenore was better off without him.

Sound advice it might have been, but it was easy for Karen to say. She mightn't be divorced yet, but she had gone through the breakdown of her marriage – all that was left was to tidy things up and get the settlement she wanted. Elenore might not be married to Donnacha but, if this meant the end of their relationship, it would be every bit as traumatic as a divorce. It would mean abandoning all that was familiar and starting from scratch: this time alone. The only time she'd been alone before was after her parents died and before she met Donnacha. She had been lonely and heartbroken. She didn't want to go back to feeling like that again.

She knew what Leslie would say if she were here now. She'd tell her it was better to be in no relationship at all than to be in a bad one. Elenore wasn't sure if she had the strength to face either of those options right now.

The phone ringing was a welcome escape from the endless thoughts in her head. Walking over to the dresser, she picked up the receiver. 'Hello, Cavendish Hall.'

'Hello, Elenore, is that you? It's Seán Saunders here, from the library. Is this a good time?'

Was this a good time? If only he knew! She could tell him she was busy, it wasn't a good time, and she'd call him back tomorrow. But what was she going to do then – sit at the table for the next three hours torturing herself with unanswered questions?

'Elenore?'

'Sorry – fire ahead, Seán – I'm not at all busy.'

'Oh great, I'm glad to hear it and I think you're going to be glad to hear from me. I have some news about the diary.'

Elenore could hear the excitement in his voice and it made her smile. How lovely for Seán to be still in a world where you could get excited about a diary! She'd give anything for such a luxury now. Nevertheless, no sooner did she have that thought but she felt a stirring of interest.

'Really?'

'Yes – after I left you the other day, I decided I'd try and find out some more information, so I called in to the rectory to see Reverend Myles. He proved to be very helpful. You know, he has full records of births, deaths and marriages going back to the late 1800s in his office.'

'Now you definitely have my attention.'

'Okay, well, I only had time to have a quick look, but it looks like a baby girl called Edith was born to Lord and Lady Edward Cavendish in June 1906. It was fairly easy to scan through the records because there were so few Protestant families in the area.'

'So, they did have a daughter? Well then, now we know!' At least there was one question in her world with a straightforward answer.

'Yes, and she'd have been sixteen in 1922, so that fits. That's not all though, there's more. The Reverend says there's a woman in the village who used to work at Cavendish – a Mrs. Russell. He says he has spoken to her a couple of times as she used to be in the historical society. According to him, the society was always asking her to do a talk about her time in Cavendish, but she always refused, saying some things are best left in the past. He said she must be over ninety by now and he's not sure how her health is as she no longer goes to the historical society meetings.'

'That all sounds great, Seán! I remember Mrs. Russell. I used to see her around the village when I was a child. I don't think I've seen her in years.'

'So, should we try and have a chat with her?'

'But if she wouldn't talk to the historical society, what's the likelihood she's going to talk to us?'

'Ah here, think positive! I've phoned her already. I spoke to her granddaughter and she said we can call up to see her on

Wednesday evening. She said she's not in the greatest of health physically but mentally she's fine.'

'I don't know, Seán. Do we want to be imposing ourselves on an elderly woman?'

'Yes, well, I imagined that might be your answer, but you're seriously underestimating the effect I have on old women. They love me! She'll probably have willed her entire estate over to me by the time we leave. Anyway, imposing or not, don't you want to find out what happened to Edith?'

She really did and this diary seemed to be giving her the only small amount of light relief in her life at the moment. She told herself to put her apprehension aside and just agree. But Wednesday seemed like an eternity away. She couldn't tell Seán that she had no idea what developments would have occurred in her life by then, that planning anything even a few hours ahead seemed an impossibility.

'OK, Seán – but I can't say for definite I'll be able to go on Wednesday evening – can I give you a call on Tuesday afternoon to confirm?'

Seán said that he was happy enough with that arrangement and hung up, but not before she thanked him for his interest in the diary.

Putting the receiver back on its cradle, her eyes were drawn again to the drawings on the dresser. She was going to have to make a decision. Should she shove the drawings in Donnacha's face and demand answers or approach it more gently? She decided the gentle approach was the only way to get the answers she needed. She gathered up the drawings, rolled them up and took them upstairs. There she hid them in the back of one of her clothes drawers.

Now she needed something to fill her mind for the next few hours until Donnacha arrived home, so she set about giving the house a good clean. That was one thing she could always depend on: cleaning Cavendish was a never-ending task. Downstairs she grabbed some cloths, polish and a duster from a cupboard in the basement corridor and made her way to the main hall. She reckoned if she polished the furniture there, including the stair bannister, and the furniture in the morning room, that would kill the required time until Donnacha got home.

Glancing up, her reflection stared back at her from the antique gilt mirror and it was not a pretty sight. She looked awful but was not surprised by this. She hadn't washed her hair or changed her clothes in two days. She also hadn't slept. Her skin looked pale and drawn which was no wonder. She hadn't ventured outside, except to go to the library the day before yesterday. She hadn't gone riding or even taken Alfie for a walk.

The cleaning could wait. When Donnacha walked through the door, she couldn't give him any reason to think that there was anything wrong. She needed him to be comfortable and open to conversation – that was the only chance she had of getting any information out of him. She was never one for wearing make-up around the house or dressing up She saved that for when they went out together – but at home she always washed her hair and had on fresh, clean clothes. If Donnacha came home and found her in this state, he'd immediately know something was up.

She needed to shower, put on something presentable to wear, get out into the fresh air and get some colour back in her cheeks.

She went back upstairs and savoured a scalding shower, then dried and brushed her hair until it fell around her shoulders in a silky sheet. She put a tiny bit of make-up on – something she'd normally never do when at home, but a touch of concealer under her eyes to hide the dark circles worked wonders. Then she pulled on a clean pair of jeans and a polo shirt, tying a cardigan loosely around her waist in case it was chilly outside.

Downstairs she pulled on her boots in the porch, whistling for Alfie who came running, and the two of them had made their way outside.

Walking down the steps, she stood for a moment and surveyed

the view. Beyond the gravel driveway, the terraced lawn stretched out in front of her, and she savoured for a moment the peaceful gurgle of the water bubbling up from the fountain in the ornamental pond. Further on, a herd of cattle grazed in the parkland, above them a cloudless, blue sky filled with birdsong. She drew in a breath of the clean country air. The sounds and sights were like a soothing balm to her soul and she reminded herself this was Cavendish as it had always been. No matter what was going on in her life, this remained a constant. She could always depend on this view and this sense of peace. She reminded herself just how lucky she was to live here.

On a whim, she decided to go to the woods, walking around the side of the house and to the back. Walking briskly, she made her way through the formal garden, past the walled garden, over the stile and into the shady woods. All the while she walked, she thought about Edith. She imagined what it would have been like to walk in the woods in 1922. Would a young girl from the house have been in danger, would rebels have been watching? The thought of being watched made Elenore shiver and she took her cardigan from her waist and threw it over her shoulders.

Alfie was scratching at something on the ground and Elenore reminded herself that, if there was anyone around watching her, they wouldn't be able to hide their presence from Alfie for too long. Her thoughts turned to what it must have been like to walk the path she was currently walking, heading to meet an illicit lover. How exciting that must have been for the young girl who had led such a cossetted life!

Thinking back to the diary, Elenore really hoped Tadgh turned out to be a good man. That he hadn't run away with Edith's money or, worse still, run away with the maid from the house. If Edith was still alive, she'd be approaching one hundred now. Elenore wondered had she got to America, and if she had, had she ever come back to Cavendish?

She thought about the differences between herself and Edith, aside from age. Here was someone desperately trying to escape from Cavendish. Meanwhile here *she* was – having never wanted to leave it from the time she was a little girl.

She hoped Edith got what she wanted in the end and thought, not for the first time, how strange it was her father hadn't known anything about the last Cavendish daughter.

After a brisk forty-minute walk, Elenore left the woods, and this time made a right after crossing the stile and made her way into the stable yard. This part of the estate always made her feel down, as in her opinion it was the area of Cavendish most in need of investment. Donnacha didn't agree with her and said it was something they could focus on at a later date.

The cobbles were covered in moss, grass was growing around the edges and the roof along the west side of the stables was missing tiles. Elenore had concentrated on keeping one block of stables in good repair and she had achieved this. This was where she kept her own horse, Jasper, who at the moment was feasting on the grass of the Long Paddock. Elenore sighed as she realised she had really ignored Jasper in the last two days and needed to pull herself together. She was happy to pay the €20 a week for Kevin Donnelly, a kid from the village, to feed and water the horse. He loved Jasper, and Elenore believed he'd come up to feed him every day even if she didn't pay him his princely wages. But she was responsible for keeping her horse exercised and she promised herself that, no matter what way the rest of the day went, Jasper and she were going for a long hack first thing the following morning.

By the time Elenore got back to the house, she was happy to see that some colour had returned to her cheeks. Returning to the cleaning she had set out to do earlier, she was soon alerted to Donnacha's return as she heard a car pull to a halt at the front on the house. She tried to remember what she'd have done back when things were normal – would she have gone out to greet him with a hug and a kiss or would she have waited inside until he came to her? Before she had a chance to decide, Donnacha came through the front door.

He looked great – relaxed and stress-free. He was handsome, in an open-necked white shirt, jeans and expensive Italian loafers.

'There you are! Come here to me – I missed you so much!'

He walked with his confident stride across the room and enfolded her in his arms.

Now, Elenore remembered, he'd start kissing her and he'd expect her to go to bed with him, seeing as they had been apart for almost a week. She couldn't do that – not now. But, if she refused, she'd raise suspicions that something was wrong.

'Oh Donnacha, it's so good to see you – I'm glad you're home.' At least that wasn't a lie: it was good to see him, and she was glad he was home. He looked the same as he always had, but what else had she been expecting? That he'd suddenly have grown horns because of all she had uncovered in his absence?

He was now rubbing his hands up and down her back and nuzzling her neck. She knew it was only a matter of time before he took her hand and tried to lead her up the stairs. She decided to pre-empt him.

Kissing him lightly on the lips, she said, 'Now, come on you. You might have been wheeling and dealing in Warsaw, but I'm guessing you haven't had a decent meal since you left here. Come downstairs with me and I'll serve up something gorgeous.'

'That sounds great, but I was thinking more that you might serve me up something gorgeous in the bedroom,' he said, pretending to take a bite out of her neck.

'I'm afraid we'll have to save that for later – my stupid period arrived this morning and I'm crippled with cramps – sorry, love.'

What she was saying wasn't strictly untrue. Her period had arrived that morning, but it was light and far from painful. Taking his hand, she led him downstairs to the kitchen.

'Are you very hungry?' she asked.

'I'm actually fine,' he said curtly. 'I'll eat alright but don't go to any trouble – just some salad will do.'

He's going to sulk for a little while now, Elenore thought. He thinks I've rejected him because I said no to sex. She decided to continue being bright and breezy, knowing it wouldn't take him long to return to normal.

'Fair enough and how about a nice cold glass of white? I have some chilling in the fridge. Why don't I throw together a salad and we can go upstairs and sit outside on the back terrace? It's still fairly warm out there. What do you think?'

'Fine.'

Grabbing the bottle of wine and two glasses, he left the kitchen. Elenore soon followed, with some crusty bread and a Greek salad.

They sat on the terrace and ate the food. Donnacha commented on how lucky they were with the weather and how unfair it was that they didn't get to sit out that often.

Elenore agreed it was a pity to have such a gorgeous place to sit and eat, with magnificent views over the formal garden and its stately old trees, but that was the sacrifice they made for living in Ireland.

Their small talk ground to a halt and Elenore knew she was going to have to say something but found herself not quite ready. She wanted to enjoy, just for a few minutes more, the feeling of having her normal life back.

'Tell me all about Poland then – did all go as well as you were hoping?'

Donnacha told her about the three potential deals and how two looked to be of interest. He said they had made very good headway over the course of the trip and that it had definitely been worthwhile.

He told her how they had planned this trip much better than the previous one. They had left plenty of time to fit in visits to see completed projects similar to the ones they hoped to invest in. He said this had been a real eye-opener – seeing the potential of what was available.

When he finished talking about the business side of things, Elenore asked him if he and Jerry had got to do anything nice and touristy while they were away. He said no, unfortunately they hadn't. Aside from a few nice meals in the evenings, they had been flat out working.

There was a pause in conversation and Elenore focused on her food, knowing it was only a matter of time before he'd start asking her about the previous few days. What should she say? Lie and tell him nothing of any note had happened or tell him snippets of the truth. Just to see what his reaction would be like?

Sure enough, it didn't take him long. 'Enough about me. Tell me, anything exciting happen with you while I was gone?'

Right, it was now or never. She'd have to dive in. 'Actually, I had a visitor when you were away. Karen was here.'

She could see the blood drain from his face.

'What? Karen? What the hell did she want and why are you telling me this only now?'

'I didn't want to be throwing it at you when you'd just come in the door. I thought you might be tired. I just wanted you to relax for a while.'

'But what did she want and why the hell didn't she just ring me?'

'She was here to talk about money. She said she's tried to talk to you about it a lot of times before, but when she calls you always hang up on her. She said when you go to her house Aaron is always there, and she doesn't want to be talking about money to you in front of him.'

'And, of course, you believe her, don't you?'

His voice had risen, reminding Elenore that she must stay calm at all costs. Otherwise this had the potential to blow up dramatically in her face.

'I don't think it really matters what I believe. This isn't anything to do with me, it's between you and Karen. She did raise a few things that I've concerns about though. I wouldn't mind talking to you about them, if that's okay?'

'Of course she did,' he said sarcastically. 'Please go on.'

'As I said, she was here to talk about money and the bottom line is that she's worried about her future and what you're prepared to give her in the divorce settlement. You've told me many times that she's coming after you for all you're worth but, according to her, that's not the case. She says she appreciates the maintenance you pay but she's worried about looking after her mother and her future. I'm wondering, as she stood by you while you made your money, isn't it within your means to be just a little more generous?'

'Right, let me get this straight. My crazy ex-wife comes over here, when she knows I'm out of the country, pretending to look for me but instead finds you. She then proceeds to tell you some sob-story about how hard-done-by she is, how I'm lying to you and how she needs more money from me. That's it in a nutshell, isn't it?'

'Well —'

'*That's fucking great, Elenore, and let me guess — you believe her, right?*' He was shouting now.

'To be honest, I don't know what to believe — and there's no need to shout, Donnacha.'

'*No need to shout!* You, who are supposed to love me, and my bloody ex-wife are ganging up on me. There's no need to shout? I think this is the best time to shout, to be honest!'

'I do love you, Donnacha, but I just wanted to raise it with you. Please. There's no need for any drama.'

He took a deep breath and there was a pause before he spoke. 'I'm sorry. It's just that bloody Karen rubs me up the wrong way. I shouldn't be taking all this out on you. I know exactly why she did what she did. It's plain old jealousy. She knows the divorce is coming ever closer and she'll do anything she can to ruin my life. She's trying now to create a problem between you and me. This is nothing to do with money, or fears for her future. I pay my fair share and I'll continue to do so after the divorce is finalised. She's not getting some big lump sum. She doesn't get to live off me for the rest of her life.'

Elenore sat there, trying to figure him out. He wasn't making any eye contact with her.

'Did she say anything else?' he demanded then.

Elenore thought she might play him at his own game and make him sweat a bit. Before he'd arrived home, she wished this whole situation could simply disappear so she could go back to normal life and being in love. Now that he was here in front of her, she felt very differently. She was growing angry. In fact, at this point she felt she wanted to smack him hard on the face. She counted slowly to ten in her head, trying to instil calmness. She realised she needed to keep drawing him out, so she would see just how big his ambitions for Cavendish really were.

'Well?' he said impatiently.

'Yes, actually, she said a whole lot more but let's not talk about that now. Let's calm down and forget about Karen for a while. We can deal with her later.' She wanted him to know that this conversation was not over, not by a long shot. 'I've been thinking a lot about Cavendish while you were away and I'm not sure if we're making the right decision, doing the work we've planned.'

'Ah Elenore, please don't start at this again! I know your idea is great, but you have to think big, otherwise we won't make a penny. We have to make Cavendish work for us, otherwise there's every chance we might lose it.'

'That's not what I'm saying. Wait a second. I've been thinking about it and I think you might be right. Let's think big – let's not limit ourselves.'

Donnacha's face lit up. 'Seriously? That's fantastic, Elenore. I think it really is for the best. I know you're apprehensive, even with what you've agreed to so far. But, honestly, there's no limit to what we could do here if we set our minds to it.'

'Calm down there, darling – there may be no limits in your head, but of course there are limits. No matter how big we dream, we'll be limited by money. But I'll indulge you – let's pretend for a minute that money is not an issue and there are no limits to what we can do. Where would you go with Cavendish, what would you do?'

She didn't have to wait long for Donnacha to outline to her, in well-thought-out detail, exactly what he'd do. She sat and listened as he described how he'd turn Cavendish into exactly what she had already seen outlined in the drawings: extensions, a golf course, a leisure centre, a housing development. Donnacha's plans were endless.

'Wow, you've really put a lot of thought into this! And what if I were to say yes and go for it? How long would all that take and how much would it cost?'

'That's difficult to say.'

Elenore was assuming it wasn't going to be difficult at all if he was already well-progressed with planning it.

'Well, ballpark?'

'Okay. Well, before we put a final price on it, we'd have to think about planning. If we were able to build, say, a fifty-unit housing development, that would make everything easier. We could build that fairly quickly. As soon as we got the planning sorted, we'd sell the units to free up capital and then we'd be home free. I'd say we'd be looking at a timeframe of just about two and a half years to complete the whole thing.'

As soon as he mentioned getting planning sorted, Elenore knew he was up to his old tricks again. He really had planned this, and she was assuming he had already investigated the practicalities of seeking planning permission to get it done.

'But how would we do it? I mean, you and I as a couple?'

'I'm hoping that won't be a problem. It won't be long now until the divorce is through and I'm assuming, with none of our parents with us, we'll have a nice low-key wedding that won't take long to plan. Once we're married, say in the next six or seven months, all you'll need to do is put my name on the deeds for Cavendish. That will free me up to deal with all the boring paperwork and we'll be home and dry.'

Home free indeed and putting his name on the deeds! He really had it well planned. The more he talked, the more she believed that everything Karen had said about his past was true. It seemed that he hadn't left his ruthless ambitions behind when his marriage to Karen ended. It looked as though he was prepared to go through with another marriage just to make more money.

She hadn't even started thinking about whether there could be any truth to the rumours Karen had heard about his infidelities. But that would have to wait for another day. The knowledge that Donnacha was prepared to ask her to hand Cavendish over to him was enough for now. He wasn't the man she'd thought he was. Cavendish was a business to him and he'd have no problem ripping it apart and destroying it in order to make money. What a fool she had been.

Karen's final words from the day before came into her head, 'If I could get Charlie Redmond to agree to support me, all it would take is one phone call. One phone call to the media about Donnacha trying to bribe Charlie would be enough to cast a shadow of doubt and to start some sort of investigation. We'd have it within our power to put a halt to all his great plans.'

CHAPTER 15

Cavendish Hall,
January 1st 1923

Dear Diary,

I cannot believe it, I simply cannot believe it. All our plans are in ruins. We now have to start over and I do not know how we are going to do that. Today was the day I was finally due to leave Cavendish, and tomorrow Tadgh and I are due to sail to America but now I no longer know if that can happen. Lord and Lady Carbery sent a message to Mama and Papa yesterday that their ball tonight is cancelled, and I am not to travel to Queenstown to visit them.

They did not give any reason why, but Papa said it was most likely a very sensible decision. He said now was the not the time for balls and parties and the Carberys were stupid to be planning such a thing in the first place when the homes of people like us and the Carberys are being burned to the ground every day.

I have not been able to tell Tadgh. He told me he would not leave for Queenstown until first light tomorrow, but I do not know where he is. I last spoke to him two days ago when he gave me my ticket for passage on the ship. He told me to leave Castle Carbery at midday tomorrow, make my way to the harbour in Queenstown and he will be waiting for me there. I have gone down to the stables so many times in the last two days, but he has never been there. This morning I left a note in our hiding place, under the stone in the loose box, but just now I checked and the note was still there. I have no idea what I should do. I need to find out where Tadgh is so that I can tell him I need to go to Queenstown with him when he is leaving.

I also went to the woods three times today, to the places where Tadgh and I meet, waiting for as long as I dared and hoping that he would be there, but alas he was not. Mama noticed my absence from the house and I suppose my agitation, and now she is watching me and so I cannot do anything. She is following me around the house. Each time I get up and leave a room she follows me. I even went to my bedroom earlier. I told her I was tired and needed to lie down and she came and sat with me. I will never be able to get word to Tadgh if I cannot get away from Mama.

Dare I ask May Ryan to pass on a message to Tadgh for me when she is leaving to go back home? She passes Mrs. Carey's cottage on her way to the village. But can I trust her? I do not think that I can. If she is in love with Tadgh, as I think she might be, she is the last person who will want to help me. She might betray me by telling Mrs. Carey or even Mama. Even if I could trust her, how can I talk to her unless I can get away from Mama?

Why has this happened? It had all seemed to be going better than I had imagined. I got through all of Christmas without raising any suspicion. I was a good and dutiful daughter. I played along with the illusion, for the sake of Mama and Papa, that I was enjoying myself. I showed lots of excitement when they presented me with their gifts and when we sat down to eat our dinner together on Christmas Day. It now seems it was all for nothing.

When I think of not being able to get word to Tadgh and him arriving to the harbour in Queenstown tomorrow and finding that I am not there, my heart feels as if it is going to break. I cannot bear to think what he will do. Will he come back to Cavendish to look for me? That is what he must do. He loves me, as I love him, and I would not dream of travelling to America without him. But what if that is not what he does? What if he leaves without me? I cannot bear to think about that. I must trust that he will wait for me, that he will wait for days if he has to — that is what I would do for him.

I will have to find a way to get out of the house and get to him before he leaves for Queenstown. We could take Taffy together in the early hours of the morning. Tadgh has cousins in Queenstown. They could bring Taffy back to Cavendish after we set sail.

And now Mama and Papa have told me we are to have visitors this evening. I do not know why they have invited people here when Papa just said how foolish the Carberys were for having a ball tonight. He is a hypocrite. He says some friends of his from Cork are coming here, they will stay for dinner and overnight. He says I have never met them before, but I must be kind to them and perhaps after dinner play the piano for them, for entertainment. When the ball was still going ahead Papa had said he was having his solicitor friend over tonight but now he is having a large group of people. It makes no sense. I do not know what has got into him.

May has laid my best dress out on my bed. It is not the new dress that I had wanted but it is still the dress that I will wear when I marry Tadgh. She has taken all the dresses she had packed for my visit to Castle Carbery and placed them back in the wardrobe. I could cry when I look at them hanging there. Though I do realise by now that I could have taken only a few to America. How silly of me to think I could have carried all my clothes from Castle Carbery to Queenstown — on foot!

I feel like the dress laid on the bed is mocking me. I do not want to put it on for strangers and eat dinner and play the piano as if everything is normal. Everything is not normal.

There is a strange atmosphere in the house, unlike anything that I have ever felt before and it is not simply because my plans have been ruined. There is a feeling of uneasiness throughout Cavendish today. I can feel it when I am talking to Mama and Papa. It is as if they are waiting for something to happen, as if they know something, but will not tell me what it is.

Papa has spent most of the day pacing up and down the drawing room, his eyes constantly looking towards the windows. I do not know what he is waiting for. It is too early for his visitors to arrive, so he cannot be waiting for them.

I overheard Mama tell him she is going to send Mrs. Carey and May home immediately after dinner. I have never heard of such a thing. Mama hardly thinks she is going to clear the dining room after dinner herself! This is turning out to be the most unusual day I have ever witnessed. Why, why did it have to be like this today? Why can it not have been just a normal day — well, a normal New Year's Day? I should be at Castle Carbery by now. I should be getting ready for the ball, laughing and excited, and all the time holding the secret close to my heart that my excitement is really because of the adventure I am to start tomorrow.

I will have to do as Mama and Papa have told me to. I am going to put on my dress, and I will go downstairs and ask Papa questions about who the visitors are. That will make him believe all is normal with me. That is what I would be doing if Tadgh and I were not running away together. I will greet the visitors and I will sit through dinner and be the most delightful company. Nobody will suspect for a moment what is really going on inside me.

Then I will wait until the right time. I will wait until everyone has gone to bed. Even Mama will not stay in my bedroom all night. I will pack a few things, I will go downstairs, I will go through the tunnel that leads to the farmyard. I will take Taffy and find my way to Mrs. Carey's cottage. There's a full moon tonight, and that will make it easier. I will find Tadgh. I will tell him all that has happened, how I could not go to Castle Carbery, how we had guests I had not expected and how Mama has been following me. I will tell him that we must leave together, now while it's dark and nobody will follow us.

I feel very much better, now that I have a plan. Perhaps all is not lost — all I need to do is get to the cottage and somehow wake Tadgh without alerting Mrs. Carey or his brother. That should be easy, I hope. I know Tadgh will be awake in his bed, dreaming of tomorrow and our lives beyond.

Now, I can hear horses on the avenue, our visitors have arrived. I must get ready to greet them. It will only be a few more hours. A few more hours and I will be with Tadgh forever.

TRHLEC

CHAPTER 16

Wednesday had arrived – the day Elenore and Seán had planned to visit Mrs. Russell. She wondered how likely it was that Mrs. Russell would talk to them about her time in Cavendish. In any case, at over ninety years old it was unlikely she'd remember much of her time at the house.

It was three days now since she'd had the conversation with Donnacha about his plans for Cavendish and he still believed she wanted to go along with them. She had convinced him that she had changed her mind completely about how she saw the future of the house. He now believed that, over the course of a week, she had gone from wanting to maintain the house in a condition as close as possible to its original self to suddenly viewing it only as a business opportunity. A convenient inheritance that could see them reap financial benefits for the rest of their lives. How could he believe that of her? Had he not listened to a word she had said since the first day they met?

She still had no real answers. The only thing she now knew for certain was that Donnacha had no idea who she was. How could he get her so wrong? How could he possibly believe that she was capable of such a sea change?

Elenore had spent the last few days walking around Cavendish like a ghost. She had never thought before of how unsettling uncertainty could be. She needed information, but she had no idea how to get it. Another person would have sat Donnacha down and asked him straight out: are you only with me because I own Cavendish – have you cheated on me? Not her though – she couldn't ask the questions that needed to be asked. Nor, in any case, would such blunt questioning extract the truth.

Perhaps it was better to keep things as they were, pretend she wanted changes at Cavendish, but change her mind at the last minute. Maybe if she went far enough with Donnacha's plans to placate him, at least she'd still have him. And then there it was again, that little voice in her head that wouldn't go away, constantly questioning: but is he worth that price? She was now avoiding him when possible, and she knew he was beginning to suspect that something was wrong.

The only real conversation they'd had since the evening he came home was relating to Karen's visit. She'd tried to bring it up with him again, taking the approach that if he made sure Karen had no financial concerns for her future that could only be positive for Aaron. She had asked him again why he wouldn't agree to making some sort of a lump sum payment to Karen as part of the divorce settlement, given that there was no family home to split between them. Donnacha side-stepped the question and again referred to the massive cost of Aaron's school fees. She had kept at him until he lost his temper completely.

'Jesus Christ, Elenore, why do you keep harping on about this? You seem to know everything, or at least the Gospel according to that bitch! I can't believe you're asking me that stupid question again!'

With that, he had stood up and stormed out of the kitchen, her question still hanging in the air – unanswered.

The only person she had been able to confide in was Leslie, that very morning. She had told her friend everything over the phone. About Karen's visit and how it had added hugely to her suspicions about Donnacha, about Karen's allegation of how Donnacha had cheated his way through their marriage and how there were rumours circulating that he was still cheating.

Leslie was livid, telling her friend to get out of the house immediately. 'You can't stay there with him, you'll go insane – come stay here with me, for a while at least. Just to clear your head.'

But Elenore would not agree to that. She needed to be at home in Cavendish. It didn't make sense to her to be anywhere else at the moment. Besides, since she'd questioned Donnacha again about the divorce settlement and he had stormed out, she'd barely seen him. He was gone to work when she woke up in the mornings, and last night it was after twelve when she'd heard his car pull into the driveway. He hadn't come to bed, so she assumed he'd slept in one of the spare rooms.

While taking Leslie up on her offer to stay at her house was not an option, Elenore did have one favour to ask her friend. As always, Leslie said she'd do anything that was needed.

'The rumours Karen referred to, about Donnacha cheating on me, have you ever heard anything like that?'

To her relief, Leslie said she never had but, as quickly as she felt some comfort, Leslie managed to take it away.

'But, El, that doesn't mean anything. I mean, anyone who knows me and knows Donnacha, also knows how close you and I are – that we've been friends for years. I'm hardly the most likely candidate for someone to confide in about my best friend's partner cheating on her.'

'I know, you're right. I was just hoping you'd chime in there and say "Absolutely not, I've never heard anything and if anyone would know about that it would be me".' Elenore was grasping at straws now.

'I'm afraid not, lovie, but I think I know what you're going to ask me now.'

As was often the case, it seemed Leslie knew what she was thinking before the words came out of her mouth.

'I want you to find out for me. I don't know anyone in the whole of County Cork better connected than you are. You'd be able to find out straight away.'

Her friend laughed. 'I think you have fairly exaggerated ideas about my importance. I might have been well connected back in the day when I was a high-flying PR girl, but not so much any more.'

'Please, Leslie, I need you to do this one thing for me.'

'Of course I'll do it for you, you don't have to ask again. If there is anything to find out, I'll keep digging until I find it.'

'Oh God!' and with that Elenore began crying her eyes out down the phone.

'Please, El, please calm down, it's going to be okay.'

'I don't think it is going to be okay,' Elenore said between sobs. 'You haven't said the one thing I was expecting you to say.'

'I'll say anything you want me to, but please, please, stop crying. What is it you want me to say?'

'I thought you'd tell me not to be silly. I thought you might say Karen sounds like she's insane, and you know there's no way Donnacha would cheat on me in a million years.'

'Oh, that! Ah, Elenore. I want that to be the case so very much. I want this all to go away and I don't want you to be feeling any pain – but I just don't know. I promise you one thing though – no matter what happens, I'm here. I'll help you in any way I can and, if the worst scenario does materialise, which I'm praying it won't, we'll get through it together.'

Not for the first time Elenore felt a surge of love for her loyal friend.

'Thanks, Leslie – and one more thing – if you do find out anything, you'll have to tell it to me straight. I've spent the last few days doing nothing, but I think I was somehow buying myself a bit of time to deal with it. Whatever is going to come my way, I am ready for it now. If it's the worst, I am going to face it head on.'

'Those are fighting words, my girl!'

She could hear Leslie smiling down the phone.

They might be fighting words, and she definitely felt stronger just by saying them, but they still didn't make the dull ache in her heart disappear – nor the desire to go upstairs, pull the curtains and crawl into bed.

Deciding it was time for a subject change, she told Leslie about Seán's call and the plan to visit Mrs. Russell. Leslie was intrigued but seemed more interested in Seán than she did in the updates about the diary.

'Tell me about this Seán character – this mystery man coming to your rescue in the library – this knight in shining armour!'

'I wish,' Elenore scoffed.

'Is he good-looking?' Leslie wasn't going to give up.

'No, Leslie, and stop that. I'm sorry to tell you, he's totally not my type. He's scrawny and wears a big jumper that looks like his mother knitted it. I'll tell you one thing though – if my worst fears about Donnacha O'Callaghan are confirmed, I'll never go near another man for the rest of my life.'

'Steady on there, girl – the rest of your life is a very long time. Don't be making sweeping statements like that. Anyway, you're presuming the worst is about to happen – it might not. Now I'm sorry, but I'll have to love you and leave you. My beloved husband is bellowing for his dinner here.'

'Okay, Leslie, thanks – for everything.'

CHAPTER 17

At twenty to seven Elenore went in search of her car keys. She'd told Seán she'd meet him outside the library at seven o'clock. Donnacha had not come home, nor had he phoned her all day. She contemplated leaving a note telling him where she was gone, but then thought better of it. If he wasn't concerned about informing her of his whereabouts, why should she bother? Feeling marginally better having made that small decision, she finally located her keys, left a doggie treat down for Alfie and made her way up to the front door.

Driving into the library car park, empty but for one car, she was glad to see she was just on time. She saw that Seán occupied the other car which he swiftly exited as soon as he spotted her. Parking beside him, she got out.

'This all feels a bit illicit, meeting in deserted carparks, under the cover of darkness. Hello there, Elenore.'

'Hi, Seán, nice to see you again – and for the record, it's still bright and this isn't illicit in any way.'

Given her state of mind for most of the day, she felt absurdly glad to see him again and reckoned anything that took her away from thinking about all her unanswered questions had to be a good thing.

'Right, the mysterious Mrs. Russell lives in one of the old cottages on the main street. Her granddaughter says she usually stays up until the wee hours of the morning, or at least until nine o'clock, so we have a good two hours to go all Miss Marple on her.'

This made Elenore laugh as together the two of them crossed the main street, to the row of cottages directly opposite the library.

'Number 8 I believe it is.' Seán was already knocking on the door.

A young woman answered almost immediately and introduced herself as Cliona Russell. Seán and Elenore both introduced themselves and Cliona and Elenore did what all people who've grown up in the same small town do – said they recognised each other from school and mentioned who they knew in common.

Elenore wondered, not for the first time, what impression most people in Ballycastle had of her. Leslie had been her closest friend in school, in fact Leslie was her only close friend. Aside from her, she hadn't really mixed with many other children in Ballycastle when growing up, mostly due to shyness. When not with Leslie, she had much preferred to be with her dogs, her pony or reading a book. She understood why some of her peers might consider her aloof. This opinion was no doubt further cemented by the fact she had grown up in what the people in the village called 'the Big House'. It lent her an air of mystery that she certainly didn't feel.

Cliona invited the two of them into her grandmother's house, cautioning them, 'She's a bit deaf, you'll have to speak up. She doesn't get out much anymore. She's not able to walk too well but she does like to chat.'

She led them from the hallway through to the back of the house and into a cosy kitchen. The heat of the room hit them, and they soon saw that the source of it was a stove, in which burned a blazing fire. A room of this size wouldn't have needed it in the depths of winter, never mind on a warm summer's evening.

'Sorry about the heat,' Cliona said. 'She insists we light the fire for her every day, no matter what the temperature is outside. I'm afraid you'll have to put up with it.'

Sitting in an armchair beside the stove, as close as she could possibly get to it without actually burning, was an old woman wearing glasses – tiny and frail with a thin, grey plait trailing down her back. She was dressed in black trousers and a cardigan and had slippers on her feet.

Cliona addressed her loudly. 'Nan, say hi to Seán and Elenore. These are the people I was telling you about earlier.'

Looking up from the book she was reading, and pulling her glasses up on to her head, Mrs. Russell smiled. 'Hello there, it's good to meet you. Has Cliona offered you a cup of tea, or maybe you'd like something stronger?'

Seán and Elenore couldn't help but grin at each other.

'A cup of tea would be lovely, please – it might be a bit early for anything stronger.' Elenore would not have said no to strong whiskey at this stage but thought it might not give the right impression. Seán thought she was crazy as it was. She didn't want him to think she had a drink problem too.

Seán and Elenore took the only other available seats in the kitchen which they pulled out from under the kitchen table. At least this put them at some remove from the stifling heat billowing from the stove.

They didn't have to worry about where to start their questioning of Mrs. Russell. It appeared that she was more than willing to lead the conversation.

'So, you've found a diary up in Cavendish, Cliona tells me.'

'Yes,' said Elenore. 'As you know, Mrs. Russell, I live up there and we're getting some work done.' The use of 'we' almost made her flinch. 'It was found in the old tunnel leading from the house to the farmyard. It was almost thrown out, never to be seen again. I rescued it, I suppose. I was puzzled about the writer because I didn't think there was a Cavendish daughter living in the house in the early 1920s. Then Seán here did some investigation and confirmed that there was a daughter called Edith. The only problem is it ends very abruptly, and we're trying to fill in some gaps. We thought you might be able to help us with that.'

Mrs. Russell was nodding, but a silence descended when Elenore finished her explanation. Perhaps this wasn't going to be as straightforward as they thought.

'Yes, yes,' she said at last. 'I probably can help you with that but first, Cliona dear, will you make a pot of tea and then maybe you should be on your way.'

'Fair enough, Nan, I'm boiling the kettle – but shouldn't I stay? In case you need anything? Besides, you never talk to us about your time in Cavendish. I'd love to hear what it was like, just once.'

'No, dear, I don't want to talk to the family about it – but I don't mind talking to strangers.'

Cliona looked disappointed but nodded and went about making the tea. Mrs. Russell filled the silence with small talk about the weather until her granddaughter served them tea and biscuits and said her goodbyes. She promised to check back in on her grandmother in an hour.

Once she was gone, Mrs. Russell wasted no time. 'There's something I need to say before I begin. I'm happy to answer any questions you two have about the diary, but anything I tell you is private. I don't want what went on up there ever getting back to my grandchildren.'

Seán grinned at her as he raised his teacup. 'Don't worry, Mrs.

Russell, your secrets are safe with us. It's more for our own curiosity that we want to know. I think Elenore has a rare find here and Cavendish is hers now. She's just hoping to learn a little bit more about the history of her house.'

Elenore couldn't have put it better herself but, as she sipped her tea, she couldn't help but wonder what salacious secrets the old lady could possibly have to share with them.

'I meant what I said, you know,' Mrs. Russell said seriously. 'I've never spoken about my time up there to anyone, not even to my husband. I didn't tell him anything about what went on. I married late in life, so people had forgotten what happened, or maybe they hadn't known in the first place. Lord Cavendish tried that hard to keep it quiet, but either way I never spoke about it, mostly out of fear.'

Elenore was astonished, feeling that they were going to get a lot more than they had bargained for. 'Fear, Mrs. Russell? What do you mean?'

'They were different times. You don't understand the hold those people had over us. They owned most of the village. They had people who couldn't pay their rent evicted. Good, hardworking families, left on the side of the road because of them.'

'They certainly were different times,' said Seán. 'I'm a history teacher and when I tell my students about what happened back then, in what is fairly recent history, they find it hard to believe. Was your family evicted, Mrs. Russell?'

She shook her head. 'No, Seán, my family was never evicted but what happened to me up there was every bit as bad. If it happened now, you'd have support. You'd be able to stand up to them, but I was just a child. I worked there for two years. I started working when I was only fourteen. I carried the fear about saying anything until now, but I've been thinking a lot about it lately. As I said, I never told my family and I don't want them to know, but I want to tell someone. I want to be able to say out loud what happened to me, but I need to know it won't go any further.'

Elenore was growing concerned about the old lady. They hadn't intended to come here to upset her. Maybe this had been a bad idea.

'Honestly, Mrs. Russell, don't feel you have to tell us anything. It doesn't matter all that much – it's just a diary.'

The old lady shook her head. 'It matters to me. Do you have the diary with you? I'd like to see it.'

'Oh, of course.' Elenore reached over into her bag, pulled out the diary and handed it to Mrs. Russell.

The old lady took the diary and turned it over in her hands, studying it carefully. Gently she opened the cover and, pulling her glasses back down onto her nose, began to read the first page.

When she looked up a few moments later there were tears in her eyes.

'Are you alright, Mrs, Russell?' said Elenore. 'Can I get you a tissue?'

'I'm absolutely fine, dear. It's just bringing back memories of things I've not thought about in a long time. This diary belongs to Lady Edith Cavendish – but you know that already. Look how she signed it – TRHLEC – that stands for The Right Honourable Lady Edith Cavendish. Of course that wasn't her right title but she liked to use it. In fact, as a mere daughter she didn't have a title but to the staff and villagers she was always 'Lady Edith'. She was the same age as me. Speaking of names, I suppose if I'm going to tell you this story you'd better stop with the "Mrs. Russell" and call me "May".'

Elenore and Seán looked at each other in unmasked disbelief. This was May, the very May that Edith had referred to in the diary. It was almost like climbing into the diary. They'd be able to ask her directly if she had been in love with Tadgh and what had become of Edith.

'You're May?' Seán was barely able to contain his excitement.

'But you're in the diary, Mrs. Russell! You were the maid, you were there during the Civil War and you remember it! This is amazing!'

'I was there alright, but I'm afraid I was just a young girl. I won't be able to tell you anything about the Civil War. I was just trying to get by.'

'Of course.' Seán fell silent, a sheepish look on his face, and took a gulp of his tea.

'I remember Lady Edith well. She was so full of life and spirit, a bit spoilt and silly definitely, but a nice girl. I suppose I was always envious of her – she had so many lovely dresses and nothing to do all day but read books and play with her dog and her pony. It was different for me. I was spending my days, from six in the morning until late at night, climbing stairs, cleaning floors, lighting fires and helping old Mrs. Carey prepare the food for them. The only bit of luck I had was that I got to go home at the end of the day. Things would have been a lot worse for me if I'd had to sleep there – like some girls did in big houses like Cavendish. As I said, my parents sent me up there when I was only fourteen years old. I can't blame them, of course. They were delighted that I was bringing in some money, small and all as it was. I was delighted with myself too. I remember heading up there on the first day, walking up the long avenue, thinking how great it was going to be, spending my days in this beautiful big house, which would be warm and where I'd get fed too. It was like that at first. It was hard work, but I was prepared for that. I came from a family with five brothers. I was used to helping my mother cook and clean for them, so looking after one family of just three people was in many ways easier than what I was used to at home. Old Mrs. Carey was lovely too. She really looked out for me, telling me what the family did and didn't like and how things should be done.'

'Mrs. Carey was Tadgh Carey's mother,' Elenore said.

'Yes, that's right. It broke her heart what happened to Tadgh.'

Elenore and Seán looked at each other in dismay, but before they could ask any questions May continued.

'Now, where was I? Yes, Lady Edith. I remember the first time I met her. I had barely laid eyes on her before. Imagine that! She lived so close to me and we were almost the same age, but any time she was in the village she was in a carriage – there was no mixing with us. She'd never even gone to school – her education was from a live-in governess up at the house. I think I might have felt a bit sorry for her – thinking how lonely it must have been for her, with no one her own age to pal about with and only her parents for company. I do remember her that first day – her beautiful long hair, so fair it was almost white, her flawless pale skin. He had the tiniest little waist – I felt like a heifer beside her.' She paused and gestured to their neglected teacups. 'Drink up – it's going cold. And eat the biscuits.' She raised her own cup and drank deeply.

They followed suit and dutifully took a biscuit each. The tea was indeed lukewarm.

May sighed as she put down her cup. 'Everything seemed like it was going well for me at the start, although Lady Cavendish was a nasty woman, shouting at me and Mrs. Carey. I suppose that's how they were allowed to carry on, back then. Lady Edith's father, the Master as we used to call him, seemed kind enough at first. I remember he used to always say hello to me and ask me how I was getting on and if I needed anything. I said to Mrs. Carey once how nice I thought he was, and I remember thinking her response was very strange. She told me to be careful with him and try not to go into the rooms to clean them when he was in them alone.'

'Oh!' Eleonor gasped and shot a look at Seán.

'I was that naïve and stupid. I thought it was some kind of rule for his benefit, so that he wouldn't be disturbed by me cleaning. How silly I was, when I look back on it now.' May fell silent for a few moments. 'It started with him giving me things – a sweet, or the leftovers of one of Mrs. Carey's cakes. I never imagined it was anything but harmless. I was only a child. It wasn't too often we got cake, so I felt I was special, that the Master was being kind to me. And then one day it all changed. I was in the drawing room, dusting down the curtains and he came in. I wasn't finished my work, so I couldn't leave the room as Mrs. Carey had told me to do. I didn't acknowledge him or say anything to him – I never would, unless he said something to me first. I had my back to the room and I could hear him coming over to me. He put his arms around my waist and pulled me tight up against him. I didn't know what to do I got such a fright. We stood like that, in silence, for what seemed like forever and then finally he pulled away and all he said was, "You're a good girl, May". I was shaking with fear. No one had ever touched me like that before, except for my mother, and certainly not a man. He hadn't done anything more than put his arms around me, but it felt so sinister. I couldn't tell anyone. I was fearful that I'd be dismissed in disgrace if I did.'

Elenore shook her head in disbelief, imagining the frightened young girl, and how confused and afraid she must have felt. 'I'm so sorry, May, that must have been terrible for you. I understand now why you don't like to talk about your time at Cavendish.'

'I wish I was able to say that was it, that it never happened again, but I'm afraid I can't. That was just the beginning of it. I spent the next two years in a daily bid to avoid being alone with him, but he knew what he was doing. It was easy for him. I managed to fend him off sometimes but, each time he managed to get to me, it got worse and he took it further. I had nowhere to go and no one to turn to. When I think about it now, I wonder should I have confided in my mother – she might have listened to me. Things were changing by then. I think now if I had told my brothers they'd have taken the situation into their own hands and taken care of him. Because I was still a child, I didn't realise that it was a time of massive change. They were losing their power, the landed classes, but of course I didn't see that. I was still of the same opinion as previous generations: they were kings of all they surveyed, and we were there to obey them, no matter what they asked.'

May took the diary up again and turned to the last entry. Elenore and Seán gave her the time to read it, thinking it was best to give her some time to recover from having told her story.

After some time had passed, she looked up and pushed her glasses back onto her head again. 'January 1st, 1923: that would be the last entry alright. I was pregnant by then, scared and with no idea what to do.'

'Oh God, May! You got pregnant!' said Elenore. 'What age were you then?'

'I was sixteen. I'm surprised that I got away without falling pregnant for that long but somehow I did.'

'May, if this is too much for you, please don't feel that you have to keep going,' Elenore said. 'It doesn't matter if you don't want to talk about this. It's all very personal and I don't want you to feel like you have to talk to us.' She was growing increasingly concerned about the impact on the old woman of talking about such a traumatic time in her life. She glanced at Seán and saw that he looked equally troubled.

'No, dear, I want to talk about this,' said May. 'I know it's hard to understand but for some reason I feel better talking about it, as if a weight has been lifted off my shoulders.'

'Okay,' said Seán, 'but any time you want to stop, please do.'

'Thank you, you're very kind, but I want to continue. Let me see, where was I? Ah yes, the fire. I wasn't sure I was pregnant, there was no way to tell – we didn't have pregnancy tests like they do now – but my mother had, thankfully, explained the facts of life to me. When I think about it now, it was very forward-thinking for a woman of her time. So I thought I must be – and that I was probably three months gone. When I first suspected it, I'd gone to the Master and asked for more money. I can't believe that I was ever so brave, when I was in such fear of him. In my stupid childish head my only thought was that if I had to leave the house in disgrace I was going to need money. I thought, as he paid such special attention to me, he might give me something. I didn't, of course, tell him the reason why and he refused anyway.'

Elenore was so appalled she wasn't even able to voice her sympathy. Seán, too, looked stricken but stayed silent.

'As it happened fate stepped in, and I didn't need the money in the end. At the end of 1922 Tadgh Carey had come to me and asked for my help with something. He said he and the local group of rebels needed information and, as I had access to the house, I might be able to get them what was needed. I didn't do much for them really. I just informed them of the movements of the family: when they were going to be home, who was coming to visit them – that type of thing. I didn't know what they intended to use the information for, but I knew it couldn't be good. Since then, I've often felt very guilty – considering what happened . . . But, you see, by that time I felt such hatred for Lord Cavendish I'd have done anything to cause him harm. Feeding information to Tadgh felt like a small act of revenge and it made me feel better.'

'That's very understandable,' Elenore said gently.

'Well, I suppose I ended up helping the family. If it wasn't for me, they might have lost Cavendish altogether. I couldn't go through with exacting the final revenge. My brothers were aware of what the rebels were planning and, although they didn't count themselves amongst them, they had information, probably overheard in the pub.' She paused and tapped the diary. 'That was also how I found out about Edith and Tadgh. I heard it from my brothers, talking about it when they thought I wasn't listening. Edith and Tadgh were planning to run away together to America. Of course, it was a completely stupid idea – at least on Lady

Edith's part – even at my young age I knew that much! But she was such a silly young girl and had no idea of the hardships facing her. I heard that Tadgh had got money off her to buy the tickets for passage on the ship from Queenstown, or Cobh as it is now. I don't know if Tadgh's intentions towards Edith were ever real, or if he was just using her for what she could provide him with, but either way him and the other rebels were planning to burn her house to the ground before he fled the country. He had bragged to my brothers that the fire would be burning at Cavendish and he'd be halfway across the Atlantic with the daughter of the house.'

Elenore was horrified. 'So, all the time he was planning this new life with Edith, and leading her to believe that he cared for her, all he wanted was to use her?' A comparison with Donnacha flew into her head.

'I don't know. He clearly intended to go to America with her. So maybe he did care for her – but, if he did, how could he burn her house down? I just don't know. But, in any case, Tadgh didn't make it to Queenstown and the ship – not then anyway.'

'What happened to him?' Elenore asked.

May waved a frail hand at her. 'Wait and let me tell you the story as it happened.' She paused and collected her thoughts. 'I didn't know what to do. I wanted my revenge on Lord Cavendish – if they had stormed the house and killed him, I'd have rejoiced. But, to save Edith, to prevent her from ruining her life, I would have to betray Tadgh. How could I do that? What was the right thing to do? Then everything changed. The message came from Castle Carbery. The ball was cancelled. Tensions were heightened at that time – five big houses had been burned in the county over Christmas. The Carberys were nervous and rightly so. But this meant Edith would not be travelling after all. She would be there when the rebels attacked and when the house was burned down. That meant she could die.' May paused. 'I couldn't let that happen. Even though nobody had protected me, I couldn't bear the thought of that for her. I didn't realise the risk was small – normally people were removed before houses were burnt. So I went to Lord Cavendish and I told him. It was terrible for me, having to do that. I hated that man but there was no way I was going to let Edith die – no matter how awful a person her father was. I didn't tell him anything about my helping the rebels. I just told him I was walking through the woods on the way from work and had seen the rebels meeting there. I told him I had stopped and hid behind a tree and heard them say they'd burn the house on the night of New Year's Day. He believed me but, when I finished talking, he just grunted and told me to get back to my work. That man was an ignorant pig. He didn't even deem it necessary to say thank you, after all he had done to me and me just after saving his house and family. He left the house not long afterwards. I assumed he was going to alert the Civic Guard. I was relieved. They might be able to issue a warning, if they suspected who the rebels were – but they'd at least be able to guard the house and their presence would prevent the attack taking place.'

Seán leaned forward and said, 'So you didn't tell him their names, May.'

She shook her head. 'He asked me, but I told him it was dark and I was afraid to look out from where I was hiding. No, Seán, I couldn't name them – not young men I'd known all my life.'

'I see.'

She sighed. 'As it turned out, Lord Cavendish hadn't alerted the Civic Guard after all – instead he'd sent a message to have some men travel from Cork to spend the night in the house. I think he may have paid them to stay and protect the family. I heard him tell them that it would have been a waste of time to alert the Civic Guards – that the bloody paddies weren't likely to go out of their way to protect him. I remember Lady Edith mooning about the house all day and the feeling of tension in the air. I was terrified. I didn't know what was going to happen. Dinner was served late and it went on for even longer than usual. Then Lady Cavendish came down to the kitchen and told Mrs. Carey and me to go home. She normally never came down and she certainly never told us when it was time to go home – we always left as soon as all the work was done and we knew they didn't want us to do anything else. I remember she told us to be careful on the way home and to walk together for as long as possible. It was just then we heard screaming coming from upstairs. I ran upstairs to the front door, where Lady Edith was screaming for her father. The rebels were running towards the house, carrying blazing torches. I ran to Edith and tried to drag her inside. They kept coming towards the house. They were like an angry mob. A few of them had broken off from the main group and made it to the front of the east wing and had smashed a window. We watched, horrified, as they poured petrol in through the window and then threw one of the torches in behind it. The main group of them were almost upon us now. But then Lady Edith and I were pushed aside as the men visiting Lord Cavendish ran out the front door armed with shotguns. They took aim and the shooting began. The rebels immediately realised that they were in no position to fight back, what with their limited supply of guns, and I suppose they felt they might have inflicted enough damage. There was smoke billowing out of the east wing and flames could clearly be seen through the windows. They ran for the hills, but not before Lady Edith saw Tadgh amongst them. But he hesitated, staring at the house, and so he was the last to run. I remember Edith screamed his name just as one of the men wrestled him to the ground. Lady Edith collapsed in the hall in sobs. She was inconsolable. She kept saying, "Why, why would Tadgh do that?" but nobody paid any attention to her, as chaos took hold.'

May fell silent, shaking her head, and Elenore had to quell the urge to prompt her to go on. She glanced at Seán, marvelling at how for all his enthusiasm he was able to be so patient.

Eventually May continued. 'The baby that was growing inside of me died that night and by the next morning it became apparent that Lady Edith was nowhere to be found. That night was the last time I ever saw her. One of the men rode down to the village and alerted the fire brigade – they came but it took hours to get the fire under control. The Civic Guard arrived too but the rebels were gone. The east wing was nothing but a shell, but at least the fire hadn't spread to the main house. Tadgh Carey ended up in prison after that. When he finally got out, he did leave Ireland and, I assume, made it to America. Lord and Lady Cavendish, when they saw that I was bleeding kept me at the house until the bleeding stopped. The fact that a baby had existed was never mentioned. I often wonder if Lady Cavendish suspected anything or if she simply assumed I had allowed one of the boys from the village to make me pregnant. It was a terrible time for me.'

May fell silent and bowed her head, tears threatening. After a while, she continued.

'It was during the following days, when they were still searching for Lady Edith, that they found her packed travelling bag. So then they knew she had intended to run away. But they were mystified by this. Run to where? And, if she had run away, why had she not taken the bag? Where was she now? They contacted the Carberys and some other families in the county, but they all said they had not seen her. Had she been abducted? They were distraught. But then they found the note.'

'The note? She left a note?' asked Sean, surprised.

'Yes, but not for them. For Tadgh. It came to light when they were cleaning out one of the loose boxes, which had been used by the carriage horses belonging to the armed men who had stayed in the house the night of the fire. The note was hidden there, under a stone. I never knew what she had written in the note but, as soon as Lord Cavendish read it, he was furiously angry and called the search off. I knew by now he wanted me out of the house, probably so that he could forget about what he had done to me. I remember, when I was leaving to go home, he told me I was never to come back to the house and I was never to mention anything that had happened to anyone. If I did, he said, my family and I would be made to pay. He also said I was never to utter Lady Edith's name again, and that someone who had behaved in the way she had was no daughter of his. And that was that. I told my mother that they no longer needed me at the house.'

'Did she ask why?' said Seán.

'No. She didn't question me – not then, not ever. But she did talk to Mrs. Carey and who knows what might have been said. Of course, Mrs. Carey lost her position too, because of Tadgh. So my mother might have thought Lord Cavendish connected me to Tadgh and the burning of the house too. I never knew what she thought.' May shook her head. 'Nobody ever mentioned Lady Edith again, not for a long time. Rumours circulated years later that she had gone to America on her own. I couldn't imagine how she could have done that – she was barely able to tie her own shoelaces. But then came the news from the Reillys who used to live next door. They had a son who went to America in the 1930s. He sent a newspaper clipping home to his mother at one stage. The clipping was a picture of Lady Edith on her wedding day. It called her Edith Cavendish and the young Reilly lad had recognised the name. He sent it home as he thought his granny might like to see it. Mrs. Reilly showed me the picture. Edith looked as beautiful as ever. She had married the heir to some newspaper fortune. I wish I could show you the clipping, but Mrs. Reilly is long dead now and a different family lives next door. It's probably difficult for you to understand all of this now but they held all the power back then, and they felt she had betrayed them. It was easy for them to wipe her out of their history. As it turned out, the damage done to the east wing was what finally broke them. Apparently, they were in massive debt before the fire and trying to repair the damage finished them completely. In the end, I suppose the rebels got their way. Lord and Lady Cavendish moved back to London a few years later and Cavendish eventually was put up for sale.' She paused and lay back in her armchair, now visibly exhausted. 'Elenore, I assume you know the rest of the story of the house from there. It's a strange sad story and so few people know about it. I'm the last one now. Anyone else who was there is long dead.'

CHAPTER 18

On waking early the next morning, Elenore had a split second where she forgot about all the events of the last few days and she felt calm and peaceful. Then, suddenly, it all came flooding back to her and she felt the familiar heaviness in her heart that she was becoming accustomed to.

On leaving May Russell's house, she had accompanied Seán to the local bar where they had a drink and spent time dissecting the information May had shared with them. They both felt enormous sympathy for the old woman and wondered at her ability to continue with her life after the traumatic events at Cavendish. She had eventually married, raised children and was now surrounded by her grandchildren and great-grandchildren. What a remarkable woman she was, they agreed. Her resilience was inspirational.

They had spent much time discussing her revelations about the Cavendish family, especially Lady Edith. They imagined the young girl, betrayed by the boy she loved. They both agreed it must have been an innocent first love, but sometimes that was the most painful. They wondered yet again what the rest of her life had been like. It now seemed she had indeed made it to America, but why had she left the security of Cavendish? Surely, when she discovered Tadgh's betrayal, she'd have wanted to stay at home? Her diary did not hint, at any time, that she had fallen out with her mother or father. Her writing showed an amount of disregard for them, but they both agreed that was not an unusual way for a teenage girl to feel about her parents – especially when she was caught up in the headiness of falling in love and eager to escape the confines of her sheltered life.

They talked about themselves. Seán shared more about his background, telling her about his upbringing on a farm in West Cork and how this had instilled in him a love of the outdoors. His love of history had led him to his chosen career, but he sometimes fantasised about a different life – running the family farm, being outside all day, and the satisfying exhaustion that came with manual work. Alas, that was not to be, as he was the second son in his family and he would not inherit the farm when his father died. He spoke too about his family, telling Elenore about the idyllic childhood they had provided for him. He'd always be thankful for that, especially now that he was a teacher and had learned about the awful homes that some of the kids he taught came from. Both his parents were still alive. By the way he spoke about them, Elenore could see that he was very close to them.

She shared some of her story with him: her own lovely childhood, how close she had been to her parents, and the pain she had felt when she lost them both within a relatively short space of time. She told him about meeting Donnacha not long after her father died and alluded to the fact that he was now living with her in Cavendish, but she didn't refer to the events of the last few days. Nor did he pry into the cause of her unusual behaviour on their first meeting – and for that she was thankful.

Before she knew it an hour and a half had passed, and she was glad to think that she had been able to forget her woes even for that short time.

Seán walked with her back to the car park, but before they parted ways asked her what she now wanted to do about the diary.

'What do you mean? Is there more we can do?'

He seemed surprised. 'Well, yes. I think there's a lot more we can do. Don't you want to know what happened to Edith? It seems she did make it to America. That can't have been easy for her. Yet it looks as if her life turned out well, if what May said about the wedding picture in the newspaper is true. I, for one, am dying to find out the rest. We can't just leave it at that.'

'No, I suppose not, but where would we start? All we have is that she apparently did end up in America and married the heir to a newspaper fortune. May doesn't even remember what the man's name was. It's vague at best.'

Seán was shaking his head. 'Oh, such little faith you have, honestly! That's enough information to find her telephone number.'

Elenore smiled. 'Really, is it?' She was teasing him now. 'Ah, come on, I know you did well to track May down but even you'd have to admit we've so little information it would stump a professional detective.'

'Let me do this, Elenore. Honestly, I want to. There must be some record of her, somewhere in the world, on the internet, somewhere. Even if not her, then her family – where did they disappear to? May said they left a few years after the fire – don't you want to know if Edith ever saw them again?'

He was right – she desperately wanted to know. 'You're right – I do want to know.'

Seán smiled. 'Good, I'd say it will take a while, but I guess there's no hurry. I'm going to get on it. As soon as I find anything, I'll let you know.'

'Great, thanks, Seán. Now I'd better go. Thanks again for everything and hopefully we'll chat soon.'

Elenore had left him then and driven home. There had been no sign of Donnacha's car at the house. She'd let Alfie out for a while and then put him to bed and gone to bed herself.

Surprisingly, she'd slept well, for the first time in weeks. Perhaps it was the fact that no builders had materialised this week. Not having spoken properly to Donnacha, except for the day he returned from Poland, she had no idea why. Seeing them in the house would have been a constant reminder of the lack of control she now had at Cavendish and what was being done to it. The longer they stayed away the better, as far as she was concerned.

But now she was awake – to another day of uncertainty and confusion. This time two weeks ago she'd have been planning for the future: picking out carpets and curtains for the house and planning trips to other country houses that had successfully been transformed from family homes to guest houses and hotels. None of that was a priority for her now.

She had never had what could be classed as a proper job. She had studied English and sociology at university, not exactly arming her with a degree that was going to lead to a lucrative career. Her plan, on returning home to Cavendish after university, was to spend some time at home, maybe go travelling for a year and then figure out exactly what she wanted to do with her life.

That was not how it had materialised though. She had never left Cavendish again. Her father, on the pretence that he was desperate for her help, roped her into helping him in Stacks, even though she knew nothing about running a business. She had learned quickly, and he had ensured she got as valuable an education over those ten years as she had at university.

He had moved her from department to department – the accounts office, the buyers' office, the planning office, human resources: making her stay in each one, until she understood the workings of it, inside out, no matter how much she hated it.

In the end she became his right-hand woman, advising him and eventually helping him to reach the decision that they must close the store. Their profits were dropping year on year and keeping it open any longer would have been detrimental to her father's finances.

Not long after that, her mother became sick, suffering a long and painful illness, and Elenore had cared for her through it all, ensuring she never needed to leave her beloved Cavendish. Violet had died peacefully in the bed she had shared with Elenore's father for so many years.

Less than a year later Elenore lost her father, and after that tried to figure out what to do with the rest of her life. That was when the idea of turning Cavendish into a guest house had planted itself in her head.

The time spent working with her father had ensured she knew how to run a business and it occurred to her that maybe that had been his plan all along. So, she decided to make it work, but instead of jumping straight in and making it happen, she had procrastinated. She could see now that setting up a business just after losing both her parents had not been the best idea and she might have even been suffering from mild depression at the time. Then Donnacha had come along and changed all that – bringing her around to his way of thinking but also bringing some joy back to her life.

But now look where she was. She had no idea of what the future might hold and, if everything went sorely wrong, what would she do? She still had some of the money her father had left to her, but it wasn't a lot. She needed to pull herself together and fast.

Telling herself the first thing to do was to get out of bed, she swung her legs to the floor and stood up. She threw on some clothes and went downstairs. She made some tea and toast and then fed Alfie.

Once the little dog had devoured his breakfast, she took him outside with her. Stopping at the courtyard, she picked up Jasper's saddle and tack. She was going to keep the promise she had made to herself a few days earlier to get some exercise. A good gallop around the demesne would work wonders to clear the cobwebs.

The plan worked, and two hours later she was feeling refreshed, having showered off the sweat she had worked up galloping Jasper across the acres of parkland surrounding Cavendish.

Her improvement was short-lived. As she went down to the kitchen to make a coffee, her phone beeped. For a second she thought it might be a message from Donnacha.

It wasn't. It was a message from Leslie.

'Free for a coffee, my house, 11.30?'

She immediately knew her worst fears were about to be confirmed. If her friend had found out nothing, she knew she would have simply called her and said that. She had also chosen the location to meet: her own house. If there was no bad news and Leslie wanted to meet for coffee, she'd have invited her to one of the cafés in Ballycastle. Leslie loved getting out and about, always eager to see what was going on in the village. But there'd be no privacy if they met in the village. If Elenore got upset, it would be the subject of gossip for days to come. Her friend had definitely discovered something.

Preparing herself for the worst, she decided it was better to get it over and done with. It was only a quarter to eleven and she'd drive to Leslie's house in less than fifteen minutes, but she couldn't wait.

Leslie greeted her at her front door before she even had a chance to knock. She looked grim and pulled Elenore into a hug. 'Come on in, girl, the kettle is boiling.'

There was no need for small talk between them. Leslie didn't drag the suspense out.

'I have news. I decided to get on it straight away – I didn't want you mulling over something which I was hoping was nothing. Unfortunately, that's not the case. It's not good news, I'm afraid.'

It wasn't a shock to Elenore at this stage and she felt strangely calm. 'Go on, tell me everything.'

'I rang Martin Cunningham – you remember him? I think you met him here once or twice?'

Elenore nodded, the name sounding vaguely familiar.

'He used to work in that legal firm Donnacha uses. He left a few years ago to set up a practice of his own. Apparently they don't have the greatest reputation and Martin is that very rare thing: an ethical solicitor. Anyway, he still moves in the same legal circles and would know everything that's going on. Also, he's not one for gossip – solicitors rarely are. I knew he wouldn't tell me anything unless he knew for certain it was true. I won't go into the details, but bottom line is yes. Donnacha is having an affair. Her name is Siobhán Ellis. She's the solicitor Karen told you about.'

'But how does Martin know this? Has he seen them together?'

'Are you sure you want to hear this? You could just take his word for it. I wouldn't be telling you this unless I trusted his word absolutely.'

'No, I need to hear it all. Otherwise I'll be coming up with all sorts of reasons in my head as to why it's not true.'

'Right, Martin told me it's common knowledge around Cork – apparently they are not at all discreet. I put it to him that it could still just be rumour. There must be any number of people Donnacha has pissed off over the years. Who's to say someone who doesn't like him didn't start spreading rumours just to make his life difficult? Martin agreed that could be the case except that, though he's never seen them together, his wife has. He said his wife and her friend went on a girlie trip to Paris earlier this year and in the airport on the way home they saw Donnacha and this Siobhán, acting like a loved-up teenage couple. Martin's wife said she saw them walking towards the executive lounge in Charles De Gaulle, holding hands and eating the faces off each other. She was out with the plebs in the normal departures area. She didn't see them on the plane – they must have flown business class.'

'But was it definitely them? She might have been mistaken?' Elenore wanted so desperately for the information to be wrong.

'It was definitely them, El – her friend saw them too – she recognised them straight away.'

'But Donnacha didn't go to Paris – if he'd gone to Paris I'd have known – when was it?'

'He said it was in February.'

Elenore remembered. 'Rome.'

'Paris – not Rome.'

'No, he told me he was in Rome – he went to Rome. Ireland was playing Italy in the rugby. He went with Jerry. He can't have lied about that, he wouldn't have risked it. If I had asked Jennifer what Jerry thought of Rome, his whole cover would have been blown. Much as she annoys me, I do see her fairly often. I could have easily mentioned it to her.'

'I know, but think about it, El – is Jerry Reynolds really a watertight alibi? You know what he's like. He's hardly the faithful type himself. Jennifer probably believes Jerry was in Rome and God only knows where he was the weekend – but let's not concern ourselves with that.'

'Oh God, you're right. I know you're right. I think I knew from the minute Karen told me about the rumours. Stupid me – I never suspected a thing before that. What sort of a bloody fool am I? How could I not have noticed something?'

Leslie jumped in immediately to defend her. 'You're not a fool, far from it. He's the one who's a fool and I'd hang the bastard out to dry if I could. You know I could ask Ben to beat the shit out of him – he could do it in the dark, so Donnacha wouldn't know it was him.'

'Thanks, Leslie, that's a nice offer but I don't think having Ben engaging in criminal acts is going to help.'

'No, of course not, sorry. I was just trying to lighten the mood. For the first time in my life I've no clue what to say to you. How are you feeling, I suppose?'

Elenore thought about it for a moment. 'I don't know, to be perfectly honest. I don't feel angry. I think I just feel numb. Numb and like a fool.'

'Will you stop that, Elenore! I told you, you're not a fool. Do you know what you're going to do now?'

Shaking her head, Elenore said, 'I haven't the foggiest. What do you think I should do?'

'I know what I would do! I'd get a scissors and cut every one of his designer suits to shreds. Then, I'd throw them out the window. I'd wreck everything he loves – I'd take a golf club to that stupid fucking Porsche he drives.'

'Steady on there – I don't think I've the energy to do any of that. Can I not just ask him to move out. He'll go quietly, and we can forget about the whole thing?'

Leslie was looking at her with pity on her face.

'No?' said Elenore. 'Now you're going to tell me something else I don't want to hear, aren't you?'

'I'm afraid so. He's paid for the work done on the house so far, hasn't he? If you kick him out, he's going to want the money back.'

'Oh shit, you're right. Fuck, what am I going to do? I don't even know how much he's spent so far. Getting the bloody roof fixed alone probably ran into tens of thousands – not to mention the rest. I don't have that sort of money.'

'You do have something on him though, El, don't forget that.'

'What have I got on him? If you mean Karen's word that he bribed politicians, sure what good is that? That's just Karen's word against his. Everyone would believe him, what with him being such a well-respected businessman and all that.'

'That's as may be, but even so you could pretend you have proof, even just hint at it – you could use it as a bargaining tool, you know? You'd promise never to say anything as long as he walked away from Cavendish without looking for his money back.'

'I'm not ready, Leslie. I can't do this. I can't be in the same room as him. I don't want to talk to him. I want to go to bed.'

'Alright, here's what we're going to do.' Leslie had shifted into practical mode. 'I'm going to make you a stiff whiskey, a large one. I know it's not even midday, but you're going to drink it, slowly. Then, when you're finished, I'm going to take you upstairs to the spare room. I'm going to close the curtains and you're going to get into bed. I don't know if you'll sleep, but you'll close your eyes and rest and I'll stay with you the whole time – until you're ready to get up.'

All Elenore could do was nod. Inwardly she marvelled at the absolute, unfaltering loyalty of her oldest friend. Donnacha might be a piece of shit, but she knew she wasn't alone.

Leslie poured her a drink, along with one for herself. 'I can't let you drink alone, that would just be bad.'

As soon as they had finished the not unsubstantial drinks, Leslie directed Elenore out to the hall and up the stairs to the bedroom. Going to the chest of drawers, she pulled out a pair of fleece pyjamas and helped Elenore undress and put them on. She then peeled back the duvet, fluffed up the pillows, and put Elenore to bed. In the exact same way her mother used to do. She then sat by the bed, reading a book and keeping watch as the effects of the whiskey took over, and Elenore dozed off.

When she finally woke up, Elenore felt no better but was glad her friend was still there with her.

'How long was I out for? I can't believe I slept, given the circumstances.'

'That was a reaction to shock – and the whiskey. You were out for almost three hours. It's just after three. How are you feeling now?'

'The same. Still just numb, but maybe it's better to deal with this when I'm numb. Better than dealing with it when the anger sets in – which no doubt it eventually will.'

'What are you going to do, El? You know you're more than welcome to stay here for as long as you need.' Leslie was determined to look after her.

'Thanks for the offer, Leslie, but I need to confront Donnacha as soon as possible. Let me think …'

Leslie nodded and waited silently.

Eventually, Elenore sat up and looked directly at her friend. 'Right … I have a plan. I need to rehearse what I'm going to say to Donnacha when we meet, the questions I need answers to. But I'm going to ring him now in a little while. I'm going to act like everything is okay and tell him I'm making dinner and ask him what time he'll be home.'

'Seriously, is that a good idea?' Leslie looked baffled.

'Yes, it is. I must get him to come home if I'm to find out what he plans to do. I need to end the relationship, Leslie, that's a given. I'll deal with my broken heart later, but for now I have to be sensible. I need to talk to him and tell him what I know. Only then will I see what's going to happen next. It all depends on whether he's willing to go quietly, in light of what I know – or, as you said, if he'll fight for the money that he's already put into the house. So, I'm going to ring him and act as normal as possible. If he thinks there's anything wrong he won't come home, and I'll have to spend another day not knowing where I stand. This way he'll be delighted with himself. He'll think I'm over fighting with him about Karen and that we're ready to go on putting his plans for Cavendish into action.'

'Well, if you're sure . . .' Leslie didn't look sure at all.

'I'm sure.'

'Right – I'll go and put the kettle on.'

Elenore got up and dressed. After splashing cold water on her face to wake herself up properly, she went downstairs to get her phone and call Donnacha.

The phone only rang once before he answered it, which surprised her.

'Hi.'

A one-word greeting – he was obviously still sulking.

She tried to sound as normal as possible. 'Hey, Donnacha, I'm just wondering what time you'll be home this evening? Will you be home for dinner?'

'I don't know. I'm not sure if I'll make it in time.'

He was going to make her beg. If that's what she must do, then she'd do it – she had no choice.

'I know things have been strange between us the last few days.' That was an understatement – the fucking bollox hadn't come home last night – ah, there it was, the first sign of anger. 'But I want things to go back to normal. Let's sit down and have a nice dinner and a chat. Just about normal things. We don't need to talk about Karen or any of that. That's your stuff, Donnacha, and I'll leave you to it. I know you're handling it the right way.'

With this he seemed to soften a bit, probably because he was used to her giving in to whatever he wanted. He was back in familiar territory.

'Fair enough, I've missed your cooking the last few days. It's a date. I'll be home by about half seven.'

'Grand – I'll see you later then.' She put down the phone.

Leslie was staring at her, a look of admiration on her face. 'I'm praying that was really an act and, if it was, the Oscar for best actress in a lead role goes to you. *Wow* is all I can say.'

'Thanks, and now I need your help. Can you get a pen and a piece of paper? I need to figure out all the questions that have to be answered about the house. Little does Donnacha O'Callaghan know that I'm on to him. He's not getting his hands on my house that easily. And you know what, you're right, I'm prepared to use the information Karen gave me to get what I need from him. Hopefully I won't have to but, if I need to, I will.'

The two women spent the next hours plotting out all possible scenarios, listing all the questions Elenore needed answered. The most important one being how much money Donnacha had spent on Cavendish to date. Elenore tried to estimate the cost of the work he'd had done so far – the work on the roof, the new heating system, not yet fully installed but presumably paid for, the new plumbing system – it was quite an extensive list and, with a house the size of Cavendish, there was every likelihood it could run beyond a hundred thousand.

Thinking of this made her panic but Leslie calmed her down as much as possible, saying there was no point panicking just yet – not until she had the facts.

By the time she arrived back at Cavendish at seven, her heart was thumping in her chest. She could only imagine how angry she was going to be when she saw him, given her strong reaction on the phone earlier. But she had to admit to herself that a part of her still wanted all this to go away. She wanted him to come home, take her in his arms and for things to be as they used to. If he could go back to the person he was when they had first met, say sorry for any wrongs he had done – wouldn't that be much easier?

Giving herself a mental slap, she did her best to pull it together. He couldn't go back to being who he was when they first met, because clearly that had all been an act. She had spent the last two years with a man she didn't know at all. An article she had once read about the various stages of love came to mind. The first was the honeymoon stage, where serotonin levels peaked in a similar way to a cocaine high. You couldn't get the person out of your mind, believed they had absolutely no flaws and that they were the only person capable of making you happy. This was the time most couples got married. Nature created this phase to make it easy to avoid the flaws that all human beings have, in order to procreate. By the time you figured out what the person was really like, it was too late.

Thankfully not for her. At least she hadn't married him or had his baby. She had to be grateful for small mercies.

She thought about the other couples, the ones who stayed the distance. Apparently the second phase involved a power struggle – this usually went on for years. She couldn't remember what the other phases were, but she knew that love, real love, took time and effort – a lot of effort. The heady romance at the beginning of a relationship was not love. How could it be? When you didn't even know the person?

She'd done all the work in their relationship, submitting to his every request – well, that was over with now. She was going to claim herself back. Cavendish was hers and she was no longer going to be dictated to by a man who deceived her and cheated on her. She wanted him to go quietly away and leave her in peace and she felt a sense of relief when she thought about that.

He arrived into the kitchen at twenty past seven, a look of surprise on his face that there was no smell of food wafting from the oven.

'What's going on? I thought we were having dinner?'

'No, Donnacha, we're not having dinner. We're going to have a conversation and making dinner was not my priority tonight.'

'But you said!'

Elenore thought he sounded like a child but didn't regret her decision not to cook. If she had gone to the trouble of making dinner for him, it would have caused her real pain. She wasn't confident that she'd not have spat in it or mixed some dog food in – just so she could watch him eat it. She had promised herself she'd remain dignified no matter what and dignified she'd be.

'I know what I said, but I changed my mind. I need to talk to you. It won't take long.' If he knew it wasn't going to take a long time, then maybe he'd be more likely to engage. 'Just give me a minute. I have something to show you.'

She walked out of the kitchen and went upstairs where she took the blueprints from the drawer where she had hidden them. A minute later she walked back into the kitchen, carrying the drawings in her arms.

She laid them out on the kitchen table in front of him.

'I found these when you were in Poland.'

His face gave nothing away.

'I want to know what they are, Donnacha.'

He paused and, for a few seconds, she thought he wasn't going to answer her at all.

'They're nothing, Elenore – what do you mean?'

'I mean, you obviously went to considerable effort to have these drawn up. I want to know what they are. Why were you planning all this work without telling me? Did you expect I'd just go along with all these plans, or were you going to go ahead with them once we were married and not bother to tell me at all? What sort of a fool do you think I am?' Despite having promised herself she'd stay calm, she felt that she was already losing it.

And so was Donnacha. 'Christ, I thought I was coming home to have dinner and a nice relaxing evening! Now I feel like I've walked into some sort of inquisition! I don't know what your problem is. We discussed these plans a few days ago, and you said you were happy for us to go ahead with them if we had the money. *What the fuck is going on here, Elenore?*'

His voice was rising to dangerously high levels.

'I'll tell you what's going on here. You had these drawn up long before we had that talk. You were planning all this when you still believed I wanted to keep the changes here to a minimum. *That's* what the problem is.'

'So what exactly are you saying, Elenore, aside from acting like a crazy woman? Has it escaped your notice that you agreed to all of this? What are you saying? Were you lying to me? Because if you were, I think we have some major issues.'

This comment finally made Elenore see red. 'We have issues if I was lying to *you*? Really, Donnacha, is that why we've issues? I'd say that's not the only reason – what about our other issues? What about Siobhán Ellis?'

Even the mention of her name didn't cause him to flinch, as Elenore expected he would.

'I really don't know what you're talking about, Elenore. All I know is you spend an hour in the company of my stupid bitch of an ex-wife and your whole personality changes. If you're going to carry on like this, I'm going out. I'm not sitting here after a hard day's work listening to this shit!'

With that he got up and walked towards the door but Elenore got there before him and blocked his exit.

'You *bastard*, you're not walking out on me! I know everything. I know about your affair, I know about your little trip to Paris in February and you know what else I know, Donnacha? I know you've been doing dodgy deals for years, bribing people to get what you want!'

Fuck, she hadn't meant to blurt it all out like that.

'You're crazy, Elenore. You've gone completely fucking insane. Pull yourself together.'

He grabbed her and tried to physically move her out of his way, but she dug her heels in. She wasn't going anywhere.

'I'm not crazy, Donnacha, and you can go wherever you want, but not until I get the information I need from you. Cavendish is mine, it's always been mine and it always will be mine. It's not yours to do whatever you want with. I want you out of here tonight but, before you go, you had better sit down, because I need some answers.'

'Right, that's it. I've had it with you. I'm sorry to tell you,

Elenore, but Cavendish is not yours. I've already spent over a hundred grand trying to rescue your beloved home. You needn't think I'm going anywhere. I'm staying right here until I see some return on my investment.'

There it was. She hadn't needed to ask the question. He'd volunteered the information. But oh God, one hundred thousand euros! It really was that bad.

'You won't get a penny of your money back, Donnacha. I know all about you. If you try to stay here, I'll go to the police. I'll tell them about your bribery. There are developers being investigated up and down the country for dodgy dealings. I just didn't think you were one of them.'

'Please spare me the dramatics, Elenore – do whatever you want. I haven't done anything wrong. If you think I'm going to walk away from all of this and leave you to reap the benefits, you're sorely wrong. Now get out of my way – you can have your Cavendish, you can live here and sleep here on your own – but, my God, this is my business now and I'm going to see it through. No matter what stupid threats you throw at me.'

With that he managed to push her aside, leaving her in the doorway shaking with anger.

He walked towards the back stairs and Alfie, noticing her distress, ran after him and growled. Donnacha took aim to kick the dog, who deftly managed to jump out of his way before his foot made contact.

She stood there for a few minutes, listening to his footsteps ascending the stairs, the bang of the front door and the roar of his car as he pulled out of the driveway.

She hated him, she hated him more than anything. There was no way she was going to let him hold her hostage like this. Picking up her handbag, she fished out the piece of paper on which she'd scribbled down Karen's number the day she'd come to visit. She dialled the number into her phone, her hands shaking.

'Hello?'

'Hi, Karen, it's Elenore here. I want you to make that call. I want you to call somebody from the paper, I want it all to come out. Everyone has to know what Donnacha O'Callaghan has been up to.'

CHAPTER 19

It had been almost two weeks since Karen had picked up the phone to hear Elenore demand that she go to the newspapers about Donnacha's wrongdoings. While nothing would have given her greater pleasure than to see him squirm, she had cautioned Elenore to be careful. Yes, she had told her that it would take just one phone call, but they needed someone to back up the claims. They also needed to think seriously about the possible negative side effects taking action might have for them both.

Now that they had done it, Karen was unsure if they had done the right thing.

When she had visited Cavendish a few days previously, Elenore had listened to her but Karen felt that she was taking everything she said with a pinch of salt. That was to be expected. It was perfectly reasonable that Elenore would view her as the hard-done-by ex-wife, wanting to cause trouble at all costs. Now, something had clearly shifted dramatically. Elenore was out for blood, and while Karen hadn't told her anything that was untrue, she also had to be mindful of her own situation. Elenore would always have the massive asset that was Cavendish to fall back on, and probably a significant amount of money in the bank too. Karen didn't have that sort of luxury. Before doing anything as radical as making it common knowledge that her ex-husband was a crook, she needed to ensure that she wasn't going to find herself in any worse a situation than the one she was already in.

When Elenore had phoned she had tried her best to calm her down, asking her what was wrong and telling her, whatever it was, it would be okay. She had managed to get out of her, between sobs, that she now knew everything Karen had told her was true. He was having an affair and, not only that, now it looked like losing Cavendish was fast becoming a certainty.

She couldn't figure out the rest of what she was saying, Elenore was that upset, so she told her to sit tight – she was going to drive over to her and would be there as soon as she could.

She called on her neighbour Maggie to keep an eye on Aaron and her mother, and soon she was travelling the road back to Cavendish. She'd have to stop taking advantage of her neighbour's kindness, but this situation was unique. If anybody had told her a month before that she'd be visiting Donnacha's home twice in as many weeks, she'd have laughed.

However bad Elenore had looked on their first meeting, she looked a hundred times worse now. Not only were the dark circles under her eyes considerably more pronounced, but her eyes were bloodshot too. Slim as she was, Karen was shocked to see she looked like she had lost quite a lot of weight in the short space of time since she had last seen her.

Clearly not in the mood for niceties, Elenore got straight down to business. She filled Karen in on the conversation she'd had with Donnacha when he'd returned from Poland – how she'd persuaded him she was fully on board with making dramatic changes to Cavendish – how she'd done this to gauge how he would react. She had hoped that this would give her some clarity on just how serious he was about the plans he had committed to paper. It had. He was rearing to go.

Then she told her about Leslie, how she was her oldest friend, and really the only person in the world that she trusted without question. She explained how she had told Leslie about the rumours and Karen's own allegations about Donnacha cheating his way through their marriage. She had asked Leslie to find out if there was any truth to the rumours.

Elenore had broken down again when she had talked about what Leslie had discovered and how her friend, as always, had been so kind to her. Then she'd brought her up to speed on her meeting with Donnacha that evening. How he had denied everything, told her he'd put a hundred thousand euros into the house so far. As far as he was concerned this gave him a claim over it. He didn't intend to go quietly and leave her in peace. He hadn't responded to her accusations about Siobhán Ellis, but he had tried to kick her dog on the way out of the house. This, for Elenore, had been the most upsetting thing of all that had happened over the past few days, even though the dog had managed to sidestep him: it had truly revealed Donnacha's character.

Finally, up to speed, Karen could see why Elenore wanted to go public with Donnacha's illegal activities. She understood, but nonetheless she had to raise her own concerns.

'I don't know what to say to you, Elenore – as far as I can see you've been to hell and back over the last few days. I'm really sorry about that, and I'm sorry for being the one to bring much of that hell to your door. Honestly, that was never my intention. I know you're worried now about losing your home, even more than you were before, but please listen to me. You've got to be careful. I know I said that all it would take is one phone call to the papers and Donnacha's world would fall apart, but we must be smart here. The sad truth is that my world, and possibly most of yours, is reliant on that bastard. We need to be sure, if we make that call, that our worlds won't come crashing down too. Do you understand me?'

Blowing her nose violently, Elenore said she agreed they needed to be careful, but surely Donnacha being made accountable for his wrongdoing could only work in Karen's favour.

'Don't you see,' she said, 'if this became public knowledge and we had that politician you mentioned corroborate the story, it would have to be good for you. If Donnacha's financial dealings were investigated, do you think he'd be able to hide anything from you? Of course he wouldn't – they'd go through every penny he has, and when it came time for your day in court, for your divorce, he wouldn't be able to hide a thing.'

Karen supposed she had a point. It certainly would put her in a stronger position if Donnacha's wrongdoings and finances were common knowledge – but what if he lost everything? If he had nothing to give her, she'd be in no better situation than she was now. What's more, that situation would last indefinitely.

But Elenore had reasoned with her. 'Look, no matter what might be taken off him, a judge is always going to ensure a child and a single mother are provided for. Besides, that business is worth far more than he's claiming it is – and he owns half of it.' She wasn't going to stop there. 'Aren't you sick of this, Karen, aren't you sick of him getting his way all the time, doing whatever it is he pleases? Taking all the time and never giving anything back? It's damn well ridiculous. I'm telling you, the chickens have come home to roost for that bastard. We've got to do something.'

Karen didn't have the heart to point out to her that if Donnacha did become the focus of an investigation, they had no way of knowing what might or might not happen. But, as things stood now, she was only going to get the minimum of what she felt she was entitled to, so maybe it was worth giving it a shot.

The other issue concerning Karen was Charlie Redmond. If

they decided to go to the papers, she'd have to be sure Charlie would support any allegations she made. She wasn't sure how likely this was, given that he was no longer in politics and that he much preferred staying out of the limelight since his illness. But she promised Elenore she'd contact him, explain all that had happened and see if he could be of any help.

'And, if by some miracle everything lines up and we've got our story straight, who are we going to tell it to? It's all very well saying we'll call the newspapers, but who exactly will we call? Who'd take us seriously?'

'Don't you worry about that. I know exactly the person who can advise us on that.'

It seemed Elenore had already put a lot of thought into this.

Karen had left her soon afterwards, and the following day had called Charlie Redmond and arranged to meet him for lunch. He was delighted to hear from her and agreed to a lunch that very day. She told him she'd travel out of the city and down to meet him in Clonakilty where he lived. Charlie said if that was the case, she might as well come to his house. It was a Saturday in August, every bar and restaurant would be full of tourists, enjoying what was left of the summer. Karen was happy at the suggestion as Charlie's house would afford them the privacy needed to discuss a very sensitive subject.

Following the directions he gave her, she located his house, outside the town, set on a height overlooking the sea. Charlie was at the door waiting to greet her and hugged her tightly. When he stood back Karen was delighted to see that he looked the picture of health. Instead of bringing her into the house, he brought her around the side, to a small picturesque courtyard which, open on one side, commanded the most amazing views out over the Atlantic. Karen thought it was no wonder Charlie looked so well: being retired and living in such a beautiful place could only be good for your health.

She sat down on one of the wicker chairs there. Charlie offered her a glass of wine and, reasoning that she'd only have one and would stay long enough for the effects to wear off, she took him up on his offer.

Charlie went into the house, leaving Karen alone. Spread out before her, the ocean was calm as a pond. She watched seagulls circling in the clear blue sky overhead and swooping down onto the surface of the water. Charlie's house was an old cottage that he had bought many years ago and lovingly refurbished, mostly at weekends, while he and his wife were still living in Cork City and he was travelling up and down to Dublin to sit in Leinster House. Built of sandstone, it was a neat little house, double-fronted with four sash windows and a pretty front door. Old outbuildings enclosed the courtyard on the other side, which really made the little space feel like another room.

She imagined what it would be like to live here, waking up to that view every day. It certainly would be a very different life to the one she lived. Leaning back in her chair, she breathed in the fresh sea air. She mightn't be here for the most pleasant of conversations, but that didn't mean she couldn't enjoy the holiday feeling that being this close to the sea always gave her.

Charlie returned with two large glasses, filled to the brim with icy-cold white wine. Taking in the size of the glasses, Karen thought she might have to stay the night. It would take that long to work that amount of alcohol out of her system before she'd be safe to drive again.

Handing one of the glasses to Karen, he sat down on the chair beside her and raised his glass.

'Here's to being retired!' he said.

Karen clinked her glass against his. 'Bring retired is right – this is amazing, Charlie. I'm so glad for you, that you get to live here – you deserve it after all you've been through.'

They went on to talk about Charlie's wife Marie, who was out playing golf as they spoke, had a catch-up on the whereabouts of his children, who were all adults now. Karen filled him in with updates on Aaron and how well he was doing at school, despite her reservations about some of the practices there.

She asked after his health and he explained how he and Marie would be on a knife-edge every three months, when he had to go back to the hospital for a check-up but, thank God, everything was going well and it seemed it was staying away for good.

Finally, Karen decided she had to move the conversation on and get down to what she had come here to talk about.

'You were probably a bit surprised when I called you this morning, looking to meet you at such short notice.'

Charlie was polite as always. 'Not at all, girl. You know I'm delighted to see you whenever the opportunity presents and that's the great thing about being retired – I've all the time in the world to catch up with old friends.'

Karen smiled at him and went on. 'It's great to see you, Charlie, but unfortunately I'm not here just for a catch-up. Nice and all as this is.'

'I had hoped you might just want to enjoy the pleasure of my company, but I'm guessing your call may have something to do with Donnacha – am I right?'

'Yes, I'm afraid it has.' Karen then proceeded to fill him in on the full details. Donnacha's thoughts on what he saw as a fair divorce settlement, her meeting with Elenore, Elenore's discovery of Donnacha's plans for Cavendish and how Donnacha was now saying that Elenore owed him a huge amount of money. Elenore simply didn't have that kind of money and feared that she was in danger of losing her home.

She had to think for a moment about whether to share with him the details of Donnacha's infidelities, but then decided she would. If Charlie was going to help them, he needed to know exactly how big a bastard Donnacha was.

When she finished her story, she gave Charlie a while to digest it.

'I can't say I'm surprised by any of this,' he said at last. 'I have my suspicions that every single building project he has ever been involved in has been in some way illegal. You know, Karen, I've said it to you before – the country may be booming now, but I'm telling you, sooner or later, this is all going to come crashing down around us. I hear he's now involved in straight land sales. He's not even building on some of the sites. He's making his money without building a thing – doesn't that strike you as a bit unusual for a developer?'

Karen wasn't sure what he meant.

'I've heard rumours that Tim Collins, the TD, is the one helping him now,' he went on. 'Donnacha and that partner of his buy the land, at a reasonable price – it's just farm land after all. Collins rows in, does whatever it is that needs to be done to rezone the land, so now it can be used to build houses or commercial units or whatever, and then *boom* – the value of the land sky-rockets. Of course, Collins is an auctioneer so I can only imagine what he's bringing as the latest addition to the partnership. Of course, I can't prove any of this and Marie keeps telling me to forget about it. She says I'm out of politics now, and why would I get involved in all of that again?'

That was what Karen had expected to hear. Who in their right mind would put themselves forward to get involved in this? Charlie was leading a peaceful, quiet life. Why bring unwanted attention upon himself? But what he said next surprised her.

'I think I know what you're here to ask me, Karen. You're wondering if I'd go on the record, say that Donnacha tried to bribe me – that's what you want, isn't it?'

'I'm not putting you under any pressure, Charlie. I honestly came here just to talk to you, to get your advice. It's Elenore that wants to go after Donnacha. She's the one who wants to go public. I'm still not completely convinced.'

She put her concerns to Charlie about what would happen to her if Donnacha lost everything. Where would she be then? She was facing an uncertain financial future as it was.

Charlie listened but, in the end, he was of the same opinion as Elenore. 'You know, we mustn't forget something very important here, and that's doing the right thing. You've no proof of what Donnacha does, but I do. He did approach me about getting land rezoned for him, saying he was going to make it worth my while. That would be my word against his, but that is all it would take. It would be enough to put him under investigation and if anyone decided to investigate Donnacha and Jerry Reynolds, and I imagine Tim Collins, there'd be no going back.'

'That's all well and good, Charlie, but, as I said, where would that leave me?'

But Charlie echoed Elenore's opinion again. 'You'd be looked after. No court is going to leave you and your son unprovided for. I'm also guessing Donnacha has money stashed somewhere – well hidden from you. He's not stupid. Those guys might act like they are invincible, but unless they're very stupid it must enter their heads that all this is going to end at some stage. It cannot continue indefinitely. He'll have something hidden – a court investigation would find it.'

Karen hoped what he was saying was true.

'And, aside from yourself, Karen, what about the other people involved in this? What about the people selling land to them, good honest people, selling farmland that may have been in their families for years? Convinced they are getting a great price. Then the likes of Donnacha and his cronies come along, manage to get planning permission to build on it and what was once farmland becomes a bloody housing estate in the middle of nowhere.'

Karen saw his point, but still . . . 'They are getting well paid for the land though – it's not as if they are walking away empty-handed, is it?'

'No, Karen, it's not. But do you think these farmers are happy now that they've gone from living in rural areas where they know everyone, to suddenly living on the edge of housing estates with an influx of people not from the area, and no proper amenities for them? This ridiculous building, with no thought for proper planning, is destroying the countryside in Ireland – not to mention the social problems it's going to cause in the future. Imagine those young couples moving out of urban areas to live in a 3-bed semi-detached house in rural Ireland, thinking they are going to be living the dream – how will it be for them in fifteen years? I'll tell you how – they'll have produced gangs of teenagers who'll be roaming those estates, with nothing to do and nowhere to go, no football pitches to play on, no community centres, no sense of community even. It's a disaster waiting to happen and the powers that be are just letting it continue regardless.'

Karen wished, not for the first time, that he had stayed in politics. But he spoke sense and told the truth, so it was no wonder his political colleagues wanted him gone.

'So, what are you saying, Charlie? Will you help us?'

'I can't commit to anything right now, not without talking to Marie first. She's going to kill me when I suggest this, but I know I can make her see sense. It's the right thing to do.'

Having got a far better result than she was expecting, Karen felt she had done enough for one day. It was up to Charlie now whether they'd be able to continue or not and she was not going to put any pressure on him. He was a good, kind man. If he wanted to continue with his quiet life here, the last thing she wanted was to get in the way of that.

With that out of the way, she decided she was going to sit there for the rest of the afternoon, sipping on her glass of wine while she enjoyed the view – and Charlie's good company. It was not often she found herself in such a pleasant situation as this and she was going to make the most of it.

Maggie had told her to take her time. She was happy staying in Karen's house, chatting to her mother and watching soap operas on the television.

Hours later, before she pulled out of Charlie's driveway, she called Elenore, explaining that she was leaving Clonakilty, and would she call in to her to update her on her visit?

Elenore agreed, explaining that her friend Leslie was with her, and she'd very much like for the two of them to meet. Especially as Leslie would be able to help them in finding the best journalist to tell the story to.

CHAPTER 20

By seven o'clock Karen was sitting at Elenore's kitchen table for the third time, having met Leslie and brought the two women up to speed on how her meeting with Charlie had gone. She told them how she believed that he'd help them, but that he needed a little bit of time. He was a man in his mid-sixties who'd had cancer. Helping them would have an impact on his life, one way or another, there was no denying that. He also had to take into account his wife and her thoughts on the whole thing.

Leslie agreed. 'You're right – if he does this, it'll be like he's back working as a politician. If he was a normal run-of-the-mill person making these accusations, the media would be interested but their focus would be on Donnacha. The fact that he's a retired politician means the media will see *him* as fair game. I hope he has good security down in Clonakilty – they'll be chasing him down.'

Karen hadn't thought of this. 'I'll have to talk to him about that. I did notice electric gates on the house when I got there. At least he'll be able to close himself off from the outside world until the media moves on to something else.'

'That's something I haven't thought about before either,' said Elenore, concerned. 'If this happens, will they come after me?'

Leslie nodded. 'I'm afraid so. They'll probably come after both of you, as well as Charlie, but don't worry – it won't be for long – a day or two of chasing ye and they'll go away and move on to the next story. Don't worry. Donnacha will be the one they'll be most interested in – they'll hound him for weeks, and they'll hound him every single time there's a development in his case.'

Leslie was going into further detail of what awaited Donnacha if his dealings became public knowledge when she was brought to an abrupt halt by the doorbell ringing. The three women stared at each other, each thinking the same thing: was it Donnacha?

Elenore was the first to break the silence. 'It's not him, he has a key.'

Breathing a sigh of relief, Karen watched as Elenore went upstairs to answer the door, returning a few minutes later accompanied by a tall, handsome man with auburn hair, who looked like he was overdue a shave but the stubble lent to his overall look of unkempt sexiness.

'Karen, Leslie, this is Seán – you remember I told you about him? He's helping me find out more about the diary?'

The two women immediately noticed that, aside from his rugged good looks, there was an energy about this man. It was as if the room became immediately smaller simply because he was standing in it. He filled up the space around him and he appeared to be brimming with excitement.

Elenore made the introductions. Seán took a seat in one of the armchairs beside the Aga, stretching his long legs out in front of him, and they all engaged in small talk for a while. Then Leslie said she needed to get home and she and Karen left – Karen promising to contact Elenore as soon as she heard from Charlie again.

After walking them to the door, Elenore returned to Seán in the kitchen.

'I'm sorry about that,' he said. 'I hope they didn't feel like they had to leave.'

'Not at all. Now tell me – have you had a chance to find out anything else about Lady Edith?' She knew his answer was going to be 'yes' by the look of excitement on his face.

'Yes! I have news, really good news. I could have phoned you, but it's too good. I had to come up here and tell you in person. I've found her. I've found Lady Edith.'

'Found her?'

'Yes! You're never going to believe it. I've spent the last few evenings in the library, doing online research. You can basically find out anything about anyone, it's amazing. So, I started by trying to find information about Edith's family. They were members of the aristocracy – if there were going to be records on anyone, there'd be records on them. Sure enough, I found records of their deaths from old newspapers, which turned out to be a stroke of luck. The father died a few years after the fire – he must have not been long back in England at that stage. His death notice was run-of-the-mill, and no mention of him ever having had a child. His wife was the only other person mentioned in the notice.'

Elenore nodded. 'That's not really surprising – according to May, the father basically denied ever having a daughter – after he read the that note and found out about her and Tadgh.'

Seán continued. 'What is surprising though is the mother's death notice. She died ten years after her husband, but on her death notice it said: "Mother of Edith Bruxby, née Cavendish".'

Elenore gasped after he delivered his punchline, but he wasn't done yet.

'The Bruxby family are – and thanks again to the internet – old-school WASPs. I think that's what you'd call them. They were the owners of, amongst other things, a number of newspapers and radio stations on the east coast of America. They're not exactly in the league of the Hearsts or the Rockefellers, but they're not far off it. So, I contacted them.'

'What do you mean you contacted them? Who exactly did you contact?'

'I was able to find the first name of the Bruxby man she married and trace her descendants. She had three children, and she has a grandson who took over the business. He's a multi-millionaire. So I emailed him.' Seán beamed, clearly chuffed with himself for being such a genius.

'How did you get his email address?' Elenore asked incredulously.

'I rang the headquarters of his company, explained I was Irish and told them about the diary. They didn't seem that interested in it, so they told me to put the information in an email, to some generic email address. So, I did what I was told, and yesterday got an email back from Robert Bruxby's personal assistant asking if I could email Robert directly and provide more information. So, I did that too. He wanted to know what condition Cavendish was in, what this Elenore person that I had referred to did, what exactly my connection to her was. All those types of questions. I replied, answering to the best of my ability everything he needed to know. I suppose I hadn't explained myself all that well in the first email that I sent so I went step by step in this one. I explained who everyone was, how I had met you, what you do and how much you love the house. Anyway, he came back to me late last night, asking if I could take a call. I said, yes, of course, and he called me there and then. Lady Edith is very much alive and well, and she wants her diary back.'

CHAPTER 21

Karen was thinking what a strange group they made. She hadn't known either Elenore or Leslie a couple of weeks previously, so it was surprising that they seemed at such ease in each other's company. She supposed it must be something to do with the exceptional set of circumstances that had brought them together.

They had spent more time together since the evening at Cavendish when Seán had interrupted them. Two days later they had convened there again after Charlie Redmond had called with the news that he was willing to help them. He was willing to talk publicly about his experience with Donnacha.

Leslie had insisted that they come together so she could explain to them what they needed to do. She had pinpointed Gerard Walsh, a journalist with one of the local papers whose articles often appeared in national media and who featured regularly on national radio – particularly when it came to conversations on political issues in the country's second city. He had also covered a number of stories about planning issues in the last two years. He was smart, fair and he knew everyone. In addition to all of this, he and Leslie had a friendship that stretched back years. She had helped him when he was a struggling journalist, feeding him any information she had that needed to see the light of day. She had trusted his fresh and balanced approach to writing news stories. She had given him information back then, in order to aid herself and her own clients. He remained grateful for the trust she had placed in him when he had been so young.

They had invited Gerard over to brief him. They included Seán in the meeting. Elenore had filled him in on all that was happening in her personal life. She'd felt she owed him an explanation for the crazy way she had behaved the first time they met. She also was incredibly grateful to him for taking her mind off her problems for a while at least, with his dedication to tracking down the woman who had written the diary.

Karen loved the idea of the diary. She had been intrigued the first time Elenore had shown it to her. In an ideal universe Elenore would have been completely caught up in the amazing historical find, not reeling with shock over the revelations about Donnacha.

As it turned out, Leslie had seriously underestimated the level of interest the media would have in Elenore. It had taken Gerard a week to research and write the first article, an interview with Charlie Redmond, interspersed with a background on Donnacha. The headline that first morning had read:

'Millionaire Property Developer in Alleged Bribery Scandal'

It was accompanied by an image of Donnacha and Elenore at a charity event. Leslie went ballistic and rang Gerard, screaming at him down the phone, asking why they had printed a picture with Elenore in it. The reporter explained that that was beyond his control. He just provided the content of the article and, even then, his editor could change it. The headline and the images that accompanied his articles were looked after by someone else at the paper.

Elenore had awoken the morning of Gerard's first article to find the driveway in front of Cavendish filled with cars, reporters and cameramen. Apparently Donnacha had gone to ground, having got a tip-off from someone that the article was going to appear. Elenore was the next best thing for the media, to the extent that Karen escaped lightly enough. The focus was on Elenore, and the perceived glamour and wealth of Cavendish.

For four days they followed her everywhere. She couldn't get out of her car without someone shoving a microphone in her face. She had got the gates to the avenue at Cavendish closed, for the first time in years, and had a sign saying 'Private Property' put up. At least that way she had some peace and quiet at home, but once she left the security of Cavendish she had no choice but to deal with them.

A few days after Gerard's first article appeared, a national tabloid ran a front-page headline **'Disgraced Property Developer Playing Away from Home'** beside a picture of Donnacha and Siobhán Ellis.

Elenore had finally had enough. They were now stopping her on the street and asking her about her private life.

Karen and Leslie came to Cavendish again, to lend support. Leslie tried to calm her down. 'Honestly, it will blow over, we knew this would happen. I just didn't think it would be this intense. Where has that fucker disappeared to? No one has seen him in days. If he was around, they'd be chasing him and they'd leave you alone.'

That was of no use to Elenore. 'I swear, I can't take any more. I need to get away from here and by the look of it I need to get out of Ireland. With my bloody picture plastered all over the newspapers, no matter where I go here someone will recognise me.'

It was then that Karen had an idea. 'Why don't you go to the States for a few days? You could give Lady Edith back her diary.'

CHAPTER 22

Closing her eyes as the plane took up speed and hurtled down the runway at Shannon airport, Elenore asked herself for the hundredth time that day, what the hell was she doing? Still she couldn't answer her own question but, whatever it was, she'd have to just go with it. The plane wasn't stopping now – no matter what.

At first, she had laughed off Karen's suggestion as being completely ridiculous. She couldn't just up and leave and head off to America – that was insanity.

But then Leslie stepped in. 'Why not, why can't you?'

'There are a million reasons,' Elenore had answered. 'Firstly, I've not even spoken to Edith. The only contact has been with her grandson and that's been through Seán. Secondly, you don't take off and fly across the Atlantic when you've just split up with your boyfriend, who you've discovered has cheated on you and is a crook. Wait, I'm forgetting something – yes, that's it – apparently, I owe him a hundred grand and I have no idea where I'd get that

kind of money. Even if I had it, I don't know how I'd get it to him
– the stupid prick hasn't answered his bloody phone since the
story broke.'

'Calm down there, El,' said Leslie. 'But seriously, think about
it. You've just said yourself you need to get away. The only
moments of enjoyment and happiness you've had over the past
month are when you've been reading that diary – or talking about
that diary – or listening to Seán talk about the diary. You've found
it for a reason and the woman who wrote it wants it back – her
grandson said so. You'd be killing two birds with one stone: you'd
be doing that woman a favour and you'd be getting away from it
all, just for a week. It will have all blown over by the time you
come back, I'd bet on it.'

Elenore hated it when Leslie made sense like that.

'Leslie's right, it makes sense,' said Karen. 'If you went
anywhere else, you'd end up moping around for the week,
thinking about what is going on here. At least if you go to find
Edith and give her back her diary, you're going on a mission. You'd
have something to do, something to make you forget.'

'Couldn't I just go on a yoga retreat?'

'No bloody way,' said Leslie. 'Apparently Edith lives in East
Hampton. Who needs yoga when you can go there and hang out
for a week? She might invite you to stay in her mansion with her
hot grandson.' Leslie was being upbeat as ever.

Eventually they talked her around to their way of thinking and
soon they roped in Seán to call the grandson again – to tell him
Elenore was going to be in East Hampton in less than a week, with
the diary. Seán would check if Mrs. Bruxby – or Lady Edith, as
they still referred to her – would be available to meet her.

Elenore ended up talking to Robert Bruxby on the phone
herself. He sounded incredibly charming, and assured her that his
grandmother had talked about nothing else but her diary since the
day Seán had first called him. He knew for certain that she'd be

delighted to meet Elenore and get her diary back. He asked Elenore if she could bring some photographs of Cavendish, as he had never seen it. He explained he was dying to see it as he had listened to his grandmother talking about it throughout his childhood and felt like he somehow knew it.

He then went on to advise Elenore of the best places to stay in East Hampton. When she'd looked them up later, she was even more charmed by the fact that he had included a list of hotels ranging from high-end and scarily expensive to modest and affordable. He had never been to Ireland but understood that most flights came in to JFK. After making sure she was comfortable with driving in the US, he advised her to hire a car once she reached New York and drive out to The Hamptons. He told her if she stayed for a full week, he'd make sure to get out to East Hampton to meet her. He also suggested that maybe on the way home she could spend a night in Manhattan. He would be happy to show her around the city where he was based.

Leslie and Karen had been hopping around the place with excitement when she'd put down the phone, having listened in on the whole conversation.

'My God, he sounds amazing and he pretty much thought of everything. He's like a real-live Mr. Big.' Leslie was referring to the love interest in their favourite television series.

Seán, for once, seemed serious. 'Just be careful, Elenore. I've checked him out for you as much as I possibly could, and he seems straight enough. He's a Democrat, which is unusual for a WASP, but apparently his grandfather, Edith's husband, was a bit of a rebel. Apparently he was the one who moved the family and its old traditions kicking and screaming into the twentieth century.'

'Don't worry, Seán. I'll be fine. You're starting to sound a bit like the brother I never had.' Elenore was touched at his concern but amused that Robert's political allegiance had led Seán to believe that he might just be okay.

'You've been through a lot,' he said. 'People can take advantage of those who are vulnerable. I just want you to be safe.'

Reclining her seat now, as the fasten-seatbelt signs went off, she thought some more about Seán. He had been really kind to her since the moment they met – going out of his way to help her – though maybe that was because he was every bit as excited about the diary as she was. But he had taken on board all she had shared with him about Donnacha and said he was available to help in whatever way he could, whenever she needed him. Another man might have run a mile, but Seán had remained constant. As Leslie had said of him, after they met for the first time: 'He seems like a safe pair of hands.'

Elenore thought that was an incredibly accurate description. She had literally got to feel how safe his hands, or at least his arms were, the night before.

He had called over to make sure she had everything she needed for her trip and ended up staying for three hours.

When he was leaving, he warned her again to be careful and to call him straight away if she needed anything. Then, before he walked out the door, he hugged her, holding her tightly. It felt great, and she was disappointed when he had let her go. She thought for a moment he might try to kiss her, but then remembered he had been a spectator in her life over the past few weeks. What sort of man would try to kiss someone who had so recently split with their partner? Instead he wished her a safe trip and she watched him as he strode confidently down the steps and over to his car.

Leslie said she had seriously undersold him. He certainly wasn't scrawny as Elenore had described him. He was tall and slim, but he had lovely broad shoulders and an endearing, understated charm. There was a real warmth about him. Both she and Karen had agreed that he was very attractive.

These comments made Elenore smile. Leslie was determined

that Elenore would have a happy ending, no matter what. Unfortunately, Elenore felt in no way inclined to think about another man – it would be a long time before she'd be able to trust someone again.

There had still been nothing from Donnacha, despite her many attempts to contact him. At first his phone had been turned off and, now that it was back on, he simply did not answer it. She'd gone to his office a couple of times too, but she'd found it empty – even his secretary hadn't been there. She considered contacting Jerry Reynolds or perhaps his wife Jennifer but thought better of it. Whatever Donnacha was involved in, so too was Jerry. If they had figured out she was involved in leaking Donnacha's story to the papers, she was hardly going to be flavour of the month with either of them.

Gerard Walsh, for his part, was keeping her as much up to date as he could. He said he had heard that Donnacha was in the country, hiding out in an apartment in Dublin belonging to Siobhán Ellis. Apparently, Siobhán's husband had thrown her out of the house when the story about her and Donnacha had appeared in the tabloids. Gerard knew a few reporters in Dublin who were keeping an eye on the apartment block where Donnacha was believed to be, but there had been no sign of either him or Siobhán. He was also able to tell her that the Gardaí were taking the allegations made against Donnacha by Charlie Redmond very seriously. Elenore knew from Charlie that the Gardaí had interviewed him several times since the story had appeared. Gerard could confirm that Charlie wasn't the only one they had interviewed. A number of high-profile politicians, including Tim Collins, had been visited by them and Gerard understood that they were working on building a case.

He had also been able to tell her that they had gone to Donnacha's office and taken away files. Of course they intended to search Cavendish. They had called her a few times, looking to see if she knew his whereabouts, and she had mentioned the hidden files which they said they would need to remove.

She had called them when she'd made the decision to go to America, to let them know she was leaving the country. They had been very nice to her and thanked her for keeping them up to date. They asked her to contact them immediately if she heard from Donnacha. They also asked if anyone had a spare key for Cavendish, in case they needed access in her absence. She gave them Leslie's number, knowing her friend would be happy to handle any queries they had.

It seemed a bit ironic that she had made this massive decision to end her relationship and reveal her ex's wrongdoings, and still she was in the exact same situation as she had been this time weeks ago. Gerard told her she needed to be patient – the Gardaí needed to gather enough evidence to be able to arrest Donnacha. If they simply brought him in for questioning, they wouldn't be able to hold him for too long and he mightn't even co-operate. These things took time – a very long time – but he assured Elenore that she had done the right thing. Donnacha would be made to pay for all the illegal dealings he had undertaken.

Elenore hoped that he was right. It still didn't solve the problem of how she was going to come up with the money he was claiming she owed him. Whether he was found guilty or not, as things stood she still had to come up with it. What's more, with Donnacha gone, she had to think long and hard about her future and putting in place her plans for Cavendish. She had spent too much time allowing Donnacha to stamp all over them these past two years.

Taking the sleeping tablets Leslie had given her out of her bag, she signalled to the air hostess and asked for a glass of water. Her plan was to get some sleep on the flight and arrive in New York ready to enjoy herself. She had always hated flying. Sitting on her own for the seven-hour flight, worrying that every bumpy patch the plane encountered was going to end with her plummeting to her death, was not what she needed right now.

Elenore awoke as the plane was beginning its descent into JFK, feeling surprisingly refreshed, given that she'd slept upright in the cramped seat for at least six hours.

She was soon collecting her bag from the luggage belt, from where she headed through passport control and out into the airport. She had spent a summer in New York on a J1 visa when she was a student. Walking outside, she remembered how much she loved it. The buzz of the airport was enough to build her excitement, along with the sight of a yellow taxi. She allowed herself a minute to stand outside the front door of the airport, studiously avoiding all the men approaching her, trying to take her suitcase off her and lead her to a taxi. Elenore wanted to stand for a minute and mark that she was in New York. It was the first week of September, the perfect time to be here. She wouldn't get any time in the city for a few days but was looking forward to a day or maybe even more there towards the end of the week.

Locating the shuttle bus which would take her to the car-hire place, she was soon collecting the keys and starting up a car. She gently manoeuvred her way out of the parking lot, her heart beating in her chest. It had been a long time since she'd driven on the right-hand side of the road. At the end of her summer here during college, she'd hired a car with some friends and driven upstate. She had been the designated driver as she had been the only one with a full driver's licence. But that was a long time ago. Nonetheless, she quickly eased back into it. But she was worried about missing her exit to get on the highway. Finally, she made her way onto Route 27, the Sunshine Highway, and felt she could relax a bit as it was now a straight drive for fifty or so miles – taking her all the way into East Hampton.

Two hours later she pulled into a parking space on the Main

Street of the picturesque town. Looking at the directions for her hotel, which she had written down on a piece of paper and tucked safely in her handbag, she got her bearings. She drove down the main street, made her way out of town, past Hook Pond and towards Main Beach. Her hotel was located two streets back from the ocean.

The hotel was everything you'd expect of an East Hampton Hotel: two-storey, white clapboard, with huge sash windows and a porch running the length of one side. Elenore immediately felt a weight lift off her shoulders when she saw it. Parking her car, she took her suitcase out of the boot and made her way towards the hotel reception.

The inside certainly didn't disappoint either. Bleached floorboards, large blue-and-white striped sofas and white walls had a calming effect but the best thing about it was the windows All the windows, many of which were floor-to-ceiling, were wide open and from them came the fresh, pure smell of the ocean. Elenore felt like a small child, wanting to rush upstairs, change into her swimsuit and run down to the beach.

I'll do that, she promised herself, but first she must sleep properly – in a bed. The hours sleeping on the plane had left her stiff and sore, made worse by two hours sitting behind the wheel of her car. She desperately needed sleep.

Checking in, she was told to take the elevator to the second floor. The hotel was really a guesthouse, and probably didn't have any more than ten rooms. Elenore reminded herself to pay attention to how the owners ran it. She needed to learn everything she could about hotel management if she was ever going to turn Cavendish into a business.

Her room had the same calming atmosphere as the hotel reception. A massive bed dominated it, along with a large off-white cushioned sofa. White wood-panelled walls, with the panelling continuing onto the high pitched ceiling, striped roman blinds and the same bleached-wood floors as downstairs completed the little oasis. The bathroom contained a roll-top bath, which sat facing a massive window from which Elenore could see the ocean.

Back in her bedroom, she was further delighted to find a door which led out onto a tiny private balcony which also had a view of the ocean.

She decided she'd take the time to study all these things in detail later but for now, leaving the balcony door open, allowing the cool evening air to float into the bedroom, she removed her shoes and fell into the softness of the bed. Within seconds she was fast asleep.

She didn't know what time it was when she eventually woke up. The room was bright, which was strange, as darkness had been falling when she lay down. Reaching her hand out towards the bedside locker, she located her phone. The screen on the phone read 7.35am. She stared at it for a moment, thinking there must be some mistake. Perhaps the phone was still on Irish time. There was a television remote control on the locker. Picking that up, she found the on-button and the small television on the sideboard opposite the bed came on. She flicked through the stations until she found a news channel and, sure enough, her phone was right. It was 7.35am – she had slept right through the night.

Her stomach growled, reminding her that she had not eaten since lunchtime yesterday, or at least whatever time lunch had been served on the plane. She had no idea if that was Irish time or American time. Either way, she was starving. But, catching a glimpse of herself in the mirror, she decided she couldn't go down for breakfast in the state she was in. Her hair was stuck to her head, her eyes were bloodshot, and she felt generally sticky and unwashed.

Stepping into the shower, she found the water pressure was

high, and the temperature perfect. She scrubbed herself clean, feeling the grime built up over her journey disappear. Having washed her hair and face, she felt human again.

She dried herself off, placed a towel around her wet hair and wrapped herself in the waffle cotton robe she found hanging on the back of the bathroom door. Enjoying the simple pleasure of being so very comfortable, she padded out of the bathroom and onto the balcony. The morning sun was beaming, and the temperature was rising rapidly. The sky was cloudless and the ocean sapphire blue. There were already people out walking on the beach, determined to make the most of the last days of summer.

Elenore took it all in and exhaled deeply. Standing here, surveying this beautiful view from this lovely hotel room, she felt that she had made the right decision. The events of the last few weeks felt very far away and for that she was grateful. Looking after her own wellbeing was important, and the world wasn't going to stop if she took a week off to heal and recover.

Her stomach growled again, and she decided she couldn't put breakfast off for any longer. She went back into the room and opened her suitcase, quickly unpacking the contents. Leslie had helped her to pack, as Elenore's head had not been in a place to think about what she'd need to pack for a week-long trip, that included time in both The Hamptons and New York. She realised she didn't recognise most of the clothes in the suitcase. They belonged to Leslie. She smiled as she thought of her friend and knew immediately why Leslie had packed a lot of her own clothes. Her friend had a theory that wearing an outfit for the first time gave you the opportunity to create good memories. Leslie had certainly given her the opportunity to create a lot of good memories, with more clothes packed into the suitcase than Elenore was likely to wear in a month. When she had finally put everything away, she decided to wear a denim mini-skirt and a plain white T-shirt, along with her Converse low-tops.

Surveying herself in the mirror, she thought that Leslie would be happy with the finished product. The skirt showed off her long legs, which admittedly were pale, but a few days in this sunshine and she should be able to work up a tan. She tied her blonde hair into a high ponytail and thought, if only her teeth were bleached, she could very easily be mistaken for an East Hampton resident with her preppy American look.

She grabbed her handbag, making sure she had the key card for her room, and made her way downstairs for breakfast.

The breakfast room led out onto another porch which overlooked a beautiful garden, filled with mature trees and beautiful shrubs, alive with colourful blooms.

Before taking her seat at one of the tables on the porch she spotted some newspapers on a side table and picked out the *New York Times*. Soon she was tucking into a plate of Belgian waffles with frozen yogurt and a strong cup of coffee. She hadn't eaten properly since all the drama with Donnacha had started – it seemed her appetite had now fully returned.

Flicking through the news section of the paper, she made her way to the arts section towards the back. Perhaps there might be a nice exhibition or play on that she could get the time to attend when she went back to New York at the end of the week. A small article on the bottom of one of the pages caught her eye.

'Acclaimed Irish Artist Launches Exhibition in East Village'

The article was small, but detailed that Zee, an artist from Ireland, had just launched an exhibition in New York and the newspaper was giving it rave reviews. She laughed to herself. This was the guy who painted the picture Donnacha had spent the ridiculous amount of money on at the auction. Elenore couldn't believe it. Her knowledge of art was limited but in her opinion a child could have drawn the picture Donnacha had bought for her

– she felt it was all about the shock value of the subject rather than any artistic merit. She was still angry when she thought about the amount of money he had spent on it. Acclaimed by the *New York Times* or not, there was no way the painting was worth the money he had spent. She decided she'd have to look into it when she got home. It was currently propped up against a wall in her bedroom at Cavendish. Even if her life had been going well over the past few weeks, she didn't think she'd have got around to hanging it on a wall – it was far too ugly as far as she was concerned.

When she was satisfied that she was finally full and had ordered a second coffee, she began to think about how she'd spend her first full day in East Hampton. She had promised Robert Bruxby that she'd contact him as soon as she had arrived, in order that he could arrange the meeting between her and his grandmother, but she felt like she needed some time before jumping into that. The last few weeks had not granted her a moment of quiet and she really wanted to be alone, just for a day, in this beautiful place, doing exactly as she wished.

She promised herself she'd call Robert later that evening but for now she was taking the day as hers. She was going to get her swimsuit, walk down to the ocean and dive right in, as she had loved doing when she was a child and her parents had taken her to the beach in West Cork. She just hoped the sea here was a little bit warmer. Then she was going to walk back down to the town centre, and spend her time wandering around the shops, maybe stopping for lunch somewhere along the way. She might find her way back here later this afternoon, order a glass of wine and enjoy it while lying by the pool. The day stretched out before her with endless possibilities and she was going to make the absolute most of it.

By four that evening she was exhausted, having followed through with her plans and spending a thoroughly enjoyable day. She'd been swimming and spent a leisurely few hours strolling around the town and eating lunch.

Relaxed and refreshed, she felt it was time to get down to what she had come here to do. Back in her hotel room, she dug out Robert's number from her address book and called him.

His secretary answered, 'Hello – Bruxby's – how may I help you?'

Elenore told her who she was, and the secretary said Robert had been awaiting her call and she put her through immediately.

'Hello, Elenore! I'm so glad you called. My grandmother is calling me on the hour to see if I've heard from you. Have you made it to East Hampton?'

Thoroughly enjoying his refined East Coast accent, Elenore had hoped he'd keep talking but realised he'd asked a question and she had to answer him,

'Yes, I'm here, Robert, and it's gorgeous. I arrived just last night, and I took today to become accustomed to the place. I have to say, I love it. I was phoning to say I'm free tomorrow – but we could meet any time in the next few days – whenever it would suit Edith.'

'Are you kidding? If I tell her you've called now, she'll want to meet tonight! How would tomorrow suit, maybe around lunchtime? I'm sure she'll want to feed you. Did you hire a car?'

'Yes.'

'Right – let me give you the directions to Cavendish.'

'Sorry, what did you say, Robert? You said Cavendish?'

'Oh yes, didn't you know? That's what her house is called, same as yours. It was her idea to rename it – after she married my grandfather.'

Elenore laughed, touched that the woman wanted to keep some part of her past with her, in her new life.

'That sounds great, Robert, how about one thirty?'

'Fine.'

He gave her the directions and she jotted them down.

'Something else, Elenore – my plans have changed slightly. I'm going to be back in East Hampton on Thursday. I thought we could meet and maybe you could travel back to Manhattan with me on Friday? I can arrange for the hire-car company to collect your car. It would save you having to drive back and, besides, I want to hear all about the old country.'

'Absolutely, Robert, that sounds like a plan.'

Right, job done, Elenore thought to herself, now for dinner. Tomorrow she'd meet Edith. There were butterflies in her stomach, she was that excited at the prospect.

CHAPTER 23

At exactly one twenty the next day, Elenore pulled up to the gate of the American Cavendish. Hopping out of her car, she rang the intercom and was greeted by a female voice.

'Hello, Ms. Stack. Mrs. Bruxby is expecting you. I'll open the gates – please drive on in.'

The buzzer beeped, and the gates began to open before she had a chance to say thank you. The driveway curved, with a manicured lawn on one side and beds of mature trees and shrubs on the other. It swept up to a large area in front of the house, dominated by an ornamental pond in which gushed a large water fountain. Elenore parked her car and surveyed her surroundings.

The house was beautiful – large although not on the same scale as her Cavendish. It was three-storey, grey clapboard, with a large pillared portico to the front. A series of pitched roofs covered the many different parts of the rambling house, varying in height. White shuttered windows of various size and shape were dotted across the front exterior A white rail ran across the top of the house, behind which sat two imposing chimney stacks. Small areas of lawn with low shrubs ran right up to the walls at either end of the house, and large trees, taller than the house itself, framed it beautifully. Elenore could see the ocean to the back of the house, suggesting direct access to the beach.

Walking under the portico, Elenore was greeted at the front door by a young woman wearing jeans, a T-shirt and loafers. She shook hands with Elenore.

'Hi, I'm Cynthia. I look after Mrs. Bruxby. She's beside herself with excitement about seeing you. She's out on the terrace — follow me.'

Elenore followed the young woman into the house, taking in the dark wood flooring and the high ceiling. The large open reception area was dominated by an ornate staircase. Even though this house was younger than her Cavendish by a longshot, it somehow felt similar. Like Cavendish, it felt homely and welcoming, despite its grandeur.

Cynthia led Elenore into a large living room, scattered with soft sofas, rag-rugs and a large open fireplace. At the back of the room was a wall of glass doors, leading out onto a wooden porch. They walked through one of the open glass doors.

Sitting on the terrace with her back to them was a woman with grey hair tied into an elegant bun. She stood up and turned around when she heard Cynthia and Elenore approaching.

Finally, Elenore was face to face with Lady Edith Cavendish.

The elderly woman walked towards her and, before Elenore knew what was happening, she had wrapped her arms around her. For a moment, Elenore felt close to tears. She did her best to stay composed.

'Mrs. Bruxby, it's wonderful to meet you,' she managed to say.

She pulled herself away from Edith, in order to get a proper look at her.

Edith Bruxby might have been well over ninety years of age,

but she looked fantastic. She was tall and elegant, wearing a stylish pair of three-quarter-length trousers and a striped shirt with the collar turned up. A strand of pearls peeked from beneath her shirt collar and a heavy gold watch hung from her tiny wrist. Her skin was lined but her high cheekbones and wide mouth meant she was one of those women who would always look beautiful, no matter what her age.

'My dear Elenore, you've no idea how wonderful this is – that you're finally here. I waited so very long for news from home and now here you are. Please, call me Edith.'

Like Robert's accent, Edith's was very much refined East Coast America, but Elenore could still hear the soft undertone of an Irish accent.

'Come sit down here, dear, and enjoy the view.'

She made a sweeping gesture and Elenore saw steps leading down to a large terraced area where a swimming pool was surrounded by sun loungers, teak furniture and large parasols. The end of the terrace dipped down into a grassy area which turned into sand dunes and from there a wooden gate led directly onto the beach. Beyond, the glittering blue sea stretched to the horizon.

They sat down, side by side.

'Cynthia, get Elenore a glass of juice from the kitchen.'

Cynthia asked what type of juice she'd prefer. Elenore chose orange and the young woman left them alone.

'Now, dear, let me look at you. I feel, because you live at Cavendish, we're somehow family. It's as if I should see something of myself in you. Isn't that silly of me?'

Elenore shook her head. 'Not at all, I know what you mean. When I found your diary, even though I didn't know at first who wrote it, it soon became clear that it was written by a young girl who had lived at Cavendish. I immediately found myself becoming very protective of the writer. Protective of you, as it turned out.'

Edith smiled at her. 'Yes, the diary. I certainly never thought I'd see that again. I hadn't thought about it in years. Then last year I had a bit of a health scare, nothing too serious in the end, but at my age you have to face your own mortality. And it makes you think about the past. I've thought a lot more about Cavendish since then, more than I have for a long time. It seems as if the contact from you was perfectly timed.'

Elenore felt as if she understood. 'I think I know what you mean. I found the diary at a particularly difficult time in my life. It has really provided me with an escape, something that I've needed a lot in the past few weeks.'

Cynthia reappeared from the house and placed a glass of freshly squeezed orange juice on the table in front of Elenore.

'I'm going to go into town to get some groceries, Mrs. Bruxby. Is there anything you need?'

'No, Cynthia dear. You go along – I'm more than fine here with Elenore.'

Cynthia excused herself, telling Elenore she hoped to see her later.

'Cynthia is an amazing girl. She's studying astrophysics at Princeton but she's from here and was looking for something to do for the summer. I think she must be very bored, running after me. There's not really a whole lot of that to do. I have a lady who comes in to clean and prepare my meals. Cynthia is more to keep me company. It was my grandson's idea. I think he feels guilty he doesn't get to spend a lot of time with me and so he decided I needed a Cynthia.'

'I'm sure you're glad to have her. Do you live alone then?' Elenore was surprised.

'I live alone, but I prefer it that way. This was where Chester and I set up home after we got married and I've been here ever since. Aside from Cavendish, it's the only real home that I've ever known. That's why I insisted this house be called Cavendish too.'

There was a tenderness in her voice when she spoke of her husband and her home.

'But I mustn't get maudlin. Now, before we start talking about the diary, I want to learn everything about you. What do you do, who are the people you love and how long have you lived at Cavendish?'

Elenore spent the next twenty minutes filling Edith in on the details of her life. How Cavendish had come to be in her family, her idyllic childhood spent there, her time at university and the years after, working with her father at Stacks, the death of her parents and meeting Donnacha.

She stopped short of going into any details of what had happened in the previous weeks, but it seemed Edith was not going to let her away with that.

'So, tell me about Donnacha. Where did you meet him and was it love at first sight?'

Having felt lighter since she'd arrived stateside, away from Ireland and the troubles brought into her life by Donnacha, she now felt that old, familiar weight on her shoulders at the mere mention of his name.

'Our first meeting wasn't very exciting – we met at a charity lunch. The charity was a client of my friend Leslie. She works in public relations. She begged me to come along because she was afraid the tickets for the lunch weren't selling very well. I literally saw Donnacha across a crowded room. It all seems like such a cliché now, but he was tall, dark and handsome. I thought he'd never look at someone like me. I remember he was surrounded by women. I think he may have been the only man at the lunch but, even so, it's not too often you meet a man who can command such attention. He did look at me though. He asked Leslie who I was, and he came over and we spent the whole time chatting. He asked for my phone number and that was it. We went on our first date a week later and we were a couple from then on.'

Edith was smiling at her. 'That sounds lovely, my dear, but what nonsense – silly you, thinking a handsome man wouldn't look in your direction! You're beautiful. I know plenty of men here in The Hamptons who would be happy to look at you more than once. I hope he's kind to you and realises how lucky he is to have you?'

Elenore thought it best to avoid the truth. 'Yes, he's very kind to …' But the lie caught her out and she stopped, unsure of how to continue.

'Elenore, dear, whatever is the matter? You look very sad. Is everything alright?'

'I'm sorry.' She felt as if she was on the verge of tears again. 'It seems Donnacha doesn't think he's lucky to have me at all. In fact, Donnacha is not kind. He's an absolutely horrible person – that's partly why I'm here – to get away from him.'

'My dear, how foolish of me, making you talk about something so painful. Let's forget about that immediately and talk about something else.'

But Elenore felt she wanted to share the story with Edith. She imagined she'd see a lot of her over the coming days and it didn't feel right not being completely honest with her.

She told Edith the story. What her relationship with Donnacha had been like, how he had always made the decisions and she had gone along with them – despite not always being fully in agreement. She told Edith how she had been at a low point when she had met him, feeling lost and alone, having lost both her parents and craving the security that she had never questioned when her parents were alive. She felt now that she might have jumped too quickly into the relationship. Maybe she had been trying to grasp on to a replacement for the security she had lost. Of course, this had only occurred to her over the last few weeks, when it became apparent that things were not at all as she believed them to be.

Edith listened to Elenore with her full attention, as she outlined what had happened in her personal life – her discovery of

Donnacha's plans for Cavendish in the tunnel, the arrival of his ex-wife Karen at her door and her revelations, along with the proof of Donnacha's infidelity. She told Edith of the decision she had made with Karen. How Donnacha's illegal business practices should be made public and how, even after all of that, she still did not know where she stood. It now seemed that she might owe Donnacha so much money that she could lose Cavendish after all.

Once Elenore finished her story, Edith gave her a few moments to compose herself, obviously aware that reliving the tale had caused her quite a bit of stress.

After Elenore had drunk some juice and recovered a little, Edith spoke.

'That's quite a story, young lady, and may I say I think you're very brave to come here, after all that happened to you. I can't say I understand why you came here, to bring a silly old woman a diary – something that could have waited – when you've had such terrible things happening in your own life. Why did you come here, Elenore – why now?'

'Well, as my friend Leslie said, the only joy in my life over the past few weeks has been when I've been thinking about the diary. I thought if I came here, I might be able to forget. I'm not doing a very good job, given that all I've done since I came here is relive my troubles. Can I start over, Edith? Let me tell you all about the diary. I'm dying for you to know.'

She began the story, how the diary had been found in the tunnel, how she had rescued it when Donnacha had consigned it to the skip, read it and been so eager to discover who had written it. She talked of her chance meeting with Seán and the help he had given her, how he'd found May Ryan, or May Russell as she was now, and how they had met her.

'I think you know the rest of the story from there. So here I am, and I have the diary here – would you like to see it?'

But Edith was not ready for that yet. 'May Ryan is still alive and you've been talking to her? How extraordinary! Poor May, I think she was my age. She must be an old lady now, like me. What different lives we've led! How is she? I hope she had a happy life. Did she marry? Did she have children?'

Elenore filled her in on May – how her health was not too good but that she had lived a happy life and was now being looked after by her granddaughter.

'I'm so glad!' said Edith fervently.

Obviously she knew nothing about May's relationship with her father, Elenore judged. Nor anything about May being an informant for the rebels.

Elenore hesitated and then continued. 'May told us all about that terrible night when the house burned, Edith.'

'Oh, so you know about that. Good.' Edith looked away and fell silent.

Unsure how to proceed, Elenore took the diary out of her handbag. 'Here's the diary, Edith. Would you like to read it now?'

Edith took the diary in her hands. 'I can't believe I'm holding this. I never thought I'd see it again. Dear Diary! Isn't it amazing that it survived, after all these years! I never meant to leave it behind, you know, but I had to. I'll tell you about that later.'

Elenore nodded but couldn't resist saying, 'I'm dying to know how it ended up in the tunnel, Edith. Was it you who left it there or was it someone else at a later date?'

'All in good time,' Edith said. 'Rest assured, I'll tell you exactly what happened.' She placed the diary down on the table in front of her and stroked its cover. 'I'd like to read it when I'm alone, if that is alright with you? I've a feeling that I'll be very embarrassed. I was such a silly and naïve young girl. I had no idea of what was going on. Not even in my own house.'

'Of course – I can leave you in peace to read it now.'

'No, not at all – that's not what I meant. I'll read it later, but for now I want us to continue our conversation. We have many things to talk about. You must have thought, on reading the diary, how silly I was. If you did, you were right, but let me tell you about it. I want to tell you about that time and what happened afterwards. Would you like to take a walk with me, Elenore? I find it's always better to talk about things when walking.'

'I'd like nothing more, Edith,' said Elenore, getting up.

She was surprised to see Edith nimbly get up and, politely refusing her offer of help, begin walking briskly towards the steps that led down to the beach.

Together, they made their way down and onto the wide stretch of sand, which was mostly deserted, leading Elenore to wonder if the beach was a private haven for the houses that had access to it.

Edith led Elenore down towards the shoreline, where the sand was compacted and so easier to walk on, and they set off.

'Imagine I thought Tadgh Carey was the love of my life?' she said after a little while. 'Can you believe that, Elenore?'

Elenore thought it perfectly normal for a sixteen-year-old girl to believe the first man she fell for was the love of her life and told Edith as much.

'Yes, perhaps you're right – and I had led such a sheltered life. My parents never allowed me to mix with anyone other than those of my own class. I had seen Tadgh before, many times, when he had got my horse ready for me at the stables, but I had never thought of him in that way. It was only on that one day that suddenly it was as if my eyes were opened. He was beautiful, Elenore. He was tall, with broad shoulders, and dark eyes like a gypsy. He took my breath away and so I thought I was in love. But, of course, I had no idea what he was involved in. I was completely wrapped up in myself and how I wanted to escape my life. It never occurred to me that he might be using me as a means to escape himself. It certainly never occurred to me that he'd do any harm to my house or my family, despite all his talk of getting rid of people of my ilk.'

Elenore felt she was being too hard on herself. 'But you were just a child, Edith. How were you to know? I'm sure your parents protected you from all that was going on around you, as much as they could.'

'Yes, they certainly did. And kept me in the dark about their financial troubles too. I didn't know that my chances of making a good marriage were getting slimmer as each day passed. My parents were running out of money. Unlike other families, they only had Cavendish. Most other people like us would have had other estates around Ireland and probably one or two in England. We really were the poor relations of the aristocracy. I had hardly a penny when I arrived in New York. There were times when I had no food. I used to think that if only I had stayed at home, I'd be safe and warm. As it turned out, I'd have had as little money if I'd stayed, so in the end it turned out I made the right decision. Tadgh used to always talk to me about how money was the most important thing in the world. I'd argue that people shouldn't talk about money and he'd say that was easy for me. I didn't have to constantly worry about where my next meal was coming for. All that quickly changed when I arrived here – all I thought about for months was where I was going to get money and where my next meal was going to come from.'

Elenore pictured a young Edith, coming from such a privileged background, thrown into the middle of an unfamiliar city and battling to survive. She couldn't imagine how she had managed it.

Edith read her mind. 'You're wondering how I survived, aren't you? I'll tell you about that in a bit – but, first of all – Tadgh. There I was, all ready, our plan in place for me to travel to Queenstown and meet him there. Then the word came that the ball in Castle Carbery was cancelled and I was devastated. I remember going down to the stables and the woods so many times that day, hoping against hope that I'd meet him and be able to tell him what had happened. The atmosphere in the house had been strange all day. I think now, my parents must have known something. That's why they had organised those men to come and stay. They were coming to protect the house.'

'Yes, that was the case, Edith – May told us.' Elenore was wondering how much, if anything, Edith knew about May's crucial role in the events leading up to that dreadful night.

Edith nodded. 'It was as they were arriving that I went down to the tunnel – and everything changed for me. I had decided that once dinner was over and darkness fell, I would go to Tadgh's house and wake him up. I thought, if I left the house through the tunnel, I was less likely to be discovered. But then I remembered that sometimes the door to it was locked – and then there was the door at the far end of it, leading out to the farmyard, which might also be locked. I didn't know where the keys were kept, so I realised I needed to locate them now, instead of fumbling trying to find them in the dead of night. Looking back on it, I was highly organised – perhaps not as silly as I sometimes think. So, before I changed for dinner, I made my way down the back stairs, careful not to make any noise. I had packed a small travelling bag and I took with me – my precious diary was inside it, wrapped in a silk scarf. The visitors had started to arrive, so I knew Mrs. Carey and May would be busy preparing drinks for them and Mama would be busy welcoming them. I made my way to the tunnel, lighting my way with a candle so as not to attract attention with a stronger light. To my relief, I found the door unlocked – so I stepped in, closed the door behind me and began to walk. The tunnel was pitch black and my candle didn't throw much light – I normally would have been terrified but I was too intent on my task to be scared. When I finally got to the end, I was delighted to find the door was open. I took my bag outside and hid it in one of the sheds in the yard – ready to collect on my way out later that night. But then I had a thought – I removed my diary. I would find a better hiding place for it – I couldn't take any risk, however small, that it would be found. In the tunnel I searched until I found a small crevice in the wall and pushed the diary in its scarf inside.'

Edith halted and looked at Elenore.

'Was the scarf found, Elenore?'

'No – no scarf. The builder must have discarded it – or maybe took it?'

Edith nodded and continued. 'Then I made my way back towards the house. And then I began to hear voices ahead. I kept walking. As I neared the end, I could see a sliver of light. The door at the end was ajar. I halted and blew my candle out. Suddenly, I recognised the voices and at the same time distinguished some figures against the wall of the tunnel. It was my father and May Ryan. I was astonished and confused. Why would they be in the tunnel and what could they possibly be talking about? My father seemed to be angry and May was upset. I pressed into a little recess in the wall, my heart hammering in my breast.

What I saw and heard turned my life upside down. My father had May Ryan pushed up against the wall. His face was close to hers and I could hear him saying that there would be a lot of men in the house tonight and she was to stay away from all of them. He told her he knew exactly what girls like her were like and if she misbehaved in any way, he'd throw her out and evict her family. That was absolutely shocking to me. I had never heard my father speak like that to anyone. I remember wondering what kind of a girl she was, to make him speak to her like that? For a moment, I remembered the way I had seen her look at Tadgh and I thought she might be the type of girl who caused trouble and flirted with men – the kind my mother had warned me about – but then something even worse happened that shocked me to my core. My father started kissing her. I honestly couldn't understand what I was seeing, squinting there in the darkness. He was kissing her roughly, and then he pulled up her skirt and pushed his hand up inside it. He continued to kiss her and push violently against her.

Then suddenly he stopped. I heard him tell May he'd see her later, before she went home, and to remember what he said. Then he let her go, adjusted his trousers and walked out of the tunnel. May just stood there and then started to cry. I was too confused and horrified to go to her. I was trying to process what I had seen and heard. So all I could do was hide in the recess and listen to May's sobs. Eventually she stopped crying and walked back into the house.'

Edith stopped and Elenore noticed that she was struggling to catch her breath. By now they had walked a considerable distance. It was time to turn back.

'Should we turn around, Edith? I think we've walked far enough.'

'Yes, you're right. I'm getting tired.'

Elenore slipped her arm through Edith's as they turned and began to retrace their steps at a slower pace. Edith had stopped at such a dramatic point in the story that Elenore could hardly restrain herself from prompting her to go on.

At last Edith resumed. 'After that, I don't know how I managed to sit through dinner and chat to our guests – nor how I then played piano for them for a while. But worse was to come. Sometime later I glanced through a window and thought I saw some movement in the trees at a distance from the house. I thought it must be Tadgh, and, terrified that he might leave, I rushed to the front door to signal that I was aware of his presence. I threw the door open and raised my hand. Then I saw men running towards the house with blazing torches in their hands. I turned and began to scream for my father. Suddenly May was there, pulling me back inside the house. But we both froze as we saw some of the rebels smash a window in the east wing and torch it. Then we were pushed aside as the men from our house rushed out with shotguns. Shots were exchanged, then the rebels turned and ran. It was then that I saw him. Tadgh. Still looking towards us as he turned to run. Then one of our men brought him crashing to the ground as I screamed his name.'

Edith fell silent for a long while, her head bent as they walked.

'The boy I loved had become the enemy,' she continued at last, 'but what I had seen my father do, earlier that evening, made him the enemy too. I felt like there was no longer anyone I could trust. I had wanted to leave Cavendish for a long time – not the house but my family – because of the life I was forced to live. I loved that house, I still do. Sometimes, when I wake up in the morning, I think for a second that I'm back there. I can almost smell the damp air and see the rolling green fields all around it.'

'So, you left,' said Elenore, wondering how she had managed to leave Cavendish and make it all the way to another continent, with little money and no life experience.

'Yes, I left. I knew I had no choice. I remember collapsing on the floor, distraught, and May coming to comfort me. Poor May, she was able to comfort me, even though my father was doing God knows what to her, and I hadn't been able to comfort her earlier that evening, when she had really needed it.'

Elenore could hear the regret in her voice. 'Edith, it wasn't your fault, what happened to her.'

'Did you know what happened to her? Did she talk to you about it?'

Elenore remembered her promise to May, that she wouldn't tell anyone about her pregnancy. 'Yes, she did mention it, but she didn't go into a lot of detail and I didn't want to pry.'

'Of course – and perhaps I shouldn't be telling you this, but I want to explain to you why I ran away. It wasn't as simple as a broken heart.'

'But how did you do it, Edith, how did you escape?'

'The fire turned out to be the perfect opportunity. I was ordered out of the house and, outside, the sight of the fire devouring Cavendish brought me to my senses. It was mayhem as they rushed to try to get the fire under control and I managed to sneak back into the house. Upstairs, I tore my evening dress off and pulled on daytime clothes and ankle boots. I took the purse containing my ticket for America and my remaining money from its hiding place, frantically threw a few necessities into a bag, grabbed my coat and hat and left. Back outside, I simply walked away from the house. Nobody saw me. No one was paying any attention. That's how the diary got left behind and the clothes I had hidden away to take with me. I couldn't risk going all the way down to the farmyard and the tunnel for them. So that answers your question about the diary, Elenore.' She flashed a small smile at her companion. 'I left the demesne and set out for Queenstown. I walked all night, in pitch darkness, and most of the next morning. I'd jump off the road and into the ditch if I heard anyone on the road. I stopped a man once I got to Queenstown and asked him where the port was. Tadgh had bought us third-class tickets, as that was all we could afford, even with my money. He had been worried that I'd stand out in third class, with my clothes and the way I spoke. He needn't have worried – having walked the fifteen miles from Cavendish to Queenstown, jumping into ditches to hide along the way, and not having slept in a day – I certainly didn't look like the type of person who would be travelling first class. I remember getting to my cabin and collapsing onto the bed. It was the most uncomfortable bed I ever slept on. I shared the cabin with three other girls – they were friends, from West Cork. Tadgh and I wouldn't have been sharing the cabin if he had come, because we weren't married. I eventually woke up, a day later, and the vomiting started straight away. I was sick for the whole journey, which was a week long. The other girls were sick too, so no one really spoke to each other. It was horrendous. By the time I got to Ellis Island, I must have weighed half what I did when I left Ireland.'

She smiled ruefully at Elenore, who was trying to imagine how that cossetted young girl had manged to endure all that suffering, both mental and physical.

'The first months in America were the hardest,' Edith went on. 'I found somewhere to stay, a boarding house, but I knew it was only a matter of time before I ran out of money. I needed to act fast. I had never worked but I needed to get a job. I had a few things working in my favour: I sounded British, not Irish – a big advantage in the America of that time – I had my upperclass manners and, most important, I had my education. My governess had given me a first-class education. I spoke French and Latin fluently and had a wide knowledge of English literature. I knew I needed to use all that to my advantage and find myself a position as a governess.'

Elenore could see now the steeliness in this lady that must have been built over this difficult time in her life.

'I started going out every day, trying to figure out where the well-to-do people in the city lived. It wasn't hard to figure out. It certainly wasn't where I was living. The streets there were filthy, and the people badly dressed. But it was the Roaring Twenties, and the city was alive. It was unlike anything I'd ever seen, so I didn't mind the dirt and the poverty so much. Each day I'd go out, looking incredibly outdated in a city where women were sporting bobbed hairstyles and calf-length dresses – my coat and skirt were ankle-length. I looked the part of a governess, but I realised that I needed to invest some of my precious money in a few items of clothing. It was important to look respectable. So I bought some clothes, choosing old-fashioned rather than more fashionable clothes. Then, by sitting in coffee shops and talking to people, letting them know I was looking for work, I finally came across Mrs. Lyndsey and her family. She took me on, in a live-in position, and I looked after her children for five years. Meeting Mrs. Lyndsey was one of the luckiest things that happened to me in my life. She and her husband were a traditional upper-class family and it felt very much like being back in Cavendish. They treated me as if I were one of their children, protecting me from the outside world. I didn't see any more of the Roaring Twenties after that. I was never able to tell them about my past. I lied and told them my parents had died. If they knew they had a member of the Anglo-Irish aristocracy living under their roof, letters would have been sent to my parents immediately.'

'You were lucky, Edith – it could have been very different for you.' Elenore was relieved at the thought of the young Edith being looked after.

'I certainly was lucky, and I don't think things would have worked out as well for me if I had travelled with Tadgh. Mrs. Lyndsey eventually decided that I needed some formal qualifications and helped me enrol in a secretarial course, so I'd know how to type. She said it was important that I knew how to do more than look after children and teach them grammar. I eventually left her when the children grew older and got a job in the typing pool at a newspaper. That's where I met Chester.'

They reached the house at this point and Edith stopped abruptly.

'I don't think I can talk any more for now,' she said. 'I'd very much like a lie-down.'

Elenore was feeling guilty at this stage, noticing that Edith looked very fatigued. 'Yes, I think we've reminisced enough for one day – I didn't mean to tire you out – I'm sorry.'

'It's not your fault. I wanted to talk to you about it. And I want to tell you about Tadgh. The night of the fire wasn't the last time I saw him, you know. But we need to save that for tomorrow.'

'You saw him again?'

'I did, yes.'

But at that point Cynthia came hurrying from the house to meet them and, passing Edith over into the capable hands of the preppy girl, Elenore said goodbye and promised Edith she'd call again at the same time the next day. Edith kissed her on the cheek and told her she very much looked forward to it.

As she drove back to the hotel, Elenore couldn't wait to call Seán. She wanted to tell him every detail of her meeting with Lady Edith.

CHAPTER 24

Elenore went back the next day to see Edith and they took another walk on the beach. The two women shared stories with each other. Elenore was growing fonder of her new companion by the minute. Edith had a wicked sense of humour and she kept Elenore entertained with her hilarious accounts of the goings-on of The Hamptons' upper classes.

However, Elenore could barely restrain herself from pressing Edith to tell her about her meeting with Tadgh. She knew she shouldn't push. It had to happen when Edith was ready.

Eventually, Edith returned to the subject, quite abruptly. 'I met Tadgh, when I was out running an errand for Mrs. Lyndsey. It was 1928. I was running down 5th Avenue, it was raining, so I wasn't looking where I was going, and I ran straight into him. Imagine that! It was one of the more surreal moments of my life.'

'Oh my God, Edith, that's unbelievable!' Elenore was astounded.

'Yes, it certainly was. Of course, we recognised each other straight away. I can't remember exactly what we said to each other, but we ended up going to get a cup of tea together. I think Tadgh was surprised that I was speaking to him, but five or six years had passed since I had fled Cavendish and I was desperate for any news from home. We spent a couple of hours together that afternoon. We were cagey around each other at first, unsure what to say. I told him a bit about my life. How I had been lucky in finding work with the Lyndseys, and how they were good to me. At first, we very much ignored all that had gone between us.'

'That must have been difficult – weren't you still angry at him?' Elenore thought that, if she were in Edith's position, she'd have been very angry.

'I don't think I was. I had seen a bit more of life at that stage. I saw real poverty for the first time when I arrived in New York. That type of poverty was part of daily life for all the families that worked and lived at Cavendish, but I had been oblivious to it. I had a better understanding by then of why Tadgh was angry towards my family.'

'So, what did you do?'

'Nothing really, we did nothing. I eventually asked him about Cavendish and he said it had survived. I was glad of that. I couldn't bear to think it had burned to the ground, like so many other houses back then. He asked if I had kept in contact with my family and, when I told him I hadn't, he said they were no longer in Cavendish but had returned to England and that Cavendish was for sale. He then said, if only he had travelled with me, we might have made our money by now, and be in a position to buy it. I laughed at that. I was as far away from having that kind of money as I had ever been. Tadgh then told me that he had only just arrived in America, that he had been arrested after the fire and spent a few years in prison. That made me sad, despite all he had done. And when he finally opened up to me, I learned that his intention had not been to hurt anyone. He told me what had happened that night. He said their orders were that no one was to be hurt or injured in the burning of the house. As you know, he thought that I was in Queenstown and he was shocked when he saw me open the door and heard me scream for my father. When the men came running towards the house, he had followed them. But, he said, his only intention at that point was to save me from any harm. I felt very sad when he told me that. For all those years I had thought all he wanted to do was burn the house and use me and the money I had in his bid to get to America. After that, I knew that he had loved me. He apologised to me over and over again. He felt that he had made a mistake getting involved with the rebels in the first place. I think prison had changed him. He said he deeply regretted any pain he had caused me.'

'Did you ever see him again?'

'No, I didn't. He asked me to meet him again, the following week, in the same place. I could have but I didn't. That part of my life was over, and I knew all Tadgh had been for me was someone to fill in the space left by an empty life. I didn't love Tadgh. I was simply bored, and he came along and brought some excitement to that life. But, you know, I'll always be thankful to him. I wouldn't have lived the wonderful life I did, if it wasn't for Tadgh Carey. But I had grown up a lot in the years since we had last seen each other, and I knew he was not the one for me. Our backgrounds were too different, and there was still an anger about him. His anger had been attractive when I met him in the woods at Cavendish. It was dangerous and that was very appealing. But I didn't want anger and danger then. I wanted a life like the Lyndseys had. I saw how Mr. and Mrs. Lyndsey were to each other, kind and caring. They spent a lot of time together and were always laughing. I knew if I became involved with Tadgh again my life would always be a struggle. I didn't want that for myself. I wanted calm and peace and comfort.'

Elenore understood exactly what Edith was saying and was full of admiration for her.

'It looks like you got peace and comfort in the end?'

'Yes, I did. I met Chester when I went to work at the newspaper. He was a journalist. Of course, his family owned the newspaper, but I had no idea of that at the time. He was kind and caring and we were friends at first. He was a little older than me and so I think he understood that I was naïve and shouldn't be rushed. But eventually I fell for him and we were happy for a long time. No life is untouched by grief and our lives were no different – but we worked through it.'

Elenore was happy that things had worked out well for her, if not a little envious, now unsure if she'd ever find such contentment.

'This was Chester's parents' house, it was their wedding gift to us. It always reminded me of Cavendish. I'm not sure why. Maybe it's the homely feel it has. I loved it from the first time I saw it, the same way that I loved Cavendish.'

'And what about your parents, Edith? Did you ever contact them to let them know where you were?'

'No, Elenore, I didn't. I've never been able to forgive my father for what he did to May. She was the same age as me and yet he could take advantage of her like that. I was so glad when you told me May is still alive and that she went on to get married and live a good life. I'm glad what happened to her didn't shape who she became.'

'I think May has been very happy all these years. I'm sure like everyone she had her difficult times but, like you, she has her family around her now and I think things worked out for her in the end. But what about your mother, Edith – didn't you want to let her know you were safe?'

Edith thought for a moment before she answered. 'I know this is hard for you to understand – it sounds like you had a very close relationship with your mother, but I was raised by a nanny, not by my mother. She never hugged or kissed me. I saw her for only a small amount of time every day. She was a cold woman and, to be honest, if she suspected what my father was doing to May, I don't think she'd have interfered or tried to make it stop. She wrote to me once. I've no idea how she found me – I suppose there's always somebody who knows somebody. Chester's family were quite well-known in certain circles. The letter was addressed to me in my married name. It said she had a daughter called Edith and she thought I might be her. She said, if I was, she wanted to let me know that Papa had died a few years previously. It was then she told me about the financial problems they had been having before I left. I replied and confirmed that I was indeed her daughter. I spoke to Chester about it and we sent her some money, but I told her that she shouldn't contact me again as I had left that part of my life behind me. I never heard from her again.'

They had talked for a while more until Edith became tired and Elenore returned to her hotel to mull over all that she had been told. She was glad Edith and Tadgh had met again and that Edith had had the chance to understand what had really happened on the night the house was burned.

Edith had said she wanted Elenore to leave her hotel and come stay with her but, although Elenore was enjoying her company immensely, she still wanted a few quiet hours in the evening – when she could go back to her hotel, report to Leslie and Seán, and catch up on what was happening at home.

She called both of them that evening, Leslie first.

Leslie told her that the media coverage had died down, as Donnacha had still not emerged into the public eye. One newspaper had published some images of Siobhán Ellis that day, shopping in a supermarket in Dublin, but it seemed that was it for now. Leslie thought that once Donnacha re-emerged from wherever he was hiding, there would be a surge in coverage. Then it should die down again, at least until it became apparent how the authorities were going to deal with the allegations.

Later, she relaxed on her bed with a glass of wine and phoned Seán. He was beside himself with excitement at all the news about Edith and her life after she had left Cavendish. He had so many questions and Elenore tried to answer them as best she could – when she was unable to, she promised to put them to Edith the next day.

He was also eager to ensure Elenore was getting along okay, constantly telling her to take it easy and to get plenty of rest. He checked the details of her return flight with her and said he was available to meet her at the airport if she needed a lift back to Ballycastle.

Elenore was touched, once again, by Seán's concern and kindness, and realised it had been a long time since she had experienced such kindness from a man. Donnacha was all about expensive gifts and bold, long-term plans. Seán's simpler, day-to-day helpfulness seemed kinder and more thoughtful. She was far more comfortable being on the receiving end of it.

CHAPTER 25

Robert was returning to East Hampton on Thursday evening and, when Elenore visited earlier in the day, Edith invited her to stay and have dinner with her and her grandson. Elenore happily accepted. Edith spoke about Robert in such glowing terms that Elenore was eager to meet him.

She had learned so much about Edith over the last couple of days. She knew that Robert was her only grandchild. She'd had two children. Michael, who was Robert's father, was retired and currently enjoying a round-the-world trip with Robert's mother Alison. Edith's second child, Ruth, had died in a horse-riding accident when she was just seventeen. Edith talked openly about the loss of her daughter and the effect it had had on her marriage. She told Elenore that at one point she had feared the pain of the loss suffered by her and Chester would bring about the end of their marriage, but they had worked on dealing with it together and ultimately it had brought them closer.

Chester had died almost fifteen years before, and Edith had

fallen into a deep depression, but the love of her son and her grandson had pulled her through and now she was determined to enjoy what remained of her life. She knew that was what Chester would have wanted for her.

Cynthia needed to go into town to pick up some food for the dinner with Robert that night and Elenore asked if she could accompany her and stop off at her hotel on the way, to pick up a change of clothes for dinner. Cynthia agreed, and they set off.

Cynthia was chatty, eager to know what life was like in Ireland. She was planning a trip to Europe the following year, as soon as she graduated. She pointed out her own house, on the way into town. It was not quite as grand as Edith's house and did not have direct access to the beach but, nonetheless, it looked as if Cynthia came from a privileged background too.

'I live very close to Mrs. Bruxby,' she told Elenore. 'It's a pity – if I lived further away I might get to stay the night, which is always appealing when Robert comes to visit.'

Elenore smiled at her, not sure how to respond to this.

'Oh, you'll understand what I mean when you meet him – he's gorgeous and he's single.'

'In that case, I had better dress to impress.'

On reaching the hotel, Elenore ran up to her room and pondered on what to wear. This Robert character might be gorgeous, but she certainly wasn't interested in him and so didn't want to look like she had made too much of an effort. On the other hand, Edith did tell her that she liked to dress up for dinner. Scanning the wardrobe full of Leslie's clothes, her eyes fell on a turquoise, jersey wrap dress. She threw the dress and some fresh underwear in a bag, together with a chunky gold necklace. Picking up her gold sandals, she ran back down to Cynthia.

The two women proceeded into town, picked up what was needed for dinner and were back at Edith's house within the hour.

Edith had not emerged from her bedroom yet and so Cynthia

directed Elenore upstairs to a spare bedroom, where she told her she could shower and prepare for dinner. Elenore walked up the stairs and down the long corridor, to the fourth door on the right. The bedroom was beautiful, dominated by a massive white cast-iron bed while muslin drapes decorated the window, which had magnificent views out towards the ocean. The deep window seat, with its soft cushions, provided the perfect place to take in the view and relax for a few moments.

An hour later, having relaxed for a while and taken a refreshing shower, Elenore was ready to meet the gorgeous Robert. It was six thirty and he was due to arrive at seven, so her timing was perfect. She took one final glance in the mirror before making her way downstairs.

The turquoise dress had been the perfect solution, the colour suiting her skin tone, especially now that she had built up a tan. Tapering in to her waist and then falling to her calves, it swayed gently as she walked. The deep V-neckline further highlighted her tanned skin, enhanced by the thick gold coil around her neck.

She had left her long, freshly washed hair hang loose down her back. As she didn't have much make-up with her, she made do with a swipe of lip gloss and some mascara. Overall, she was happy with the result. If Leslie were here, she'd have told her to go borrow some make-up from Cynthia, but Elenore liked how she looked. The tired look she had worn when she first arrived first had been replaced by a tanned, healthy glow and the dark circles under her eyes were no more.

Edith pretended to do a double-take when Elenore came downstairs. 'My goodness, I knew you were beautiful, but tonight you look like a goddess. I should have warned Robert – he isn't going to be able to control himself.'

Elenore laughed off her comment but, when Robert arrived into the dining room, twenty minutes later, she wasn't so sure she wanted him to control himself. He was gorgeous – not Donnacha-gorgeous, but JKF Junior gorgeous. He was confident, amazingly so, but it was an easy confidence, not like Donnacha's. Elenore couldn't imagine Robert needing to be the centre of attention. He came across as a man who was entirely comfortable in his own skin and didn't feel the need to persuade anyone of his qualities. He also appeared to be very sincere – and very interested in Elenore.

The dinner flew by, as Elenore and Edith brought Robert up to speed on everything they had discovered about each other over the last few days.

Edith, with Elenore's permission, shared with Robert the situation that Elenore now found herself in and Robert shook his head, agreeing that Elenore's smaller plans for Cavendish made much more sense. He said he understood the hospitality industry and 5-star hotels were a massive undertaking that usually didn't work without the support of a hotel group behind them. It simply wasn't easy for a medium-sized enterprise to maintain that level of consistent luxury.

In his opinion, small meant better. You could sell exclusivity and the real country-house experience and there would always be those high-end clients who wanted that, as much as they wanted the designer bathroom products and access to a spa that came with five stars. In Robert's opinion, the American market was exactly where Elenore needed to be.

Elenore was beyond delighted to hear this and wasn't sure if it was because of Robert's belief in her plan, or the two glasses of wine she had consumed, but she felt her confidence growing. She was enjoying the night. She felt great. If someone like Robert could see the potential in what she wanted to do, then that meant there was hope.

After dinner, Edith took the diary from the sideboard where she had put it for safe-keeping and showed it to her grandson. He spent some time going through it and asking all sorts of questions.

He was particularly interested in May, but the women didn't go into the details of her unfortunate experience with Robert's great-grandfather, neither of them feeling it was necessary for him to know this.

Eventually Edith announced that she was off to bed. She told Elenore to help herself to more wine and that she was welcome to stay in the spare room – or Robert would drop her back to her hotel.

Kissing Edith on the cheek, Elenore promised she'd see her next day, as she tried to put out of her mind the fact that tomorrow would be her last day in East Hampton and most likely the last time she'd see Edith.

After Robert had seen his grandmother to bed, he returned downstairs and invited Elenore to join him on the terrace, where he poured her another glass of wine.

'I really shouldn't, Robert – tomorrow is the last day I'll get to spend with Edith and I don't want to be feeling hungover.'

Robert wasn't taking no for an answer. 'Live a little, Elenore. From what my grandmother tells me, you've had a rough time recently. You're here tonight, on a terrace overlooking the ocean in East Hampton. Let your hair down and your worries drift away. Enjoy it.'

Put that way, how could she say no? One glass turned into two and all the time Elenore was trying desperately to stay sober, conscious that Robert was not drinking, due to his commitment to drive her back to her hotel.

But it was so nice here – the sky above them was filled with stars and the ocean was lapping gently below them. It was quite possibly one of the most beautiful and most peaceful places she had ever been. It was difficult not to relax.

They talked long into the night. Robert told her all about his parents and how happy he was to take over the family firm from his father, allowing his parents to travel the world while they were still young enough to enjoy it. He told her all he knew about his grandfather, Edith's husband, how Chester had been a bit of a wild child, rebelling against his parents and causing uproar by marrying the Irish girl who worked in the typing pool.

'If they had known they had an "aristocrat" marrying into the family, it would have been very different but apparently Edith was adamant that she didn't want her parents-in-law to know her family history. I think that suited my grandfather too. He very much wanted to make his own way, despite being born into wealth. That's why he was working in the newsroom when he met Edith. He was determined not to have the family business handed over to him without having worked in it properly. They were two very strong-willed people. I like to think of them as a great power couple. Edith was devastated when Chester died. It took her a long time to recover.'

Then Elenore found herself talking about her relationship with Donnacha and boldly asking Robert about his own love life. The answer proved to be evasive, as he told her there had been a couple of serious girlfriends but currently there was nobody. He told her he'd love to settle down but somehow the right woman just hadn't materialised – but he lived in hope.

Elenore thought this was a bit of a stretch of the imagination. Robert was rich and strikingly handsome, not to mention the fact that he appeared to have no baggage like an ex-wife. It seemed highly unlikely that he was unable to find the right person to settle down with. But Elenore let it go – she was having too much fun with him.

Soon they heard the grandfather clock in the hallway strike midnight and Elenore announced that he must take her home. Standing up, she wasn't surprised to find that she wobbled slightly, and Robert rushed over to steady her.

He led her into the house and, picking up her bag along the way, steered her towards the front door and out to his car.

On the way back to the hotel he made plans for tomorrow. 'I'll come and pick you up at nine in the morning and you can come back and have breakfast with us. Then you can spend the day with Edith. I'll arrange to have the rental car picked up. Then maybe about six tomorrow evening we can head back to Manhattan. We'll be back in the city in time for dinner. I'll make reservations, if that suits?'

Elenore knew she'd be very sad to leave East Hampton, and especially to leave Edith, but a part of her could feel excitement building at the prospect of two nights and a day in New York City with this very attractive man.

'That all sounds perfect to me, Robert, but I don't want to make a nuisance of myself. I can always drive back and wander around the city on my own, as I had originally planned. I don't need to keep you away from your work.'

'Don't be ridiculous, Elenore, you're not a nuisance at all. I can't think of anything I'd rather do than spend the next forty-eight hours with you.'

He flashed her a smile and Elenore thought that had she been standing up her knees would have given way beneath her.

'You know Edith has taken a real shine to you?' he said, changing the subject.

Elenore had to concentrate to keep up. 'I've taken a real shine to her too. She's amazing. She's led such a fabulous life.

Robert nodded. 'She wants to go back to Cavendish, you know?'

Elenore hadn't known this and was amazed. 'Really? Did she tell you that? She hasn't mentioned it to me.'

'Don't worry, she's not coming to take Cavendish off you!'

'Oh, of course not, I know that. I know she does have a great affection for it – she's told me so – but it just seems strange she would want to return to the scene of such heartache.'

'I don't think so. It's where she was born and where she lived until she was sixteen. The house was in her family for generations. She's the last Cavendish. I don't think it's unusual at all that she'd want to go and see it, one last time.'

'What are you telling me, Robert? Edith's not sick, is she?'

Robert laughed. 'No, she's fine, but she's ninety-six, Elenore. If she wants to see Cavendish, she doesn't have much time to waste.'

He parked his car outside the hotel and jumped out to go open the door for her. He offered her his hand and she took it as she stepped out of the car.

'I understand why Edith has taken such a shine to you,' he said. 'I really see the appeal myself.'

He was still holding her hand and now he seemed to have his other arm around her waist. She wasn't sure how that had happened, but it felt nice.

She looked up at him, he was smiling down at her, and he was even more handsome this close-up. She could see the grey flecks in his lovely green eyes, and his jawline was chiselled and strong. Then he leaned down and kissed her, and she just let herself go with it. It didn't feel real. It was as if she was watching it happen to someone else, but it did feel wonderful.

When it was over, he looked down at her and smiled again. 'Will you be alright to get back to your room alone? I'd happily walk you back, but I'm afraid I wouldn't be controlled enough not to invite myself in. I don't want to be accused of taking advantage of such a beautiful woman.'

His little speech was probably much practised and used but delivered in his lovely accent it sounded perfect to Elenore. She wouldn't have minded if he had taken advantage, but then she got a glimpse of how she might feel the next morning, facing Edith, if she had spent the night with her grandson.

'I think you're right, Robert. It mightn't be the best idea. I'll be fine to get back to my room on my own. Thanks for a lovely evening, and a lovely ending. It was unexpected but really nice. I'll see you in the morning.'

She turned to walk away but before she could, Robert grabbed her arm, pulled her close and kissed her passionately.

'I couldn't let you get away that easily, sorry about that. I promise I'll let you go this time.'

He was grinning at her, and Elenore was sure she could have kept him there all night but instead, standing on tip-toe, she kissed him on the cheek.

'I think we've both had enough kissing for one night.' With that she turned and walked towards the hotel, but it took everything in her power not to break into a skip.

CHAPTER 26

Elenore ran, almost tripping over Alfie, and managed to get to the phone before it stopped ringing.

'Hello, Cavendish Hall.'

'Elenore dear, it's Edith – how are you?'

'Edith, it's wonderful to hear you voice. I'm doing well – how are you?'

'I'm fantastic, dear, and I have some wonderful news. I've booked my flights. Robert and I arrive on Tuesday. But that's not all – I have another surprise for you too, but I'm going to keep it to myself until I get to you.'

'That's amazing, Edith. I can't wait to see you both and I can't wait for you to see Cavendish.'

'I know, I'm beside myself with excitement at the thought of seeing it again and showing it to Robert. I know he'll love it. He's almost as excited as I am.'

Elenore was genuinely glad that Edith was coming to visit but wasn't sure how she felt about her grandson accompanying her.

After leaving East Hampton, she had spent her time in New York with him. He had shown her all the sites and brought her out for amazing dinners. Unable to resist his charm, she had allowed him to spend the two nights with her at the hotel. It had felt strange sleeping with another man after all her time with Donnacha. She soon forgot about that, however, and let the undeniable attraction she felt for this handsome man take over. It had been just what she needed, and she had returned to Ireland refreshed and ready to face whatever was to come.

She hadn't heard from Robert since and that was exactly what she had expected. The day she left East Hampton, she had spent some more time alone with Edith and was surprised at what the older woman had to say about her grandson.

'Be careful of Robert,' was how Edith had started the conversation, taking Elenore completely by surprise.

'What do you mean, Edith?' she asked uncertainly.

'Well, I can clearly see that he likes you and it's easy to see why. I can also understand if the feeling is mutual – Robert is a very handsome man. I know I'm biased, being his grandmother, but he really does present himself as a great catch and one day I hope he will be. The problem with Robert is, he's a ladies' man and has been from day one. He's left a trail of broken hearts across The Hamptons and, I dare say, in most of the boroughs of New York. He gets bored easily, that's simply his nature. And you, Elenore, you've been through a lot. I don't want you to get hurt. By all means have fun with him. You deserve as much fun as you can get, but don't go falling in love with him. You'll only get hurt and that's the last thing you need right now.'

Elenore couldn't believe how forthright Edith was and felt immense gratitude to her for her candidness. Not too many women of her generation would be able to view their own flesh and blood with such clarity – especially a handsome grandson.

The time in New York had been glorious but Elenore, perhaps

because of what Edith had said to her, remained as she had been on the night they had first kissed. She viewed the experience as something that was happening to someone else. She let herself go with it and enjoyed every second but was constantly aware that this was not real life. Instead it was a further few days of escapism.

Besides, Robert's over-the-top gestures and declarations were somewhat comical. Over the course of the two days he had declared on at least five occasions that she was the most beautiful woman in the world and told her, at least twice, that he was falling in love with her.

She smiled to herself now when she thought about it. He was falling in love with her and yet had not contacted her once since she had returned home, almost two weeks ago now. It was a good job she had taken heed of Edith's advice. Robert clearly was one for grand declarations as opposed to being on the lookout for someone to settle down with.

She wouldn't have thought about him again, except to recall with pleasure the time they had spent together – only now he was coming to Cavendish.

When Edith had told her, the day she left East Hampton, that she wanted to see Cavendish one last time, Elenore had been delighted but assumed she'd travel with Cynthia, or someone else paid to look after her. The news of Robert's arrival to stay in her home, in less than a week, was unexpected.

Edith chatted away on the phone some more, asking Elenore if there were any further updates on Donnacha. Elenore had kept her up to speed on developments since she had returned home.

On arrival back to Shannon airport, Elenore had been greeted by Leslie, Karen and Seán. She hadn't spoken to any of them for two days, between travelling and being caught up in her time with Robert. She was surprised to see that all three of them had come to meet her.

They welcomed her home, Seán relieving her of her suitcase and Leslie linking arms with her and steering her out of the airport.

'Gosh, thanks for coming, guys – I could have taken the bus, you know.'

'We wanted to be here, Elenore,' said Leslie. 'There's a few things we need to tell you, and we thought it better if we were all here together.'

Elenore's heart dropped: not a minute back in Ireland and already she was being faced with bad news.

'Go on, Leslie, tell me whatever it is you need to tell me.'

'Donnacha's been arrested and brought in for questioning. The Gardaí have been to Cavendish and seized all the documents that he had stored in the tunnel and they want to talk to you.'

She looked at her three friends and, despite what they had just told her, felt a surge of gratitude that she had them in her life.

'Okay, I think that's to be expected though, isn't it?' she said. 'We always knew that might happen and I don't mind talking to the Gardaí. I've nothing to hide.'

On the journey back to Cavendish they filled her in on the events of the last two days. Donnacha had reappeared and the reporter Gerard Walsh had got a tip-off that he was back in Cork. A picture had appeared in the paper Gerard worked for, of Donnacha outside his office. By ten that morning, the Gardaí had arrested him.

He had been held for a few hours and questioned and then let go but cautioned not to leave the country. Gerard was keeping a close eye on him and had alerted Leslie when he discovered that Donnacha was heading for Cavendish. Leslie, however, was at Cavendish already, as the Gardaí had called her, asking to get access to the house in Elenore's absence.

When Donnacha had arrived at the house he had stormed in and, making his way straight down the back stairs, had found

Leslie in the storage room locking the tunnel door. He had shouted at her to give him access to the tunnel, but she had told him he was too late – the Gardaí had already removed the files. He became angry, demanding to know how the Gardaí had known to make their way straight to the tunnel. They couldn't have known he had files stored there unless someone had told them.

Luckily for Leslie, her husband Ben arrived at that moment to check she was okay and, grabbing Donnacha by the arm, escorted him off the premises. Leslie had been quite shaken by the incident but insisted that she and Ben sleep at Cavendish that night.

'He was so angry, Elenore. I was afraid he might come back and do some damage. Myself and Seán are going to stay there with you tonight.'

Karen had her own part to add to the story. Donnacha had shown up at her door the previous day, screaming at her and threatening he was going to seek full custody of Aaron. But Karen had stood her ground.

'I told him not to come around to my house threatening me, or I'd call the Gardaí. I also told him if he didn't provide me with draft divorce papers that ensured I get a decent payout, I'd get a barring order against him and I'd be sure that the newspapers were made aware of it. That shut him up straight away. Getting a barring order is something Donnacha would see as being beneath him. He's such a snob. It would be dragging his name further into the mud. Even after all that's been revealed about him, he's still worried about his reputation. It's a bit late for that.'

Leslie had more to add. 'I don't want to worry you any more, Elenore, but I think it's only a matter of time before he comes looking for you. The phone at Cavendish has rung a few times and, each time I answer, whoever is calling hangs up. I think he wants to talk to you.'

Elenore remained calm. 'I really appreciate all you've done for me, but you know what, let him come looking for me. I'm ready.

I need to know what he wants from me and, until I do, I can't start making plans for the future.'

Back at Cavendish, Elenore had a joyful reunion with Alfie and slept soundly knowing that Leslie and Seán were in the neighbouring rooms. Karen had gone home to take care of Aaron but promised she'd be back at some point the next day. She still had not informed her son of her new friendship with his father's ex-partner. She was unsure how to best broach the topic. Elenore promised her it was something they'd figure out together.

Two days later the inevitable had happened. Donnacha had shown up at Cavendish, demanding to speak to Elenore. Luckily both Seán and Leslie were there with her and Elenore told Donnacha that she'd only speak to him in the company of her two friends.

He hadn't not been happy about this at all, wanting to know who Seán was and what he was doing in his house. Elenore had reminded him that Cavendish was not his, told him Seán was a friend of hers, and that he'd better get on with whatever it was he had to say as she was fast running out of time and patience.

Donnacha had sat down at the table. 'The simple fact of the matter, Elenore, is that I've invested heavily in Cavendish and, as I'm assuming our relationship is over, and you're forcing me to walk away from my investment, you need to pay me my money back. I have full receipts for everything here.'

He had opened the folder he had in his hand and pulled out a pile of papers, laying them down on the table for Elenore to look at.

'As you'll see from these, the work carried out comes to a total of €98, 985. That is the amount you owe me, for me to walk away from Cavendish and let you get on with your life. If you don't have this money, you do have an asset here in the house. You can always sell it. If you decide to do that, I'd obviously be an interested buyer and we can come to some arrangement on the outstanding monies.'

Elenore had relayed all these happenings to Edith in their regular phone calls.

'I honestly didn't know what to do next, I thought my legs might go from under me. He was suggesting I should sell Cavendish to him. How dare he! I can't even think about what I'd do if I were forced to sell, but I know one thing for certain: I'll never sell to him.'

'But what happened then, dear?' Edith had asked her.

'Seán stepped in, thankfully – as I literally couldn't speak. He took the folder off Donnacha, said I'd review the contents before speaking to my solicitor and I'd be in contact. Donnacha looked as if someone had shoved a gun in his face, he was that shocked. Then Seán said, "If that's all, you might leave us now so that we can get on with our evening." I thought Donnacha might have a seizure, but he got up and walked out.'

Edith chuckled. 'Seán sounds fantastic.'

Elenore could not but agree with her.

And now Elenore was updating her on the latest developments. She had been to see her solicitor who had told her she'd need to review the documents Donnacha had provided. The solicitor suggested Elenore get a surveyor in to review the work that Donnacha had carried out or, as Seán said, the works he claimed he had carried out.

Edith was relieved to hear that she had sought professional advice. She filled Elenore in on the details of their flight into Shannon the following Tuesday and hung up after telling Elenore not to worry because everything would work out for her in the end.

Over the next few days Elenore had arranged for a surveyor to come to the house so that she could properly understand the value of the works Donnacha had completed.

Then the Gardaí had contacted her – asking her to come in and answer some questions. She duly made an appointment and presented herself at the station at the appointed time. They were extremely kind to her, thanking her for her time and asking her to tell them in detail her history with Donnacha.

She told them everything, how and when she had met him, how long they had lived together and how she had been unaware of anything unusual about his behaviour until recently. She then told them about finding the blueprints for Cavendish by accident, her meeting with Karen and what had been revealed to her. She then told them about their decision to ask Charlie Redmond to go public about his experience with Donnacha.

She was then questioned about whether she had been involved in any meetings or part of any telephone conversations about the land around Cavendish or was aware of any plans to seek planning permission for the land – aside from what she had seen on the drawings. Several politicians, at both a local and national level were mentioned and Elenore was asked if she had been part of meetings with any of those named. She was able to confirm that she hadn't, but she confirmed that Donnacha had made her aware of his meetings with many of them. From what they told her, it seemed Donnacha had been putting in place plans to have the land surrounding Cavendish rezoned – illegally. He couldn't do it without owning the land and Elenore assumed that once they were married and he'd persuaded her to put his name on the deeds, he'd have taken action. This would be investigated further but it was enough to confirm Elenore's beliefs.

That had been the end of it and they had told her she was free to go.

Elenore recounted in detail her first official visit to a police station to Edith and Robert, when they were sitting at her kitchen table on Tuesday evening. Her reunion at the airport with Edith had been joyful. The two women had fallen into each other's arms as if they had been separated for months – instead of just a few weeks. The reunion with Robert had amounted to an awkward hug.

Their arrival at Cavendish had been emotional, with the elderly woman overcome by her return to the home she had left eighty years previously. She had chattered away in the car all the way from the airport and continued all the way through Ballycastle, amazed at the changes in the town. As soon as they reached the gates of Cavendish, she had fallen silent and Elenore could see tears rolling down her cheeks as they turned the final bend in the avenue and the house presented itself in front of them.

It took Edith some time to regain her powers of speech, at which point all she could manage to say was, 'I can't believe I'm here. I can't believe I've finally come home.'

At the house, Elenore put her arms around her, trying to provide her with some comfort, but this seemed to make Edith more emotional. Sensing that the combination of flying across the Atlantic and a return to her childhood home was becoming too much for her, Elenore took Edith to her room – the room she had slept in until the age of sixteen – where she'd put her to bed for a nap. There would be plenty of time to explore her old home in the coming two weeks.

She was now faced with a few hours alone with Robert and was not exactly relishing the prospect.

She was only halfway down the stairs when the doorbell rang and, going to answer it, she found Seán standing in the porch, an expectant look on his face. 'Are they here yet? I'm dying to meet Lady Edith.'

He was disappointed when she told him that Edith had gone for a nap but she took him down to the kitchen to meet Robert. The two men shook hands. Elenore made them tea and conversation was soon flowing. Seán asked Robert about his life in Manhattan, his knowledge of his grandmother's life here in Cavendish and how he felt she was dealing with her return. Robert answered all his questions, telling him how Edith had been displaying childlike excitement in the days leading up to their trip. He thanked Seán for his work in tracking them down and said he was delighted for his grandmother, if a little concerned that she might find the entire trip overwhelming, given her age.

Seán said there was no need to thank him. 'It wasn't difficult really. After May, the woman who used to work here, told us what she knew about the family Edith had married into, it was relatively straightforward to find you. We didn't have much of a problem, did we, Elenore?'

Elenore noticed that Seán had been referring to the two of them as 'we' quite a lot since he'd arrived at the house that evening and wondered if it was deliberate.

'No, Seán, we didn't.'

There was a pause in conversation and Elenore excused herself and go check on Edith.

Upstairs, she found Edith awake and sitting up in the bed, gazing out the window onto the parkland beyond.

'Thank you for this, Elenore. I can't believe I'm here. You've no idea how much this means to me.'

Elenore smiled at her. 'Stop it now. It's an honour to have you here. I hope you're feeling a bit more rested. Take your time. The bathroom is just beside you – of course you know that already! There's plenty of hot water if you want to freshen up. But don't feel under pressure. Come downstairs whenever you're ready. Leslie and Karen are coming over to meet you and have dinner with us – but not for a few hours yet. Seán is here already.'

Edith told her she'd be down soon and Elenore left her to continue enjoying the view.

Coming back down the main staircase, Elenore saw Seán heading towards the front door. 'Sean! Where are you off to? Edith's getting up in a while. Aren't you joining us for dinner? Leslie and Karen are coming too.'

But Seán was almost out the door already. 'No, thanks, Elenore, I've got to be going. I don't want to be in the way.'

'You're not in the way at all, Seán, and you have to meet her. If it wasn't for you, she wouldn't be here.'

'No, it's fine, honestly. I'll chat to you soon.'

And with that he was gone.

Bewildered, she returned to the kitchen where Robert was sitting by the fire.

'Seán left very abruptly, Robert,' she said. 'I thought he'd stay for dinner.'

'Yes, he did leave suddenly. We were talking and then he said he had to go, that he had something to take care of.'

Elenore found this strange. She was really disappointed. She couldn't wait for him to meet Edith. She decided to call him later to check that he was okay.

Edith arrived downstairs soon afterwards and later they were joined by Karen and Leslie. Both women immediately asked where Seán was but Elenore was not able to provide an adequate explanation. They were charmed by Robert and both fell madly in love with Edith instantly.

Sitting down to dinner, their spirits were high. However, when talk turned to Cavendish, Elenore told them she had something she wanted to tell them all.

'There have been some developments over the last few days, but I wanted to wait until I had you all together before I told you. I'm afraid it's not good news. I had a surveyor come out and look at the work and it seems that the work that has been carried out does come to the value of the money that Donnacha is looking for.'

'Oh Elenore, I'm sorry to hear that!' said Leslie.

'Wait, that's not all. I also got the surveyor to give me a cost of what I'd need to get Cavendish up to scratch to go ahead with the plans I have for it. He said I'd be looking at another twenty thousand euros to get it in line with standards to meet safety

requirements. He said I'd never get the insurance I need to run it
commercially unless the work is done properly. I've no idea where
I'm even going to come up with the money to pay Donnacha, never
mind doing any more work with the house. It looks as if I
really will have to sell Cavendish.'

'Oh, no!' Leslie gasped.

'But what about the banks?' said Karen. 'Surely you can get a
bank loan and be done with the whole thing?'

Elenore shook her head. 'That's what I was hoping too but
unfortunately not. I went to the bank and talked to the manager.
They'd have no problem loaning me the money to do the work I
need to do – but not when I'm in so much debt to Donnacha.
Remember I've no income and now I owe him almost one
hundred grand. I'm not exactly the best candidate for a loan.'

'But what will you do now, Elenore? Where will you get the
money from?' Leslie couldn't accept the idea that her friend
would have to sell her home.

Then Edith spoke up. 'I wouldn't despair, my dear girl.
Remember I told you I had a surprise for you, over the phone?'

'Yes, I remember.'

'I have a proposal to put to you. I want to invest in Cavendish.
I want to help you.'

'Invest?' Elenore was confused. 'Edith, there will be no
Cavendish to invest in, don't you see? I can't get a loan. I'll have
to sell.'

'My grandmother means we will loan you the money,' said
Robert.

'All the money? But I can't let you do that – it's too much!
How would I pay it back? It would take forever.'

'We've discussed this in detail over the last number of weeks,
Elenore,' said Robert, 'and, now that I've seen the place, I think
it's a sound investment. Admittedly, this news means putting more
money in than anticipated – but I can help you. I already own two

Home to Cavendish

hotels in the US and I wouldn't mind expanding into Ireland, so my help would come in the form of marketing to that American audience you're after. I wouldn't interfere in your plans in any way. I fully agree with keeping Cavendish small-scale – it's the right thing to do. For me it would be a way to learn the Irish market.'

'Robert, you can't be serious. I can't ask you to do that, nor you, Edith.' While the idea sounded like the answer to all her prayers, how could she allow them to take such a risk? And how could she contemplate going into business with a man she had slept with!

Edith was adamant. 'I want this for you more than anything, Elenore. I knew from the minute I met you how much this house means to you. I can't let you lose it. And, remember, if you lose it, it will be lost to me too. Just when I've found it again. I love it and I don't want it to go to strangers. I want you to take care of it – because you love it like I do. If you're concerned about sharing your profits, don't be. This is a long-term investment. Robert isn't going to be chasing you for fifty per cent, or anywhere near it. Looking after the marketing side is something he knows how to do. Let us help you.'

Elenore still couldn't believe what they were saying to her. Seeing that she was shocked, Robert said they didn't need to talk about it any more tonight. They could sit down later and have a proper meeting about it and go through everything.

After Leslie and Karen had left, and Edith went to bed, Elenore sat with Robert in the kitchen, chatting to him about her friends and going into further detail about what his investment offer entailed.

Elenore liked the idea of an investment in the marketing side. That was where she'd need the most help and, if she could depend on Robert to take the idea of Cavendish directly to the people she wanted as her guests, that would be half the battle. She wasn't sure about anything else, though. Taking money to pay off her debt to

Donnacha didn't feel right. She felt that Robert would have too much power over her – just like Donnacha had done. If she had no control over what happened at Cavendish, would she be better off just giving up and selling it after all? But that thought filled her with such horror she knew she had no choice but to agree to Robert and Edith's proposal.

Getting up to go to bed, Robert reassured her. 'We'd be silent partners in the venture. I promise you that. I'd be sure to have that outlined in the legal documents.'

She thanked him once again and told him they'd talk more about it tomorrow. Before she had a chance to turn and walk to the door, Robert had leaned in and was trying to kiss her.

This was what she had been afraid of. Pulling away, she said, 'Robert, I think it's best we don't do that. If we're going to be business partners, it's not the best idea.'

He smiled at her. 'Fair enough, but you can't judge me for trying – you're a very beautiful woman.

There he was with the over-the-top statements. If she hadn't been annoyed with him, she'd have found it funny.

'I'm serious, Robert – and, in any case, I don't want to get involved with you.'

Now he was laughing. 'I'm sorry, you don't want to get involved with me? Why ever not?'

'Because of what Edith told me – she said you're a ladies' man and that I should have fun with you but not to fall for you – that I'd get my heart broken. So that's what I did. I didn't fall for you and I had great fun in New York, but we need to leave it at that.'

Robert burst into uncontrollable laughter and very soon Elenore was laughing too, unable to stop herself.

'I'm sorry, Elenore, but that's just about the funniest thing I've ever heard. My ninety-six-year-old grandmother told you it was alright to have sex with me but not to fall for me, I ...' He broke into a fit of laughter again.

Eventually he composed himself enough to continue talking.

'She's right, you know. I'm a ladies' man and I've absolutely no intention of settling down any time soon. If I promise to behave myself, will you consider my offer?'

Elenore was relieved. 'Absolutely, Robert, I'll consider it. I'd like to have you on my side, but I need to know there'll be no messiness.'

'You have my word. Now come on, let's get some sleep. We have a lot to do tomorrow.'

Robert gave her a brotherly hug and the two of them headed for their rooms.

Lying in bed, Elenore pondered the events of the evening again. Was there any way she could come up with the money to pay Donnacha back on her own? She thought about the furniture in the house – was there anything valuable enough to sell? That would solve all her problems. She could take Robert and Edith up on the offer of a cash injection in the business but look after her debt to Donnacha and the upgrades to Cavendish herself. But there was nothing that valuable. If she sold a number of items she might be able to raise some of the money, but she couldn't break up the beautiful furniture collection her parents had so lovingly put together.

And just then, out of nowhere, it suddenly popped into her head – the painting by Zee.

CHAPTER 27

September 2003

Lifting her head from the newspaper, Elenore greeted Karen as she came into the kitchen.

'Hi, Karen. Have you seen the paper yet? This thing keeps going on and on.'

'Yes, I heard it on the radio.' Karen took the paper and scanned the front page. 'I wonder if he'll end up going to prison? He deserves to.'

The investigation into Donnacha's dealings had been dragging on for almost a year. The news was reporting that another politician had stepped down, due to involvement in the illegal rezoning of land. It was the third politician whose career lay in ruins as a result of involvement with Donnacha's business.

'Whether he goes to prison or not, either way his reputation is in tatters – he'll never be able to run a business again, not after this.'

For Aaron's sake, Karen didn't want Donnacha to go to prison, and neither did Elenore. The fact that no one would ever trust him to do business again, after this exposure, was punishment enough for him. She hadn't seen him in over six months. He had stopped pestering her as soon as she had paid him back the money for the work on the house.

The painting he had bought her at the action had saved the day. And he had bought it in her name. While he had paid well above the value of it at the time, only a few weeks later the exhibition of the artist's paintings in New York had been a runaway success. After some research she had discovered that due to Zee's unbridled success stateside his last painting had sold for ninety-thousand euros in Ireland. He was the new darling of the art world and Elenore had a painting belonging to him on her bedroom floor.

She'd quickly set about selling the painting, using the money to pay off Donnacha, and the bank had then been happy to offer her a loan to complete the works she wanted done on Cavendish. Robert and Edith had still come in with their cash injection and Robert had kept his word. He'd marketed Cavendish extensively in America, all the while being highly professional towards Elenore the couple of times he'd come back to Ireland to see the progress at the house.

'Hey, let's not waste time thinking of him today,' said Elenore. 'We have a busy day ahead of us – are you all set?' Karen was going to Shannon to collect Cavendish's first guests.

Karen smiled at her. 'I certainly am. I'll get on the road soon. Have you heard from Robert?'

'Yes, he called me last night to wish us luck. He's coming over next month to check up on how we're getting on.'

Robert's advice in the set-up of the business had proved invaluable. He advised her on how best to prepare for the launch of Cavendish Hall as an exclusive get-away. He had advised her on partnering with a local golf club, so that in addition to the equestrian and fishing pursuits on the estate, they could also avail of golf as part of the Cavendish offering.

The work he had done on advertising the house was the one thing Elenore would not have been able to do alone. He'd found exactly the right type of websites and magazines that would reach her wealthy target market and as a result Cavendish Hall was fully booked up until the middle of the following year.

It had been Robert who suggested she might need someone to help ferrying guests to and from the airport and ensuring they had everything they needed during their stay. That would leave Elenore free to look after the business side of things and spend time riding out with her guests. That meant they got to spend time with the owner of the house and to feel as if they were part of the Cavendish family for a short time. Karen had been the obvious choice for the role.

As part of the refurbishments, Elenore had had one of the outbuildings converted into comfortable living accommodation and Karen and Aaron had happily chosen the décor for their new home. Aaron was now attending the secondary school in Ballycastle and Karen's mother was living with them too.

Cavendish was as Elenore had always wished it to be – full of people. It was no longer the quiet house it had become after her parents died. Now there was always someone coming and going. Aaron came home from school in the evening and plonked himself at the kitchen table to do his homework, while his grandmother could usually be found sitting in front of the fire with Alfie curled up on her knee.

Karen had finally received her divorce papers and come to an agreement with Donnacha. She had received a lump sum. It wasn't the amount she had hoped for, but it was enough. Now that she had somewhere secure to live and a decent job, she no longer needed to depend on Donnacha so much. The sense of independence she felt was amazing. Her mother was happy living at Cavendish and a woman from Ballycastle came to take care of her when Karen was working. And she knew she'd be alright if her mother's health deteriorated further, now that she had a nest-egg in the bank.

She dropped Aaron over to Donnacha's apartment in Cork once a week for a visit but, as time went on, the teenager wanted to spend less and less time with his father. Karen had come to terms with this. She hoped that someday they might have a good relationship again but for now Aaron was angry with his father and so she had to put her son's needs first. Karen was so proud of Aaron and how he had adapted to their new situation.

Helping herself to a cup of coffee, Karen asked Elenore what her plans were for the day.

'I think I'm all set really. I want to give one last clean to the place and then I was thinking of taking a walk down to the graveyard. I'll be back well before your return from the airport.'

Karen smiled at her. 'If you clean the place one more time, you'll actually clean it away.'

Once she had finished her coffee, Karen said her goodbyes, promising Elenore she'd be back before lunch with the guests who would no doubt be hungry.

Left alone again, Elenore decided she'd take her walk first and tackle the cleaning when she got back. She needed some fresh air to keep her calm. Her nervous excitement was at a peak and she didn't want to appear frazzled when the guests arrived.

Calling for Alfie, she walked upstairs and out the front door. It was a perfect autumn morning, fresh and bright, and the birds were singing high in the clear blue sky. She walked down the avenue, and made her way towards the village, keeping up a brisk pace to work off some of her energy, stopping occasionally to collect the wild flowers growing in the grass verges.

Leaving the demesne, she passed the Church of Ireland chapel and turned into the graveyard beside it, making her way to the new plot at the back. She stood a moment at the grave. The headstone had only gone up the day before and she was seeing it for the first time.

Edith Bruxby née Cavendish
Born June 28th 1906
Died March 5th 2003
Beloved wife, mother and grandmother

She gently placed the flowers on the grave and said a prayer. Sadness overcame her. She wished Edith was still with her. She'd have been so excited to be here today and in the thick of all that was going on at Cavendish. But then Elenore remembered how happy the woman had been for the last months of her life – how grateful she had been to Elenore for ensuring she got to spend them at Cavendish.

Elenore thought fondly of May and the time she and Edith had spent together over the last months. They'd had a tearful reunion and Elenore had left them alone to catch up. She wasn't sure how much May had shared with Edith about her time at Cavendish or whether Edith knew she had fallen pregnant and then lost her baby. If Edith was aware, it was a secret she had taken to the grave with her. The two elderly women had visited each other frequently, Edith taking great pleasure in inviting May to Cavendish. She made sure it would be easy for May's granddaughter to wheel her into the house in her wheelchair and ensured she served her tea in the grand rooms in the main part of the house.

Deciding she had better return to Cavendish, as by the time she got back she'd need to start preparing lunch, Edith said goodbye to Edith.

'Thank you for making all this possible.'

Elenore felt strong arms wrap around her waist.

'Who are you talking to?'

She turned around into Seán's embrace.

'I was just saying thank you to Edith. I suppose I was asking for her to look out for us today. How did you know I was here?'

He smiled at her and kissed her tenderly.

'I met Karen on the road earlier. She said you had mentioned you might come here this morning. I think Edith's looking out for us alright.'

After his departure from Cavendish the night Robert and Edith had first arrived, Seán had stopped calling Elenore. It was only when she called to his door unannounced one day and insisted she was invited in for tea, that she got to the bottom of his sudden coldness.

After she'd gone to check on Edith, Seán and Robert had been left to chat in the kitchen. It turned out that Robert had spoken about the time he and Elenore had spent in New York. He'd said that now that he was in Ireland he was hoping to rekindle their romance. It had taken some time to persuade Seán that she was not interested in Robert but over the winter they had spent more and more time together and, without any grand declarations, they had become a couple. He was now spending most of his time at Cavendish and less and less time at his own house in the village.

Putting his arm around her waist, he whistled for Alfie, and they began to walk towards the road.

'Come on, girl. We've a lot of work to do – let's go home to Cavendish.'